ROSEANNA

ROSEANNA

Maj Sjöwall and Per Wahlöö

Translated from the Swedish by Lois Roth

VINTAGE BOOKS
A Division of Random House
New York

FIRST VINTAGE BOOKS EDITION, March 1976

Library of Congress Cataloging in Publication Data

Sjöwall, Maj, 1935-
  Roseanna.

  Reprint of the ed. published by Pantheon Books, New
York.
  I. Wahlöö, Per, 1926-1975 joint author. II. Title.
[PZ4.S61953Ro7] [PT9876.29.J63] 839.7'3'74 75-34370
ISBN 0-374-71779-1

ROSEANNA

1

They found the corpse on the eighth of July just after three o'clock in the afternoon. It was fairly well intact and couldn't have been lying in the water very long.

Actually, it was mere chance that they found the body at all. And finding it so quickly should have aided the police investigation.

Below the locks at Borenshult there is a breakwater which protects the entrance to the lake from the east wind. When the canal opened for traffic that spring, the channel had begun to clog up. The boats had a hard time maneuvering and their propellers churned up thick clouds of yellowish mud from the bottom. It wasn't hard to see that something had to be done. As early as May, the Canal Company requisitioned a dredging machine from the Civil Engineering Board. The papers were passed from one perplexed civil servant to another and finally remitted to the Swedish National Shipping and Navigation Administration. The Shipping and Navigation Administration thought that the work should be done by one of the Civil Engineering Board's bucket dredging machines. But the Civil Engineering Board found that the Shipping and Navigation Administration had control over bucket dredging machines and in desperation made an appeal to the Harbor Commission in Norrköping, which immediately returned the papers to the Shipping and Navigation Administration, which remitted them to the Civil Engineering Board, at which point someone picked up the telephone and dialed an engineer who knew all about bucket dredging machines. He knew that of the five existing bucket dredgers, there was only one that could pass through the locks. The vessel was called *The Pig* and happened just then to be lying in the fishing harbor at Gravarne. On the morning of July 5 *The Pig* arrived and moored at Borenshult as the neighborhood children and a Vietnamese tourist looked on.

One hour later a representative of the Canal Company went on board to discuss the project. That took the whole afternoon. The next day was a Saturday and the vessel remained by the breakwater while the men went home for the weekend. The crew consisted of a dredging foreman, who was also the officer in command with the authority to take the vessel to sea, an excavating engineer, and a deck man. The latter two men were from Gothenburg and took the night train from Motala. The skipper lived in Nacka and his wife came to get him in their car. At seven o'clock on Monday morning all three were on board again and one hour later they began to dredge. By eleven o'clock the hold was full and the dredger went out into the lake to dump. On the way back they had to lay off and wait while a white steamboat approached the Boren locks in a westerly direction. Foreign tourists crowded along the vessel's railing and waved excitedly at the working crew on the dredger. The passenger boat was elevated slowly up the locks toward Motala and Lake Vättern and by lunch time its top pennant had disappeared in back of the uppermost sluice gate. At one-thirty the men began to dredge again.

The situation was this: the weather was warm and beautiful with mild temperate winds and idly moving summer clouds. There were some people on the breakwater and on the edge of the canal. Most of them were sunning themselves, a few were fishing, and two or three were watching the dredging activity. The dredger's bucket had just gobbled up a new mouthful of Boren's bottom slime and was on its way up out of the water. The excavating engineer was operating the familiar handgrips in his cabin. The dredging foreman was having a cup of coffee in the galley, and the deck man stood with his elbows on the railing and spit in the water. The bucket was still on the way up.

As it broke through the surface of the water, a man on the pier took a few steps toward the boat. He waved his arms and shouted something. The deck man looked up to hear better.

"There's someone in the bucket! Stop! Someone's lying in the bucket!"

The confused deck man looked first at the man and then at the bucket which slowly swung in over the hold to spit out its contents. Filthy gray water streamed out of the bucket as it hung over the hold. Then the deck man saw what the man on the breakwater had seen. A white, naked arm stuck out of the bucket's jaw.

The next ten minutes seemed endless and chaotic. Someone stood on the pier and said, over and over again: "Don't do

2

anything; don't touch anything; leave everything alone until the police come . . ."

The excavating engineer came out to see what was going on. He stared, then hurried back to the relative scurity of his seat behind the levers. As he let the crane swing and the bucket open, the dredging foreman and the deck man took out the body.

It was a woman. They laid her on her back on a folded tarpaulin out on the breakwater. A group of amazed people gathered around and stared at her. Some of them were children and shouldn't have been there but no one thought to send them away. But all of them had one thing in common: they would never forget how she looked.

The deck man had thrown three buckets of water over her. Long afterwards, when the police inquiry was bogged down, there were people who criticized him for this.

She was naked and had no jewelry on. The lines of her tan made it apparent that she had sunbathed in a bikini. Her hips were broad and she had heavy thighs. Her pubic hair was black and wet and thick. Her breasts were small and slack with large, dark nipples. A red scratch ran from her waist to her hipbone. The rest of her skin was smooth without spots or scars. She had small hands and feet and her nails were not polished. Her face was swollen and it was hard to imagine how she had actually looked alive. She had thick, dark eyebrows and her mouth seemed wide. Her medium-length hair was dark and lay flat on her head. A coil of hair lay across her throat.

2

Motala is a medium-sized Swedish city in the province of Östergötland at the northern end of Lake Vättern. It has a population of 27,000. Its highest police authority is a Commissioner of Police who is also the Public Prosecutor. He has a Police Superintendent under him who is the chief executive of both the regular police constabulary and the criminal police. His staff also includes a First Detective Inspector in the ninth salary grade, six policemen and one policewoman. One of the policemen is a trained photographer and when medical examinations are needed they usually fall back on one of the city's doctors.

One hour after the first alarm, several of these people had gathered on the pier at Borenshult, several yards from the harbor light. It was rather crowded around the corpse and the men on the dredger could no longer see what was happening. They were still on board in spite of the fact that the vessel was prepared to make way with its port bow against the breakwater.

The number of people behind the police barricade on the abutment had increased tenfold. On the other side of the canal there were several cars, four of which belonged to the police, and a white-painted ambulance with red crosses on the back doors. Two men in white overalls leaned against a fender smoking. They seemed to be the only people who weren't interested in the group out by the harbor light.

On the breakwater the doctor began to gather his things together. He chatted with the Superintendent who was a tall, grayhaired man named Larsson.

"There isn't much I can say about it now," said the doctor.

"Does she have to remain lying here?" Larsson asked.

"Isn't that more your business," replied the doctor.

"This is hardly the scene of the crime."

"Okay," the doctor agreed, "See that they drive her to the mortuary. I'll telephone ahead."

He shut his bag and left.

The Superintendent turned and called, "Ahlberg, You're going to keep the area blocked off, aren't you?"

"Yes, damn it."

The Commissioner of Police hadn't said anything out by the harbor light. He didn't usually enter investigations in the early stages. But on the way in to town, he said: "You'll keep me informed."

Larsson didn't even bother to nod.

"You'll keep Ahlberg on it?"

"Ahlberg's a good man," said the Superintendent.

"Yes, of course."

The conversation ended. They arrived, left the car and went into their separate offices. The Commissioner placed a telephone call to the County Authority in Linköping who merely said: "I'll be waiting to hear from you."

The Superintendent had a short conversation with Ahlberg. "We have to find out who she is."

"Yes," said Ahlberg.

He went into his office, called the Fire Department and requisitioned two frogmen. Then he read through the report on a burglary in the harbor. That one would be cleared up soon. Ahlberg got up and went to the officer on duty.

"Is there anyone reported missing?"

"No."

"No notification of missing persons?"

"None that fit."

He went back to his office and waited.

The call came after fifteen minutes.

"We have to ask for an autopsy," said the doctor.

"Was she strangled?"

"I think so."

"Raped?"

"I think so."

The doctor paused a second. Then he said: "And pretty methodically, too."

Ahlberg bit on his index fingernail. He thought of his vacation which was to begin on Friday and how happy his wife was about it.

The doctor misinterpreted the silence.

"Are you surprised?"

"No," said Ahlberg.

He hung up and went into Larsson's office. Then they went to the Commissioner's office together.

Ten minutes later the Commissioner asked for a medicolegal post-mortem examination from the County Administrator who contacted the Government Institute for Forensic Medicine. The autopsy was conducted by a seventy-year-old professor. He came on the night train from Stockholm and seemed bright and cheerful. He conducted the autopsy in eight hours, almost without a break.

Then he left a preliminary report with the following wording: "Death by strangulation in conjunction with gross sexual assault. Severe inner bleeding."

By that time the records of the inquiry and reports had already begun to accumulate on Ahlberg's desk. They could be summed up in one sentence: a dead woman had been found in the lock chamber at Borenshult.

No one had been reported missing in the city or in neighboring police districts. Thre was no description of any such missing person.

It was quarter after five in the morning and it was raining. Martin Beck took more time brushing his teeth than usual to get rid of the taste of lead in his mouth.

He buttoned his collar, tied his tie and looked listlessly at his face in the mirror. He shrugged his shoulders and went out into the hall, continued on through the living room, glanced longingly at the half-finished model of the training ship *Danmark*, on which he had worked until the late hours the night before, and went into the kitchen.

He moved quietly and softly, partly from habit and partly not to wake the children.

He sat down at the kitchen table.

"Hasn't the newspaper come yet?" he said.

"It never comes before six," his wife answered.

It was completely light outside but overcast. The daylight in the kitchen was gray and soupy. His wife hadn't turned on the lights. She called that saving.

He opened his mouth but closed it again without saying anything. There would only be an argument and this wasn't the moment for it. Instead he drummed slowly with his fingers on the formica table top. He looked at the empty cup with its blue rose pattern and a chip in the rim and a brown crack down from the notch. That cup had hung on for almost the duration of their marriage. More than ten years. She rarely broke anything, in any case not irreparably. The odd part of it was that the children were the same.

Could such qualities be inherited? He didn't know.

She took the coffee pot from the stove and filled his cup. He stopped drumming on the table.

"Don't you want a sandwich?" she asked.

He drank carefully with small gulps. He was sitting slightly round-shouldered at the end of the table.

"You really ought to eat something," she insisted.

"You know I can't eat in the morning."

"You ought to in any case," she said. "Especially you, with your stomach."

He rubbed his fingers over his cheek and felt some places he'd missed with his razor. He drank some coffee.

"I can make some toast," she suggested.

Five minutes later he placed his cup on the saucer, moved it away without a sound, and looked up at his wife.

She had on a fluffy red bathrobe over a nylon nightgown and she sat with her elbows on the table, supporting her chin with her hands. She was blond, with fair skin and round, slightly popping eyes. She usually darkened her eyebrows but they had paled during the summer and were now nearly as light as her hair. She was a few years older than he and in spite of the fact that she had gained a good deal of weight in the last few years, the skin on her throat was beginning to sag a little.

She had given up her job in an architect's office when their daughter was born twelve years ago and since then had not thought about working again. When the boy started school, Martin Beck had suggested she look for some part-time work, but she had figured it would hardly pay. Besides, she was comfortable with her own nature and pleased with her role as a housewife.

"Oh, yes," thought Martin Beck and got up. He placed the blue-painted stool under the table quietly and stood by the window looking out at the drizzle.

Down below the parking place and lawn, the highway lay smooth and empty. Not many windows were lighted in the apartments on the hill in back of the subway station. A few seagulls circled under the low, gray sky. Otherwise there was not another living thing to be seen.

"Where are you going?" she said.

"Motala."

"Will you be gone long?"

"I don't know."

"Is it that girl?"

"Yes."

"Do you *think* you'll be gone long?"

"I don't know any more about it than you do. Only what I've seen in the newspapers."

"Why do you have to take the train?"

"The others took off yesterday. I wasn't supposed to go along."

"They'll drive with you, of course, as usual?"

He took a patient breath and gazed outside. The rain was letting up.

"Where will you stay?"

"The City Hotel."

"Who will be with you?"

"Kollberg and Melander. They went yesterday."

"By car?"

"Yes."

"And you have to sit and get shaken up on the train?"

"Yes."

Behind him he heard her washing the cup with the chip in the rim and the blue roses.

"I have to pay the electric bill and also Little One's riding lessons this week."

"Don't you have enough money for that?"

"I don't want to take it out of the bank, you know that."

"No, of course not."

He took his wallet out of his inner pocket and looked into it. Took out a 50 crown note, looked at it, put it back and placed the wallet in his pocket.

"I hate to draw out money," she said. "It's the beginning of the end when you start that."

He took the bill out again, folded it, turned around and laid it on the kitchen table.

"I've packed your bag, Martin."

"Thanks."

"Take care of your throat. This is a treacherous time of the year, particularly the evenings."

"Yes."

"Are you going to take that awful pistol with you?"

"Yes, no. Yes, no. What's the difference?" Martin Beck thought to himself.

"What are you laughing at?" she asked.

"Nothing."

He went into the living room, unlocked the drawer in the secretary and took out the pistol. He put it in his suitcase and locked the drawer again.

The pistol was an ordinary 7.6 millimeter Walther, licensed in Sweden. It was useless in most situations and he was a pretty poor shot anyway.

He went out into the hall, put on his trenchcoat, and stood with his dark hat in his hands.

"Aren't you going to say goodbye to Rolf and the Little One?"

"It's ridiculous to call a twelve year old girl 'Little One.' "

"I think it's sweet."

9

"It's a shame to wake them. And anyway, they know that I am going."

He put his hat on.

"So long. I'll call you."

"Bye bye, and be careful."

He stood on the platform and waited for the subway and thought that he really didn't mind leaving home in spite of the half-finished planking on the model of the training ship *Danmark*.

Martin Beck wasn't chief of the Homicide Squad and had no such ambitions. Sometimes he doubted if he would ever make superintendent although the only things that could actually stand in his way were death or some very serious error in his duties. He was a First Detective Inspector with the National Police and had been with the Homicide Bureau for eight years. There were people who thought that he was the country's most capable examining officer.

He had been on the police force half of his life. At the age of twenty-one he had begun at Jakob Police Station and after six years as a patrol officer in different districts in central Stockholm, he was sent to the National Police College. He was one of the best in his class and when the course was finished he was appointed a Detective Inspector. He was twenty-eight years old at the time.

His father had died that year and he moved from his furnished room in the middle of the city back to the family home in southern Stockholm to take care of his mother. That summer he met his wife. She had rented a cottage with a friend out in the archipelago where he happened to be with his sailing canoe. He fell very much in love. Then, in the autumn, when they were expecting a child, they got married at City Hall and moved to her small apartment back in the city.

One year after the birth of their daughter, there wasn't much left of the happy and lively girl he had fallen in love with and their marriage had slipped into a fairly dull routine.

Martin Beck sat on the green bench in the subway car and looked out through the rain-blurred window. He thought about his marriage apathetically, but when he realized that he was sitting there feeling sorry for himself, he took his newspaper out of his trenchcoat pocket and tried to concentrate on the editorial page.

He looked tired and his sunburned skin seemed yellowish in the gray light. His face was lean with a broad forehead

10

and a strong jaw. His mouth, under his short, straight nose, was thin and wide with two deep lines near the corners. When he smiled, you could see his healthy, white teeth. His dark hair was combed straight back from the even hairline and had not yet begun to gray. The look in his soft blue eyes was clear and calm. He was thin but not especially tall and somewhat round-shouldered. Some women would say he was good looking but most of them would see him as quite ordinary. He dressed in a way that would draw no attention. If anything, his clothes were a little too discreet.

The air in the train was close and stuffy and he felt slightly uncomfortable as he usually did when he was on the subway. When they arrived at Central Station, he was the first one at the door with his suitcase in his hand.

He disliked the subway. But since he cared even less for bumper-to-bumper automobile traffic, and that 'dream apartment' in the center of the city was still only a dream, he had no choice at the moment.

The express to Gothenburg left the station at 7:30 p.m. Martin Beck thumbed through his newspaper but didn't see a line about the murder. He turned back to the cultural pages and began to read an article on the anthroposophist Rudolf Steiner but fell asleep in a few minutes.

He awoke in good time to change trains at Hallsberg. The lead taste in his mouth had come back and stayed with him despite the three glasses of water that he drank.

He arrived in Motala at 10:30 p.m. and by then the rain had stopped. Since it was his first visit there, he asked at the kiosk in the station the way to the City Hotel and bought a pack of cigarettes and the Motala newspaper.

The hotel was on the main square only a few blocks from the railroad station. The short walk stimulated him. Up in his room he washed his hands, unpacked, and drank a bottle of mineral water which he got from the porter. He stood by the window for a moment and looked out over the square. It had a statue in the center which he guessed was of Baltzar von Platen. Then he left the room to go to the police station. Since he knew it was right across the street, he left his trenchcoat in the room.

He told the officer on duty who he was and was immediately shown to an office on the second floor. The name Ahlberg was on the door.

The man sitting behind the desk was broad and thick-set and slightly bald. His jacket was on the back of his chair and he was drinking coffee out of a container. A cigarette was burning on the corner of an ash tray which was already filled with butts.

Martin Beck had a way of slinking through a door which irritated a number of people. Someone once said that he was able to slip into a room and close the door behind him so quickly that it seemed as if he were still knocking on the outside.

The man behind the desk seemed slightly surprised. He pushed his coffee container away and got up.

"My name is Ahlberg," he said.

There was something expectant in his manner. Martin Beck had seen the same thing before and knew what this sprang from. He was the expert from Stockholm and the man behind the desk was a country policeman who had come to a standstill on an investigation. The next few minutes would be decisive for their cooperation.

"What's your first name?" said Martin Beck.

"Gunnar."

"What are Kollberg and Melander doing?"

"I have no idea. Something I've forgotten, I suspect."

"Did they have that we'll-settle-this-thing-in-a-flash look?"

The local policeman ran his fingers through his thin blond hair. Then he smiled wryly and took to his familiar chair.

"Just about," he said.

Martin Beck sat down opposite him, drew out a pack of cigarettes and laid it on the edge of the desk.

"You look tired," Martin Beck stated.

"My vacation got shot to hell."

Ahlberg emptied the container of coffee, crumpled it and threw it into the wastebasket under the desk.

The disorder on his desk was remarkable. Martin Beck thought about his own desk in Stockholm. It was usually quite neat.

"Well," he said. "How goes it?"

"Not at all," said Ahlberg. "After more than a week we don't know anything more than what the doctor has told us."

Out of habit he went on to the routine procedures.

"Put to death by strangulation in conjunction with sexual assault. The culprit was brutal. Signs of perverse tendencies."

Martin Beck smiled. Ahlberg looked at him questioningly.

"You said 'put to death.' I say it myself sometimes. We've written too many reports."

"Yeah, isn't it hell?"

12

Ahlberg sighed and ran his fingers through his hair.

"We brought her up eight days ago," he said. "We haven't learned a thing since then. We don't know who she is, we don't know the scene of the crime, and we have no suspects. We haven't found a single thing that could have any real connnection with her."

4

"Death by strangulation," thought Martin Beck.

He sat and thumbed through a bunch of photographs which Ahlberg had dug out of a basket on his desk. The pictures showed the locks, the dredger, its bucket in the foreground, the body lying on the embankment, and in the mortuary.

Martin Beck placed a photo in front of Ahlberg and said:

"We can have this picture cropped and retouched so that she looks presentable. Then we can begin knocking on doors. If she comes from around here someone ought to recognize her. How many men can you put on the job?"

"Three at most," said Ahlberg. "We're short of men right now. Three of the boys are on vacation and one of them is in the hospital with a broken leg. Other than the Superintendent, Larsson and myself, there are only eight men at the station."

He counted on his fingers.

"Yes, and one of them is a woman. Then too, someone has to take care of the other work."

"We'll have to help if worst comes to worst. It's going to take a hell of a lot of time. Have you had any trouble with sex criminals lately by the way?"

Ahlberg tapped his pen against his front teeth while he was thinking. Then he reached into his desk drawer and dug up a paper.

"We had one in for examination. From Västra Ny, a rapist. He was caught in Linköping the day before yesterday but he had an alibi for the entire week, according to this report from Blomgren. He's checking out the institutions."

Ahlberg placed the paper in a green file which lay on his desk.

They sat quietly for a minute. Martin Beck was hungry. He thought about his wife and her chatter about regular meals. He hadn't eaten for twenty-four hours.

The air in the room was thick with cigarette smoke.

Ahlberg got up and opened the window. They could hear a time signal from the radio somewhere in the vicinity.

"It's one o'clock," he said. "If you're hungry I can send out for something. I'm as hungry as a bear."

Martin Beck nodded and Ahlberg picked up the telephone. After a while there was a knock at the door and a girl in a blue dress and a red apron came in with a basket.

After Martin Beck had eaten a ham sandwich and had a few swallows of coffee, he said:

"How do you think she got there?"

"I don't know. During the day there are always a lot of people at the locks so it could hardly have happened then. He could have thrown her in from the pier or the embankment and then later the backwash from the boats' propellers might have moved her further out. Or maybe she was thrown overboard from some vessel."

"What kind of boats go through the locks? Small boats and pleasure craft?"

"Some. Not so terribly many. Most of them are freighters. And then there are the canal boats, of course, the *Diana*, the *Juno* and the *Wilhelm Tham*."

"Can we drive down there and take a look?" asked Martin Beck.

Ahlberg got up, took the photograph that Martin Beck had chosen, and said: "We can get going right away. I'll leave this at the lab on the way out."

It was almost three o'clock when they returned from Borenshult. The traffic in the locks was lively and Martin Beck had wanted to stay there among the vacationers and the fishermen on the pier to watch the boats.

He had spoken with the crew of the dredger, been out on the embankment and looked at the system of locks. He had seen a sailing canoe cruising in the fresh breeze far out in the water and had begun to long for his own canoe which he had sold several years ago. During the trip back to town he sat thinking about sailing in the archipelago in summers past.

There were eight, fresh copies of the picture from the photo laboratory lying on Ahlberg's desk when they returned. One of the policemen, who was also a photographer, had retouched the picture and the girl's face looked almost as if she had been photographed alive.

Ahlberg looked through them, laid four of the copies in the green folder and said:

15

"Fine. I'll pass these out to the boys so that they can get started immediately."

When he came back after a few minutes Martin Beck was standing next to the desk rubbing his nose.

"I'd like to make a few telephone calls," he said.

"Use the office farthest down the corridor."

The room was larger than Ahlberg's and had windows on two walls. It was furnished with two desks, five chairs, a filing cabinet and a typewriter table with a disgracefully old Remington.

Martin Beck sat down, placed his cigarettes and matches on the table, put down the green folder and began to go through the reports. They didn't tell him much more than he had already learned from Ahlberg.

An hour and a half later he ran out of cigarettes. He had placed a few telephone calls without result and had talked to the Commissioner and to Superintendent Larsson who seemed tired and pressed. Just as he had crumpled the empty cigarette package, Kollberg called.

Ten minutes later they met at the hotel.

"God, you look dismal," Kollberg said. "Do you want a cigarette?"

"No thank you. What have you been doing?"

"I've been talking to a guy from the *Motala Times*. A local editor in Borensberg. He thought he had found something. A girl from Linköping was to have started a new job in Borensborg ten days ago but she never arrived. She was thought to have left Linköping the day before and since then, no one has heard from her. No one thought to report her missing since she was generally unreliable. This newspaperman knew her employer and started making his own inquiries but never bothered to get a description of her. But I did. And it isn't the same girl. This one was fat and blond. She's still missing. It took me the entire day."

He leaned back in his chair and picked his teeth with a match.

"What do we do now?"

"Ahlberg has sent out a few of his boys to knock on doors. You ought to give them a hand. When Melander gets here we'll have a run through with the Commissioner and Larsson. Go over to Ahlberg and he'll tell you what to do."

Kollberg straightened his chair and got up.

"Are you coming too?" he asked.

16

"No, not now. Tell Ahlberg that I'm in my room if he wants anything."

When he got to his room Martin Beck took off his jacket, shoes, and tie and sat down on the edge of the bed.

The weather had cleared and white puffs of cloud moved across the sky. The afternoon sun shone into the room.

Martin Beck got up, opened the window a little, and closed the thin, yellow drapes. Then he lay down on the bed with his hands folded under his head.

He thought about the girl who had been pulled out of Boren's bottom mud.

When he closed his eyes he saw her before him as she looked in the picture, naked and abandoned, with narrow shoulders and her dark hair in a coil across her throat.

Who was she? What had she thought? How had she lived? Whom had she met?

She was young and he was sure that she had been pretty. She must have had someone who loved her. Someone close to her who was wondering what had happened to her. She must have had friends, colleagues, parents, maybe sisters and brothers. No human being, particularly a young, attractive woman, is so alone that there is no one to miss her when she disappears.

Martin Beck thought about this for a long time. No one had inquired about her. He felt sorry for the girl whom no one missed. He couldn't understand why. Maybe she had said that she was going away? If so, it might be a long time before someone wondered where she was.

The question was: how long?

5

It was eleven-thirty in the morning and Martin Beck's third day in Motala. He had gotten up early but accomplished nothing by it. Now he was sitting at the small desk thumbing through his notebook. He had reached for the telephone a few times, thinking that he really ought to call home, but nothing had come of the idea.

Just like so many other things.

He put on his hat, locked the door to his room, and walked down the stairs. The easy chairs in the hotel lobby were occupied by several journalists and two camera cases with folded tripods, bound by straps, lay on the floor. One of the press photographers stood leaning against the wall near the entrance smoking a cigarette. He was a very young man and he moved his cigarette to the corner of his mouth and raised his Leica to look through the viewer.

When Martin Beck went past the group he drew his hat down over his face, ducked his head against his shoulder and walked straight ahead. This was merely a reflex action but it always seemed to irritate someone because one of the reporters said, surprisingly sourly:

"Say, will there be a dinner with the leaders of the search this evening?"

Martin Beck mumbled something without even knowing what he had said himself and continued toward the door. The second before he had opened the door, he heard the little click which indicated that the photographer had taken a picture.

He walked quickly down the street, but only until he thought he was out of the range of the camera. Then he stopped and stood there indecisively for about ten seconds. He threw a half-smoked cigarette into the gutter, shrugged his shoulders and walked over to a taxi stand. He slumped into the back seat, rubbed the tip of his nose with his right index finger, and peered over toward the hotel. From under his hat brim he saw the man who had spoken to him in the lobby. The journalist stood directly in front of the hotel and stared after the taxi. But only for a moment. Then he, too, shrugged his shoulders and went back into the hotel.

Press people and personnel from the Homicide Division of the National Police often stayed at the same hotel. After a speedy and successful solution to a crime, they often spent the last evening eating and drinking together. Over the years this had become a custom. Martin Beck didn't like it but several of his colleagues thought otherwise.

Even though he hadn't been on his own very much, he had still learned a little about Motala during the forty-eight hours he had been there. At least he knew the names of the streets. He watched the street signs as the taxi drove by them. He told the driver to stop at the bridge, paid him, and stepped out. He stood with his hands on the railing and looked along the canal. While he stood there he realized that he had forgotten to ask the driver to give him a receipt for the fare and that there would probably be some kind of idiotic nonsense back at the office if he were to make one out himself. It would be best to type out the information, it would give more substance to his request.

He was still thinking about that as he walked along the path on the north side of the canal.

During the morning hours there had been a few rain showers and the air was fresh and light. He stopped, right in the middle of the path, and felt how fresh it was. He drank in the cool, clean odor of wild flowers and wet grass. It reminded him of his childhood, but that was before tobacco smoke, gasoline odors and mucus had robbed his senses of their sharpness. Nowadays it wasn't often he had this pleasure.

Martin Beck had passed the five locks and continued along the sea wall. Several small boats were moored near the locks and by the breakwater, and a few small sailboats could be seen out in the open water. One hundred and fifty feet beyond the jetty, the dredger's bucket clanged and clattered under the watchful eye of some seagulls who were flying in wide, low circles. Their heads moved from one side to the other as they waited for whatever the bucket might bring up from the bottom. Their powers of observation and their patience were admirable, as was their staying power and optimism. They reminded Martin Beck of Kollberg and Melander.

He walked to the end of the breakwater and stood there for a while. She had been lying here, or more accurately, her

19

violated body had been lying here, on a crumpled tarpaulin practically on view to anyone for public inspection. After a few hours it had been carried away by two businesslike, uniformed men with a stretcher and, in time, an elderly gentleman whose profession it was to do so, had opened it up, examined it in detail, and then sewed it together again before it was sent to the mortuary. He hadn't seen it himself. There was always something to be thankful for.

Martin Beck became conscious of the fact that he was standing with his hands clasped behind his back as he shifted his weight from the sole of one foot to another, a habit from his years as a patrolman which was totally unconscious and almost unbreakable. He was standing and staring at a gray and uninteresting piece of ground from where the chalk marks from the first, routine investigation had long since been washed away by the rain. He must have occupied himself with this for a long time because the surroundings had gone through a number of changes. When he looked up he observed a small, white passenger boat entering one of the locks at a good speed. When it passed the dredger, some twenty cameras pointed at it, and, as if to underscore the situation, the dredging foreman climbed out of his cabin and also photographed the passenger boat. Martin Beck followed the boat with his eyes as it passed the jetty and noted certain ugly details. The hull had clean lines but the mast was cut off and the original smokestack, which had surely been high and straight and beautiful, had been replaced by a strange, streamlined little tin hood. From inside the ship growled something that must have been a diesel engine. The deck was full of tourists. Nearly all of them seemed to be elderly or middle-aged and several of them wore straw hats with flowered bands.

The boat was named *Juno*. He remembered that Ahlberg had mentioned this name the first time they had met.

There were a lot of people on the breakwater and along the edge of the canal now. Some of them fished and others sunbathed, but most of them were chiefly occupied with watching the boat. For the first time in several hours Martin Beck found a reason to say something.

"Does the boat always pass here at this time of day?"

"Yes, if it comes from Stockholm. Twelve-thirty. Right. The one that goes in the other direction comes by later, just after four. They meet at Vadstena. They tie up there."

"There are a lot of people here, on shore, I mean."

20

"They come down to see the boat."

"Are there always so many?"

"Usually."

The man he was talking to took the pipe from his mouth and spat in the water.

"Some pleasure," he said. "To stand and stare at a bunch of tourists."

When Martin Beck walked back along the brink of the canal he passed the little passenger boat again. It was now about halfway up, peacefully rising in the third lock. A number of passengers had gone on land. Several of them were photographing the boat, others crowded around the kiosk on shore where they were buying postcards and plastic souvenirs which, without doubt, were made in Hong Kong.

Martin Beck couldn't really say that he was short of time so with his innate respect for government budgets he took the bus back to town instead of a taxi.

There were no newspapermen in the hotel lobby and no messages for him at the desk. He went up to his room, sat down at the table and looked out over the Square. Actually he should have gone over to the police station but he had already been there twice before lunch.

A half hour later he telephoned Ahlberg.

"Hi. I'm glad you called. The Public Prosecutor is here."

"And?"

"He's going to hold a press conference at six o'clock. He seems worried."

"Oh."

"He would like you to be there."

"I'll be there."

"Will you bring Kollberg with you. I haven't had time to tell him yet."

"Where is Melander?"

"Out with one of my boys following up a lead."

"Did it sound as if it could be anything important?"

"Hell, no."

"And otherwise?"

"Nothing. The Prosecutor is worried about the press. The other telephone is ringing now."

"So long. See you later."

He remained seated at the table and listlessly smoked all his cigarettes. Then he looked at the clock, got up, and went out into the corridor. He stopped three doors down the hall,

21

knocked and walked in, quietly and very quickly, in his usual manner.

Kollberg lay on the bed reading an evening paper. He had taken off his shoes and jacket and opened his shirt. His service pistol lay on the night table, wrapped up in his tie.

"We've fallen back to page twelve today," he said. "The poor devils, they don't have an easy time of it."

"Who?"

"Those reporters. 'The mystery tightens around the bestial murder of the woman in Motala. Not only the local police but even the Homicide Division of the National Police are fumbling around hopelessly in the dark.' I wonder where they get all that?"

Kollberg was fat and had a nonchalant and jovial manner which caused many people to make fateful mistakes in judging him.

" 'The case seemed to be a routine one in the beginning but has become more and more complicated. The leaders of the search are uncommunicative but are working along several different lines. The naked beauty of Boren . . .' oh, crap!"

He looked through the rest of the article and threw the newspaper on the floor.

"Yes, she was some beauty! A completely ordinary bow-legged woman with a big rear end and very small breasts."

"She had a big crotch, of course," said Kollberg. "And that was her misfortune," he added philosophically.

"Have you seen her?" Martin Beck asked.

"Of course, haven't you?"

"Only her pictures."

"Well I've seen her," said Kollberg.

"What have you been doing this afternoon?"

"What do you think? Reports from knocking on doors. What garbage! It's insane to send out fifteen different guys all over the place. Everybody expresses themselves differently and sees things differently. Some of them write four pages about seeing a one-eyed cat and saying that the kids in a house are snot-nosed, and others write up finding three bodies and a time bomb in a few paragraphs. They even ask totally different questions."

Martin Beck said nothing. Kollberg sighed.

"They should have a formula," he said. "They would save four-fifths of the time."

"Yes."

Martin Beck searched in his pockets.

"As you know I don't smoke," said Kollberg jokingly.

"The Public Prosecutor is holding a press conference in a half an hour. He would like us to be there."

"Oh. That ought to be lively."

He pointed to the newspaper and said:

"If *we* questioned the reporters for once. For four days in a row that guy has written that an arrest can be expected before the end of the afternoon. And the girl looks a little bit like Anita Ekberg and a little bit like Sophia Loren."

He sat up in bed, buttoned his shirt and began to lace his shoes.

Martin Beck walked over to the window.

"It's going to rain any minute," he said.

"Oh damn," Kollberg said and yawned.

"Are you tired?"

"I slept two hours last night. We were out in the woods in the moonlight searching for that type from St. Sigfrid's."

"Yes, of course."

"Yes, of course! And after we had wandered around for seven hours in this damn tourist place someone got around to telling us that the boys back at Klara station in Stockholm got the guy in Berzelii Park the night before last."

Kollberg finished dressing and put his pistol in place. He took a quick look at Martin Beck and said: "You look depressed. What is it?"

"Nothing special."

"Okay, let's go. The world press is waiting."

There were about twenty journalists in the room in which the press conference was to be held. In addition, the Public Prosecutor, the Superintendent of Police, Larsson, and a TV photographer with two spotlights were there. Ahlberg wasn't there. The Prosecutor sat behind a table and was looking thoughtfully through a folder. Several of the others were standing. There weren't enough chairs for everyone. It was noisy and everyone was talking at once. The room was crowded and the air was already unpleasant. Martin Beck, who disliked crowds, took several steps away from the others and stood with his back to the wall in the space between those who would ask the questions and those who would answer them.

After several minutes the Public Prosecutor turned to the Chief of Police and asked, loudly enough to cut through all the other noise in the room:

"Where the devil is Ahlberg?"

Larsson grabbed the telephone and forty seconds later Ahlberg entered the room. He was red-eyed and perspiring and still in the process of getting into his jacket.

The Public Prosecutor stood up and knocked lightly on the table with his fountain pen. He was tall and well built and quite correctly dressed, but almost too elegant.

"Gentlemen, I am pleased to see that so many of you have come to this impromptu press conference. I see representatives of all branches of media, the press, radio and television."

He bowed slightly toward the TV photographer, who was obviously the only press person present in the room whom he could definitely identify.

"I am also pleased to be able to say that from the outset your manner of handling this tragic and ... sensitive matter has been, for the most part, correct and responsible. Unfortunately, there have been a few exceptions. Sensationalism and loose speculations do not help in such a ... sensitive case as ..."

Kollberg yawned and didn't even bother to put his hand in front of his mouth.

"As you all know this case has ... and I certainly do not need to point it out again, special ... sensitive aspects and ..."

From the opposite side of the room Ahlberg looked at Martin Beck, his pale blue eyes filled with gloomy recognition and understanding.

"... and just these ... sensitive aspects call for a particularly careful way of treating them."

The Public Prosecutor continued to speak. Martin Beck looked over the shoulder of the reporter who sat in front of him and saw a drawing of a star on his notebook. The TV man was leaning against his tripod.

"... and naturally I want to, no, more properly said, we neither want to nor can we hide our gratefulness for all the help in this ... sensitive case. In short, we need the support of what we often call that great detective, the Public."

Kollberg yawned again. Ahlberg looked desperately unhappy.

Martin Beck finally ventured a look at the people in the room. He knew three of the journalists, they were older and came from Stockholm. He also recognized a few others. Most of them seemed very young.

"In addition, gentlemen, the collected information that we

24

do have is at your disposal," said the Public Prosecutor and sat down.

With that he had clearly said his piece. In the beginning Larsson answered the questions. Most of them were asked by three young reporters who followed each other's questions in rapid order. Martin Beck noted that a number of newspapermen sat quietly and didn't take any notes. Their attitude toward the lack of real leads in the case seemed to show compassion and understanding. The photographers yawned. The room was already thick with cigarette smoke.

QUESTION: Why hasn't there been a real press conference before this one?

ANSWER: There haven't been many leads in this case. In addition, there are certain important facts in this case that could not be made public without hindering its solution.

QUESTION: Is an arrest immediately forthcoming?

ANSWER: It is conceivable, but from the present standpoint we cannot give you a definite answer, unfortunately.

QUESTION: Do you have any real clues in this case?

ANSWER: All we can say is that our investigations are following certain distinct lines.

(After this amazing series of half truths the Chief of Police threw a sorrowful look at the Public Prosecutor who stubbornly examined his cuticles.)

QUESTION: Criticism has been directed toward several of my colleagues. Is it the opinion of those in charge of the case that these colleagues have more or less intentionally twisted the facts?

(This question was asked by the notoriously well known reporter whose article had made such a deep impression on Kollberg.)

ANSWER: Yes, unfortunately.

QUESTION: Isn't it more a case of the police leaving us reporters out in the cold and not giving us useful information? And deliberately leaving us to our own devices to find out whatever we can in the field?

ANSWER: Humn.

(Several of the less talkative journalists began to show signs of displeasure.)

QUESTION: Have you identified the corpse?

(Superintendent Larsson, with a quick glance, threw the ball over to Ahlberg, sat down, and demonstratively took a cigar out of his breast pocket.)

ANSWER: No.

25

QUESTION: Is it possible that she is from this city or somewhere around here?

ANSWER: It doesn't seem likely.

QUESTION: Why not?

ANSWER: If that were the case we would have been able to identify her.

QUESTION: Is that your only reason for suspecting that she comes from another part of the country?

(Ahlberg looked dismally at the Chief of Police who was devoting all his attention to his cigar.)

ANSWER: Yes.

QUESTION: Has the search of the bottom near the breakwater produced any results?

ANSWER: We have found a number of things.

QUESTION: Do these things have anything to do with the crime?

ANSWER: That is not easy to answer.

QUESTION: How old was she?

ANSWER: Presumably between twenty-five and thirty.

QUESTION: Exactly how long had she been dead when she was found?

ANSWER: That isn't easy to answer, either. Between three and four days.

QUESTION: The information that has been given to the public is very vague. Isn't it possible to tell us something more exact, information which really says something?

ANSWER: That's what we are trying to do here. We have also retouched a picture of her face which you are welcome to, if you want to have it.

(Ahlberg reached for a group of papers on the desk and started to hand them out. The air in the room was heavy and humid.)

QUESTION: Did she have any particular marks on her body?

ANSWER: Not as far as we know.

QUESTION: What does that mean?

ANSWER: Simply, that she had no marks at all.

QUESTION: Has a dental examination given any special clues?

ANSWER: She had good teeth.

(A long and pressing pause followed. Martin Beck noted that the reporter in front of him was still doodling with the star he had drawn.)

QUESTION: Is it possible that the body was thrown into the water at some other place and that it was brought to the breakwater by the current?

ANSWER: It doesn't seem likely.

QUESTION: Have you learned anything by knocking on doors?

ANSWER: We are still working on that.

QUESTION: To sum up, isn't it so that the police have a complete mystery on their hands?

It was the Public Prosecutor that answered:

"Most crimes are a mystery in the beginning."

With that, the press conference ended.

On the way out, one of the older reporters stopped Martin Beck, laid his hand on his arm and said: "Don't you know anything at all?" Martin Beck shook his head.

In Ahlberg's office two men were going through all the material they had gathered from the operation of knocking on doors.

Kollberg walked over to the desk, looked at several of the papers, and shrugged his shoulders.

Ahlberg came in. He took off his jacket and hung it over the back of his chair. Then he turned to Martin Beck and said: "The Public Prosecutor wants to talk to you. He is still in the other room."

The Prosecutor and the Police Superintendent were still sitting behind the table.

"Beck," said the Prosecutor, "I don't see that your presence is necessary here any longer. There simply is not any work for the three of you."

"That's true."

"In general I think that a lot of what is left to do can be done conveniently some other place."

"That is possible."

"To put it simply, I don't want to detain you here, especially if your presence is more motivated in another direction."

"That is also my point of view," the Chief of Police added.

"Mine also," said Martin Beck.

They shook hands.

In Ahlberg's office it was still very quiet. Martin Beck did not break that silence.

After a while Melander came in. He hung up his hat and nodded to the others. Then he went over to the desk, sat down at Ahlberg's typewriter, put some paper in it and knocked out a few lines. He pulled the paper out of the typewriter, signed it, and placed it in the folder on the desk.

"Was that anything?" asked Ahlberg.

27

"No," said Melander.

He hadn't changed his manner since he had come in.

"We are going home tomorrow," Martin Beck said.

"Great," said Kollberg and yawned.

Martin Beck took a step toward the door and then turned and looked at the man at the typewriter.

"Are you coming along to the hotel?" he asked.

Ahlberg put his head back and looked at the ceiling. Then he got up and began to straighten his tie.

In the hotel lobby they separated from Melander.

"I've already eaten," he said. "Good night."

Melander was a clean living man. In addition he was economical with his expense account and subsisted mainly on hot dogs and soft drinks when he was out on a job.

The other three went into the dining room and sat down.

"A gin and tonic," said Kollberg. "Schweppes."

The others ordered beef, aquavit and beer. Kollberg took his drink and finished it in three swallows. Martin Beck took out a copy of the material which had been given to the reporters and read through it.

"Will you do me a favor," said Martin Beck looking at Kollberg.

"Always ready to," answered Kollberg.

"I want you to write a new description, write it for me personally. Not a report but a real description. Not a description of a corpse but of a human being. Details. How she might have looked when she was alive. There's no hurry about it."

Kollberg sat quietly for a while.

"I understand what you mean," he said. "By the way, our friend Ahlberg supplied the world press with an untruth today. She actually did have a birthmark, on the inside of her left thigh. Brown. It looked like a pig."

"We didn't see it," said Ahlberg.

Before he left he said:

"Don't worry about it. No one can see anything. Anyway, it's your murder now. Forget that you've seen me. It was only an illusion. So long."

"So long," said Ahlberg.

They ate and drank silently. A lot later and without looking up from his drink, Ahlberg said:

"Are you planning to let this one go now?"

"No," replied Martin Beck.

"I'm not either," said Ahlberg. "Never."

A half hour later they separated.

When Martin Beck went up to his room he found some folded papers under his door. He opened them and immediately recognized Kollberg's orderly, easy to read, handwriting. Because he had known Kollberg well for a long time he wasn't at all surprised.

He undressed, washed the top of his body in cold water and put on his pajamas. Then he put his shoes out in the corridor, laid his trousers under the mattress, turned on the night table lamp, turned off the ceiling light and got into bed.

Kollberg had written:

"The following can be said about the woman who is occupying your thoughts:

1) She was (as you already know) 5 feet, 6½ inches tall, had gray-blue eyes and dark brown hair. Her teeth were good and she had no scars from operations or other marks on her body with the exception of a birthmark, high up on the inside of her left thigh about an inch and a half from her groin. It was brown and about as large as a dime, but uneven and looked like a little pig. She was, according to the man who performed the autopsy (and I had to press him to tell me this on the telephone), twenty-seven or twenty-eight years old. She weighed about one hundred and twenty-three pounds.

2) She was built in the following manner: Small shoulders and a very small waist, broad hips and a well developed rear end. Her measurements ought to have been approximately: 32-23-37. Thighs: heavy and long. Legs: muscular with relatively heavy calves but not fat. Her feet were in good condition with long, straight toes. No corns but heavy calluses on the soles of her feet, as if she had gone barefoot a lot and worn sandals or rubber boots a great deal of the time. She had a lot of hair on her legs, and must have been bare-legged most of the time. Condition of her legs: some defects. She was somewhat knock-kneed and seems to have walked with her toes pointed outward. She had a good deal of flesh on her body but was not fat. Slender arms. Small hands but long fingers. Shoe size was seven.

3) The suntan on her body showed: she had sunbathed in a two-piece bathing suit and worn sunglasses. She had worn thong sandals on her feet.

4) Her sex organ was well developed with a heavy growth

29

of dark hair. Her breasts were small and slack. The nipples were large and dark brown.

5) Rather short neck. Strong features. A large mouth with full lips. Straight, thick, dark eyebrows and lighter eyelashes. Not long. Straight, short nose which was rather broad. No traces of cosmetics on her face. Fingernails and toenails hard, and clipped short. No traces of nail polish.

6) In the record of the autopsy (which you have read) I place special attention on the following: She had not had a child and never had an abortion. The murder had not been committed in connection with any conventional act (no trace of sperm). She had eaten three to five hours before she died: meat, potatoes, strawberries and milk. No traces of sickness or any organic changes. She did not smoke.

I've left a call to be awakened at six o'clock. So long."

Martin Beck read through Kollberg's observations twice before he folded the papers and laid them on his night table. Then he turned off the light and rolled over toward the wall.

It had begun to get light before he fell asleep.

6

The heat was already trembling over the asphalt when they drove away from Motala. It was early in the morning and the road lay flat and empty ahead of them. Kollberg and Melander sat in the front and Martin Beck sat in the back seat with the window down and let the breeze blow on his face. He didn't feel well and it was probably due to the coffee that he had gulped down while he was getting dressed.

"Kollberg was driving, poorly and unevenly," Martin Beck thought, but for once he remained silent. Melander looked blankly out the window and bit hard on the stem of his pipe.

After they had driven silently for about three-quarters of an hour Kollberg nodded his head to the left where a lake could be seen between the trees.

"Lake Roxen," he said. "Boren, Roxen and Glan. Believe it or not that's one of the few things I remember from school."

The others said nothing.

They stopped at a coffee house in Linköping. Martin Beck still didn't feel well and remained in the car while the others had something to eat.

The food had put Melander in a better mood and the two men in the front seat exchanged remarks during the rest of the trip. Martin Beck still remained silent. He didn't want to talk.

When they reached Stockholm he went directly home. His wife was sitting on the balcony sunbathing. She had shorts on and when she heard the front door open she took her brassiere from the balcony railing and got up.

"Hi," she said. "How are you?"

"Terrible. Where are the children?"

"They took their bikes and went off to swim. You look pale. You haven't eaten properly of course. I'll fix some breakfast for you."

"I'm tired," said Martin Beck. "I don't want anything to eat."

"But it will be ready in a second. Sit down and . . ."

31

"I don't *want* any breakfast. I think I'll sleep for a while. Wake me up in an hour."

It was a quarter after ten.

He went into the bedroom and closed the door after him.

When she awakened him he thought he had only slept for a few minutes.

The clock showed that it was quarter of one.

"I told you one hour."

"You looked so tired. Commissioner Hammar is on the telephone."

"Oh, damn."

An hour later he was sitting in his chief's office.

"Didn't you get anywhere?"

"No. We don't know a thing. We don't know who she was, where she was murdered, and least of all by whom. We know approximately how and where but that's all."

Hammar sat with the palms of his hands on the top of the desk, and studied his fingernails and wrinkled his forehead. He was a good man to work for, calm, almost a little slow, and they always got along well together.

Commissioner Hammar folded his hands and looked up at Martin Beck.

"Keep in contact with Motala. You are most probably right. The girl was on vacation, thought to be away, maybe even out of the country. It might take two weeks at least before anyone misses her. If we count on a three week vacation. But I would like to see your report as soon as possible."

"You'll get it this afternoon."

Martin Beck went into his office, took the cover off his typewriter, thumbed through the papers he had received from Ahlberg, and began to type.

At five-thirty the telephone rang.

"Are you coming home to dinner?"

"It doesn't seem so."

"Aren't there any other policemen but you?" said his wife. "Do you have to do everything? When do they think you'll see your family? The children are asking for you."

"I'll try to get home by six-thirty."

An hour and a half later his report was finished.

"Go home and get some sleep," said Hammar. "You look tired."

Martin Beck was tired. He took a taxi home, ate dinner and went to bed.

32

He fell asleep immediately.

At one-thirty in the morning the telephone awakened him.

"Were you asleep? I'm sorry that I woke you up. I only wanted to tell you that the case has been solved. He turned himself in."

"Who?"

"Holm, the neighbor. Her husband. He collapsed, totally. It was jealousy. Funny, isn't it?"

"Whose neighbor? Who are you talking about?"

"The dame in Storängen, naturally. I only wanted to tell you so that you wouldn't lie awake and think about it unnecessarily. . . . Oh, God, have I made a mistake?"

"Yes."

"Damn it, of course. You weren't there. It was Stenström. I'm sorry. I'll see you in the morning."

"Nice of you to call," said Martin Beck.

He went back to bed but he couldn't sleep. He lay there looking at the ceiling and listening to his wife's mild snoring. He felt empty and depressed.

When the sun began to shine into the room he turned over on his side and thought: "Tomorrow I'll telephone Ahlberg."

He called Ahlberg the next day and then four or five times a week during the following month but neither of them had anything special to say. The girl's origins remained a mystery. The newspapers had stopped writing about the case and Hammar had stopped asking how it was going. There was still no report of a missing person that matched in any way. Sometimes it seemed as if she had never existed. Everyone except Martin Beck and Ahlberg seemed to have forgotten that they had ever seen her.

In the beginning of August, Martin Beck took one week's vacation and went out to the archipelago with his family. When he got back he continued to work on the routine jobs which came to his desk. He was depressed and slept poorly.

One night, at the end of August, he lay in his bed and looked out in the dark.

Ahlberg had called rather late that evening. He had been at the City Hotel and sounded a little drunk. They had talked for a while about the murder and before Ahlberg had hung up, he had said: "Whoever he is and wherever he is, we'll get him."

Martin Beck got up and walked barefooted into the living room. He turned on the light over his desk and looked at the model of the training ship *Danmark*. He still had the rigging to finish.

He sat down at the desk and took a folder out of a cubbyhole. Kollberg's description of the girl was in the folder together with copies of the pictures that the police photographer in Motala had taken nearly two months ago. In spite of the fact that he practically knew the description by heart he read it again, slowly and carefully. Then he placed the photographs in front of him and studied them for a long time.

When he put the papers back in the folder and turned off the light, he thought: "Whoever she was, and wherever she came from, I'm going to find out."

7

"Interpol, the devil with them," said Kollberg.

Martin Beck said nothing. Kollberg looked over his shoulder.

"Do those louses write in French too?"

"Yes. This is from the police in Toulouse. They have a missing person."

"French police," said Kollberg. "I made a search with them through Interpol last year. A little gal from Djursholm section. We didn't hear a word for three months and then got a long letter from the police in Paris. I didn't understand a word of it and turned it in to be translated. The next day I read in the newspaper that a Swedish tourist had found her. Found her, hell. She was sitting in that world famous cafe where all the Swedish beatniks sit . . ."

"Le Dôme."

"Yes, that one. She was sitting there with some Arab that she was living with and she had been sitting there every day for nearly six months. That afternoon I got the translation. The letter stated that she hadn't been seen in France for at least three months and absolutely was not there now. In any case, not alive. 'Normal' disappearances were always cleared up within two weeks, they wrote, and in this case, unfortunately, one would have to assume some kind of crime."

Martin Beck folded the letter and placed it in one of his desk drawers.

"What did they write?" asked Kollberg.

"About the girl in Toulouse? The Spanish police found her in Mallorca a week ago."

"Why the devil do they need so many official stamps and so many strange words to say so little."

"You're right," said Martin Beck.

"Anyway, your girl must be Swedish. As everyone thought from the beginning. Strange."

"What's strange?"

"That no one has missed her, whoever she is. I sometimes think about her too."

Kollberg's tone changed gradually.

"It irritates me," he said. "It irritates me a lot. How many blanks have you drawn now?"

"Twenty-seven with this one."

"That's a lot."

"You're right."

"Don't think too much about the mess."

"No."

"Well meant advice is easier to give than to take," thought Martin Beck. He got up and walked over to the window.

"I'd better be getting back to my murderer," said Kollberg. "He just grins and gnashes his teeth. What behavior! First he drinks a bottle of soda water and then he kills his wife and children with an axe. Then he tries to set fire to the house and cuts his throat with a saw. On top of everything else he runs to the police crying and complains about the food. I'm sending him to the nut house this afternoon.

"God, life is strange," he added and slammed the door after him as he left the room.

The trees between the police station and Kristineberg's Hotel had begun to turn and to lose some of their leaves. The sky lay low and gray with trailing rain curtains and storm-torn clouds. It was the twenty-ninth of September and autumn was definitely on the way. Martin Beck looked distastefully at his half-smoked cigarette and thought about his sensitivity to temperature change and of the six months of winter's formidable colds which would soon strike him.

"Poor little friend, whoever you are," he said to himself.

He was conscious of the fact that their chances were reduced each day that passed. Maybe they would never even find out who she was, not to speak of getting the person who was guilty, unless the same man repeated the crime. The woman who had lain out there on the breakwater in the sun at least had a face and a body and a nameless grave. The murderer was nothing, totally without contours, a dim figure, if that. But dim figures have no desires and no sharp pointed weapons. No strangler's hands.

Martin Beck straightened up. "Remember that you have three of the most important virtues a policeman can have," he thought. "You are stubborn and logical, and completely calm. You don't allow yourself to lose your composure and you act only professionally on a case, whatever it is. Words like repulsive, horrible, and bestial belong in the newspapers,

36

not in your thinking. A murderer is a regular human being, only more unfortunate and maladjusted."

He hadn't seen Ahlberg since that last evening at the City Hotel in Motala but they had talked on the telephone often. He had spoken to him last week and he remembered Ahlberg's final comment: "Vacation? Not before this thing is solved. I'll have all the material collected soon but I'm going to continue even if I have to drag all of Boren myself."

These days Ahlberg wasn't much more than merely stubborn, Martin Beck thought.

"Damn, damn, damn," he mumbled and rapped his forehead with his fist.

Then he went back to his desk and sat down, swung his chair a quarter turn to the left and stared listlessly at the paper in the typewriter. He tried to remember what it was he wanted to write before Kollberg had come in with the letter from Interpol.

Six hours later, at two minutes before five he had put on his hat and coat and already begun to hate the crowded subway train to the south. It was still raining and he could already perceive both the musty odor of wet clothing and the frightening feeling of having to stand hemmed in by a compact mass of strange bodies.

One minute before five, Stenström arrived. He opened the door without knocking as usual. It was irritating but endurable in comparison with Melander's woodpecker signals and Kollberg's deafening pounding.

"Here's a message for the department of missing girls. You'd better send a thank you letter to the American Embassy. They sent it up."

He studied the light red telegram sheet.

"Lincoln, Nebraska. What was it the last time?"

"Astoria, New York."

"Was that when they sent three pages of information but forgot to say that she was a Negro?"

"Yes," said Martin Beck.

Stenström gave him the telegram and said:

"Here's the number of some guy at the embassy. You ought to call him."

With guilty pleasure at every excuse to postpone the subway torture, he went back to his desk but it was too late. The embassy staff had gone home.

The next day was a Wednesday and the weather was worse than ever. The morning paper had a late listing of a missing twenty-five year old housemaid from a place called Räng which seemed to be in the south of Sweden. She had not returned after her vacation.

During the morning registered copies of Kollberg's description and the retouched photographs were sent to the police in southern Sweden and to a certain Detective Lieutenant Elmer B. Kafka, Homicide Squad, Lincoln, Nebraska, U.S.A.

After lunch Martin Beck felt that the lymph glands in his neck were beginning to swell and by the time he got home that evening it was hard for him to swallow.

"Tomorrow the National Police can manage without you, I've decided," said his wife.

He opened his mouth to answer her but looked at the children and closed it again without saying anything.

It didn't take her long to take advantage of her triumph.

"Your nose is completely stopped up. You're gasping for breath like a fish out of water."

He put down his knife and fork, mumbled "thanks for dinner," and absorbed himself with his rigging problem. Gradually, this activity calmed him completely. He worked slowly and methodically on the model ship and had no unpleasant thoughts. If he actually heard the noise from the television in the next room, it didn't register. After a while his daughter stood on the threshold with a sullen look and traces of bubblegum on her chin.

"Some guy's on the phone. Wouldn't you know, right in the middle of Perry Mason."

Damn it, he would have to have the telephone moved. Damn it, he would have to start getting involved in his children's upbringing. Damn it, what does one say to a child who is thirteen years old and loves the Beatles and is already developed?

He walked into the living room as if he had to excuse his existence and cast a sheepish look at the great defense lawyer's worn out dogface which filled the television screen. He picked up the telephone and took it out into the hall with him.

"Hi," said Ahlberg. "I think I've found something."

"Yes?"

"Do you remember that we spoke about the canal boats which pass here in the summer at twelve-thirty and at four o'clock during the day?"

"Yes."

"I have tried to check up on the small boats and the

38

freight traffic this week. It's almost impossible to do with all the boats that go by. But an hour ago one of the boys on the regular police staff suddenly said that he saw a passenger boat go past Platen's moat in a westerly direction in the middle of the night sometime last summer. He didn't know when and he hadn't thought about it until now, when I asked him. He had been doing some special duty in that area for several nights. It seems completely unbelievable but he swore that it was true. He went on vacation the next day and after that he forgot about it."

"Did he recognize the boat?"

"No, but wait. I called Gothenburg and spoke to a few men in the shipping office. One of them said that it certainly could be true. He thought the boat was named *Diana* and gave me the captain's address."

A short pause followed. Martin Beck could hear that Ahlberg had struck a match.

"I got hold of the captain. He said he certainly did remember although he would rather have forgotten it. First they had to stop at Hävringe for three hours because of heavy fog and then a steam pipe in the motor had broken. . ."

"Engine."

"What did you say?"

"In the engine. Not the motor."

"Oh yes, but in any case they had to stay over more than eight hours in Söderköping for repairs. That means that they were nearly twelve hours late and passed Borenshult after midnight. They didn't stop either in Motala or Vadstena but went directly on to Gothenburg."

"When did this happen? Which day?"

"The second trip after midsummer, the captain said. In other words, the night before the fifth."

Neither of them said anything for at least ten seconds. Then Ahlberg said:

"Four days before we found her. I called the shipping office guy again and checked out the time. He wondered what it was all about and I asked him if everyone on board had reached Gothenburg in good order. He said, 'Why shouldn't they have,' and I answered that I didn't really know. He must have thought that I was out of my mind."

It was quiet again.

"Do you think it means anything?" Ahlberg said finally.

"I don't know," answered Martin Beck. "Maybe. You've done a fine job in any event."

"If everyone who went on board arrived in Gothenburg, then it doesn't mean very much."

His voice was a strange mixture of disappointment and modest triumph.

"We have to check out all the information," Ahlberg said.

"Naturally."

"So long."

"So long. I'll call you."

Martin Beck remained standing a while with his hand on the telephone. Then he wrinkled his forehead and went through the living room like a sleepwalker. He closed the door behind him carefully and sat down in front of the model ship, lifted his right hand to make an adjustment on the mast, but dropped it immediately.

He sat there for another hour until his wife came in and made him go to bed.

8

"No one could say that you look particularly well," said Kollberg.

Martin Beck felt anything but well. He had a cold, and a sore throat, his ears hurt him and his chest felt miserable. The cold had, according to schedule, entered its worst phase. Even so, he had deliberately defied both the cold and the home front by spending the day in his office. First of all he had fled from the suffocating care which would have enveloped him had he remained in bed. Since the children had begun to grow up, Martin Beck's wife had adopted the role of home nurse with bubbling eagerness and almost manic determination. For her, his repeated bouts of colds and flu were on a par with birthdays and major holidays.

In addition, for some reason he didn't have the conscience to stay home.

"Why are you hanging around here if you aren't well?" said Kollberg.

"There's nothing the matter with me."

"Don't think so much about that case. It isn't the first time we have failed. It won't be the last either. You know that just as well as I do. We won't be any the better or the worse for it."

"It isn't just the case that I'm thinking about."

"Don't brood. It isn't good for the morale."

"The morale?"

"Yes, think what a lot of nonsense one can figure out with plenty of time. Brooding is the mother of ineffectiveness."

After saying this Kollberg left.

It had been an uneventful and dreary day, full of sneezing and spitting and dull routine. He had called Motala twice, mostly to cheer up Ahlberg, who in the light of day, had decided that his discovery wasn't worth very much as long as it couldn't be connected with the corpse at the locks.

"I suspect that it is easy to overestimate certain things when you've been working like a dog for so long without results."

41

Ahlberg had sounded crushed and regretful. It was almost heartbreaking.

The girl who had disappeared from Räng was still missing. That didn't worry him. She was 5 feet, 1 inch tall, had blond hair and a Bardot hair style.

At five o'clock he took a taxi home but got out at the subway station and walked the last bit in order to avoid the devastating economic argument which undoubtedly would have followed if his wife had happened to see him get out of a taxi.

He couldn't eat anything but drank a cup of camomile tea. "For safety's sake, so that he'd get a stomach ache too," Martin Beck thought. Then he went and lay down and fell asleep immediately.

The next morning he felt a little better. He ate a biscuit and drank with stoic calm the cup of scalding hot honey water which his wife had placed in front of him. The discussion about his health and the unreasonable demands that the government placed on its employees dragged on and by the time he arrived at his office at Kristineberg, it was already a quarter after ten.

There was a cable on his desk.

One minute later Martin Beck entered his chief's office without knocking even though the "Don't Disturb" red light was on. This was the first time in eight years he had ever done this.

The ever-present Kollberg and Commissioner Hammar were leaning against the edge of the desk studying a blueprint of an apartment. They both looked at him with amazement.

"I got a cable from Kafka."

"That's a hell of a way to start a work day," said Kollberg.

"That's his name. The detective in Lincoln, in America. He's identified the woman in Motala."

"Can he do that by cable?" asked Hammar.

"It seems so."

He put the cable on the desk. All three of them read the text.

THAT'S OUR GIRL ALL RIGHT. ROSEANNA MCGRAW, 27, LIBRARIAN. EXCHANGE OF FURTHER INFORMATION NECESSARY AS SOON AS POSSIBLE.

KAFKA, HOMICIDE

"Roseanna McGraw," said Hammar. "Librarian. That's one you never thought of."

"I had another theory," said Kollberg. "I thought she was from Mjölby. Where's Lincoln?"

"In Nebraska, someplace in the middle of the country," said Martin Beck. "I think."

Hammar read through the cable one more time.

"We had better get going again then," he said. "This doesn't say particularly much."

"Quite enough for us," said Kollberg. "We aren't spoiled."

"Well," said Hammar calmly. "You and I ought to clear up what we're working on first."

Martin Beck went back to his office, sat down a moment and massaged his hairline with his fingertips. The first surprised feeling of progress had somehow disappeared. It had taken three months to come up with information that in ninety-nine cases out of a hundred you had free from the beginning. All the real work remained to be done.

The embassy people and the County Police Superintendent could wait. He picked up the telephone and dialed the area code for Motala.

"Yes," said Ahlberg.

"She's been identified."

"For sure?"

"It seems so."

Ahlberg said nothing.

"She was an American. From a place called Lincoln in Nebraska. Are you writing it down?"

"Hell, yes."

"Her name was Roseanna McGraw. I'll spell it: R for Rudolf, O for Olof, S for Sigurd, E for Erik, A for Adam, N for Niklas, again N for Niklas, A for Adam. New word: capital M for Martin, C for Cesar, capital G for Gustav, R for Rudolf, A for Adam, W for Wilhelm. Have you got that?"

"Sure I've got it."

"She was twenty-seven years old and a librarian. That's all I know at the moment."

"How did you manage that?"

"Only routine. They began to look for her after a while. Not through Interpol. Via the embassy."

"The boat?" said Ahlberg.

"What did you say?"

"The boat. Where would an American tourist be coming

43

from if not from a boat? Maybe not from my boat but from some pleasure yacht. Quite a few go through here."

"We don't know if she was a tourist."

"That's right. I'll get going immediately. If she knew anyone here or lived in town, I'll know about it in twenty-four hours."

"Fine. I'll call you as soon as I know more."

Martin Beck ended the conversation by sneezing in Ahlberg's ear. By the time he tried to apologize, the other had already hung up.

In spite of his headache and his clogged up ears he felt better than he had for a long time. He felt like a long-distance runner one second before the starting gun. There were only two things that worried him: the murderer had jumped the gun and was three months ahead of him, and he didn't know in which direction to run.

Somewhere under this surface of disquieting perspective and speculations of unknown worth his policeman's brain had already begun to plan the routine searches of the next forty-eight hours, which, he knew in advance, would obtain certain results. This was as sure as the fact that sand will run down in an hour glass.

For three months he hadn't really thought about anything but this. The moment when the investigation would really begin. It had been like trying to get out of a swamp in coal-black darkness and now he was feeling the first solid piece of ground under his feet. The next one would not be as far away.

He wasn't expecting any quick results. If Ahlberg found out that the woman from Lincoln had worked in Motala, or had been visiting friends in the city, or had even been there, he would be more surprised than if the murderer walked through the door and placed the evidence of the murder on his desk.

On the other hand he was waiting for the supplementary material from the U.S.A. without feeling particularly impatient. He thought about all the different statements that would gradually be sent on from the man in America and about Ahlberg's stubborn contention, which was actually totally groundless, that the woman had come by boat. It was more logical to think that the body had been brought down to the water by car.

Immediately afterwards he began thinking about Detective Lieutenant Kafka, how he looked, and if the police station

44

where he worked resembled the ones people saw on television.

He wondered what time it was right now in Lincoln and where the woman had lived. He wondered if her apartment was empty, with white sheets covering the furniture, if the air in it was close and heavy, and filled with dust.

It struck him that his knowledge of the geography of North America was rather poor. He didn't know where Lincoln was at all and the name Nebraska was just another name to him.

After lunch he went to the library and took a look at a world atlas. He soon found Lincoln. The city certainly was inland, in fact as far in the middle of the United States as any city could be. It seemed to be a rather large city but he couldn't find any books containing information on North American cities. With the help of his pocket almanac he studied the time difference and figured it to be seven hours. It was now two-thirty in the afternoon in Stockholm and it was seven-thirty in the morning in Lincoln. Presumably Kafka was still in bed, reading his morning newspaper.

He studied the map for several minutes, then placing his finger on the pin-sized point in the southeast corner of the state of Nebraska, which was nearly one hundred longitude degrees west of Greenwich, he said to himself: "Roseanna McGraw."

He repeated the name several more times almost as if to nail it down in his consciousness.

When he got back to the police station Kollberg was sitting at the typewriter.

The telephone rang before either of them had time to say anything. It was the switchboard.

"The Central Telephone Office has advised us that there is a phone call coming from the United States. It is coming in about thirty minutes. Can you take it?"

Detective Lieutenant Kafka was not lying in bed reading the newspaper! Once again he had drawn too hasty a conclusion.

"From America. Well, I'll be damned," said Kollberg.

The call came after three-quarters of an hour. At first there were only confused noises and then a lot of telephone operators all talking at once, and then a voice came through, amazingly clear and distinct.

"Yeah, Kafka speaking. That you Mr. Beck?"

"Yes."

45

"You got my wire?"

"Yes. Thank you."

"It's all clear, isn't it?"

"Is there not any doubt about that it is the right woman?" asked Martin Beck.

"You sound like a native," said Kollberg.

"Nope, sir, that's Roseanna all right. I got her identified in less than one hour—thanks to your excellent description. I even double-checked it. Gave it to her girlfriend and that ex-boyfriend of hers down in Omaha. Both were quite sure. All the same, I've mailed photographs and some other stuff for you."

"When did she leave home?"

"Beginning of May. Her idea was to spend about two months in Europe. It was her first trip abroad. As far as I know she was traveling alone."

"Do you know anything about her plans?"

"Not very much. In fact no one here does. I can give you one clue. She wrote a postcard from Norway to her girlfriend, saying that she was to stay one week in Sweden, then proceed to Copenhagen."

"Did she not write anything more?"

"Well, she said something about boarding a Swedish ship. For some sort of lake cruise through the country or something like that. That point is not very clear."

Martin Beck held his breath.

"Mr. Beck, are you still there?"

"Yes."

The connection was getting worse rather quickly.

"I understand she was murdered," shouted Kafka. "Did you get the guy?"

"Not yet."

"I can't hear you."

"In a short time, I hope, not yet," said Martin Beck.

"You shot him?"

"I did what? No, no, not shot . . ."

"Yeah, I hear, you shot the bastard," screamed the man on the other side of the Atlantic. "That's great. I'll give that to the papers here."

"You are misunderstanding," Martin Beck roared.

He heard Kafka's final reply like a weak whisper through ethereal noise.

"Yeah, I understand perfectly well. I've got your name all

right. So long. You'll be hearing from me. Well done, Martin."

Martin Beck put down the receiver. He had been standing up during the entire conversation. He was panting and perspiration had broken out all over his face.

"What are you doing?" asked Kollberg. "Do you think that they have speaking-tubes to Nebraska?"

"We couldn't hear very well toward the end. He thought that I had shot the murderer. He said he was going to tell that to the newspapers."

"Great. Tomorrow you'll be the hero of the day over there. The day after, they'll make you an honorary citizen and at Christmas time they'll send you the key to the city. A gilded one. 'Shoot-em-up-Martin, The avenger from south Stockholm.' The boys are going to have a good time with this one."

Martin Beck blew his nose and wiped the perspiration from his face.

"Well, what did he say? Or did he only go on about how clever you are?"

"It was mostly you that was praised. For your description. 'Excellent description,' he said."

"Was he positive of the identification?"

"Yes, definitely. He had checked with her friend and with some sort of former beau."

"What else?"

"She left home in the middle of May. She was to spend two months in Europe. It was her first trip out of the country. She sent a postcard from Norway to her girlfriend and wrote that she would be here for a week and then continue on to Copenhagen. He said that he had mailed some pictures of her and some other things."

"Was that all?"

Martin Beck went over to the window and gazed out. He bit on his thumbnail.

"She wrote on the postcard that she was going to take a boat trip. Some sort of cruise through Sweden on the lakes and inland waterways . . ."

He turned around and looked at his colleague. Kollberg was no longer smiling and the teasing look had left his eyes. After a while he said, very slowly:

"So she did come with the canal boat. Our friend in Motala was right."

"It seems so," said Martin Beck.

47

9

Martin Beck took a deep breath when he came out of the subway station. The trip, with its crowded subway cars, had made him feel slightly ill as usual.

The air was clear and light and a fresh breeze swept in over the city from the Baltic. He crossed the street and bought a pack of cigarettes in a tobacco store. He walked on toward Skepps Bridge and stopped, lit a cigarette and stood with his elbows on the bridge railing. A cruise ship bearing an English flag was anchored at a pier in the distance. He couldn't make out the name but guessed that it was the *Devonia*. A group of seagulls screeched as they fought over some garbage which had been thrown overboard. He stood for a while looking at the ship and then continued on toward the pier.

Two dismal looking men sat on a pile of wood. The first one tried to light a cigarette butt in a wooden holder and when he didn't succeed the other one, whose hands shook less, tried to help him. Martin Beck looked at his wristwatch. Five minutes to nine. "They must be broke," he thought, "otherwise they would be waiting by the door of the liquor store at this time of day."

He passed the *Bore II* which was tied up at the pier loading freight and stood on the curb directly across from the Hotel Reisen. It took a few minutes before he managed to break through the unending line of automobiles and get across the street.

The passenger list for the *Diana*'s trip on July 3 was not in the canal boat's shipping office. It was in the Gothenburg office but they had promised to send it as soon as possible. However, a list of the crew and other personnel was given to him immediately. When he left, he took a few brochures with him which he read on the way back to the office.

Melander was already sitting in his visitor's chair when he arrived.

"Hi there," Martin Beck said.

"Good morning," said Melander.

48

"That pipe smells dreadful. But by all means sit here and poison the air. You are most welcome. Or was there something special you wanted?"

"You don't get cancer as quickly if you smoke a pipe. Your brand of cigarettes are said to be the most dangerous, by the way. At least that's what I've heard. Otherwise, I'm on duty."

"Check with American Express, the Post Office, banks, the telephone company, other contacts, you understand, don't you?"

"I believe so. What was the woman's name again?"

Martin Beck wrote the name on a piece of paper, ROSEANNA MCGRAW, and gave it to Melander.

"How do you pronounce it?"

He left and Martin Beck opened the window. It was chilly and the wind blew through the tree tops and swept up the leaves on the ground. After a while he shut the window again, hung his jacket over the back of his chair and sat down.

He picked up the telephone and dialed the number of the National Office for Aliens. If she had registered at a hotel she ought to be on file there. Some record of her ought to be there in any event. He had to wait a long time before anyone answered and then it took ten minutes before the girl came back to the phone. She had found the card. Roseanna McGraw had stayed at the Hotel Gillet in Stockholm from June 30 until July 2.

"Please send me a photocopy," said Martin Beck.

He pressed down the buttons on the telephone and waited for the disconnected signal with the receiver still in his hand. Then he telephoned for a taxi and put on his jacket. Ten minutes later he got out of the taxi, paid the driver, and entered the hotel through its glass doors.

In front of the reception desk stood a group of six men. They had name tags on their lapels and were all talking at the same time. The desk clerk looked unhappy and threw up his arms in a complaining gesture. It looked as if the discussion would take some time, so Martin Beck sat down in one of the armchairs in the lobby.

He waited until the discussion was over and let the group disappear into the elevator before he went up to the desk.

The desk clerk looked stoically through the register until he found the name. He turned the book toward Martin Beck so that he could read it. She had printed with attractive, even letters. Place of Birth: Denver, Col. USA. Home Address: Lincoln, Nebr. Last Place Visited: Nebr. USA.

Martin Beck checked the guests who had registered on June 30 and the days immediately preceding and following. Above Roseanna McGraw's name were the names of no less than eight Americans. All except the two names on top of the list had given some place in the U.S.A. as their last place visited. The first one had written Phyllis with the rest of the name illegible. She had written North Cape, Sweden, as the last place visited. The person who had registered just beneath her had written North Cape, Norway, in the same column.

"Was it a group tour?" asked Martin Beck.

"Let's see," said the desk clerk and turned his head to look. "No, I don't really remember, but it is very likely. We sometimes have American groups here. They arrive with the 'dollar train' from Narvik."

Martin Beck showed the man a photograph but he shook his head in reply.

"No, I'm sorry, we have so many guests here . . ."

No one had recognized her but the trip to the hotel had some results. Now he knew where she had stayed, he had seen her name in the register and had even looked at the room she had stayed in. She had left the hotel on July 2.

"And then? Where did you go?" he said quietly to himself.

His temples were throbbing and his throat hurt. He wondered how much fever he had, and went back to the office.

She could have traveled with the canal boat and gone on board the night before it left Stockholm. He had read in the brochure from the shipping office that passengers could go on board the night before the boat left. He was more and more convinced that she had been on the *Diana* in spite of the fact that there was still no evidence of it.

He wondered where Melander was and reached for the telephone. Just as he was about to dial the number he heard a distinct pecking at the door.

Melander stood in the doorway.

"No," he said. "Neither American Express nor any other such place knows anything about her. I'll go and get something to eat now if you don't mind."

He had no objection and Melander disappeared.

He telephoned Motala but Ahlberg wasn't in.

His headache was getting worse. After looking for some headache pills for a while he went up to Kollberg's office to borrow a few. Just inside the door he started coughing so badly that he couldn't say anything for a long time.

Kollberg cocked his head and looked at him worriedly.

"You sound worse than eighteen Ladies of the Camelias. Come here and let the doctor look at you."

He looked at Martin Beck through his magnifying glass.

"If you don't listen to the doctor you won't have much time left. Go home and creep into bed and drink a real large glass of toddy. Preferably three of them. Rum toddies. That's the only thing that will help. Then go to sleep and you'll wake up like new."

"What do you think it is? And, by the way, I don't like rum," said Martin Beck.

"Take cognac then. Don't worry about Kafka. If he calls, I'll take care of him. My English is excellent."

"He won't call. Do you have any headache pills?"

"No, but you can have a chocolate praline."

Martin Beck returned to his office. The air in the room was thick and smoky but he didn't want to open the window and let the cold air in.

Ahlberg still wasn't there when he telephoned a half hour later. He took out the list of the *Diana*'s crew. It contained eighteen names and addresses from different parts of the country. Six of them were in Stockholm and there were two names without an address. Two of them lived in Motala.

At four-thirty he decided to take Kollberg's advice. He cleaned off his desk and put his hat and coat on.

On the way home he stopped at a pharmacy and bought a box of pills.

He found a drop of cognac in the pantry, poured it into a cup of bouillon, and took the cup with him into the bedroom. By the time his wife had come in with a heat lamp he was already asleep.

He awoke early the next morning but stayed in bed until a quarter to eight. Then he got up and got dressed. He felt a great deal better and his headache had disappeared.

On the dot of nine he opened the door to his office. An envelope with a red special delivery sticker lay on his desk. He opened it up with his index finger without taking the time to take off his overcoat.

The envelope contained a passenger list.

His eyes caught her name immediately.

McGraw, R., Miss, USA: Single cabin A 7.

51

10

"I knew that I was right," Ahlberg said. "I had a feeling. How many passengers were there on the boat?"

"According to the list there were sixty-eight," said Martin Beck and filled in the number on the paper in front of him with a pen.

"Are their addresses listed?"

"No, only nationalities. It's going to be one hell of a job to find all these people. We can cross off some of them, of course. Children and old women, for example. Then too, we have the crew and other personnel to get hold of. That makes eighteen more but I have their addresses."

"You said that Kafka thought that she was traveling alone. What do you think?"

"It doesn't seem as if she was with anyone. She had a single cabin. According to the deck plan it was the one farthest back toward the stern on the middle deck."

"I must admit that it doesn't tell me very much," said Ahlberg. "In spite of the fact that I see that boat several times a week every summer I don't really know what it looks like. I've never been on board any of them. All three seem alike to me."

"Actually, they are not really alike. I think we ought to try and get a look at the *Diana*. I'll find out where she is," said Martin Beck.

He told Ahlberg about his visit to the Hotel Gillet, gave him the address of the pilot and chief engineer both of whom lived in Motala, and promised to call again when he found out where the *Diana* was now.

After he had finished the conversation with Ahlberg, he went into his chief's office with the passenger list.

Hammar congratulated him on the progress and asked him to go and have a look at the boat as soon as possible. Kollberg and Melander would have to worry about the passenger list for the time being.

Melander didn't seem very enthusiastic about the task of locating the addresses of sixty-seven unknown people spread out over the entire globe. He sat in Martin Beck's office with a copy of the passenger list in his hand and made a fast tabulation:

"Fifteen Swedes, of which five are named Andersson, three named Johansson, and three named Petersson. That sounds promising! Twenty-one Americans, minus one, of course. Twelve Germans, four Danes, four Englishmen, one Scot, two Frenchmen, two South Africans—we can look for them with tom-tom drums—five Dutchmen and two Turks."

He tapped his pipe against the wastepaper basket and put the list into his pocket.

"Turks. On the Göta Canal," he mumbled and left the room.

Martin Beck telephoned the canal boat office. The *Diana* was at Bohus for the winter, a community on the Göta River about twelve miles from Gothenburg. A man from the Gothenburg office would meet them there and show them the boat.

He called Ahlberg and informed him that he would take the afternoon train to Motala. They agreed that they would leave Motala at seven o'clock the following morning in order to be in Bohus around ten o'clock.

For once he missed the rush hour going home and the subway car was almost empty.

His wife had begun to understand how important this case was to him and only ventured a mild protest when he told her that he was leaving. She packed his suitcase in sullen silence but Martin Beck pretended not to notice her demonstrable sulkiness. He kissed her absentmindedly on the cheek and left home a full hour before train time.

"I didn't bother to reserve a room for you at the hotel," said Ahlberg, who was waiting with his car in front of the railroad station in Motala. "We have a formidable sofa you can sleep on."

They sat up late and talked that evening and when the alarm clock rang the next morning they felt anything but rested. Ahlberg telephoned S.K.A.* and they promised to send two men to Bohus. Then they went down to the car.

The morning was cold and gray and after they had driven a while it began to rain lightly.

---

* Statens Kriminal Teknista Anstalt—the federal criminal technical bureau.

"Did you get hold of the pilot and the chief engineer?" Martin Beck asked, when they had left the city behind them.

"Only the chief engineer," said Ahlberg. "He was a tough guy. I had to drag every word out of him. In any case he had very little to do with the passengers. And on this particular trip he was obviously fully occupied due to the trouble with the motor ... sorry, the engine. He was in a bad mood the minute I mentioned that trip. But he said that there had been two boys helping him and that as far as he knew, they had signed on a boat which was going to England and Germany right after the *Diana*'s last trip."

"Oh, well." Martin Beck replied. "We'll get hold of them. We'll have to go through all the shipping company lists."

The rain increased and by the time they reached Bohus the water was pouring over the windshield. They didn't see very much of the town because the heavy rain blocked their view but it looked rather small with a few factories and a large building which stretched out along the river. They found their way to the edge of the river and after they had driven slowly for a while, they caught sight of the boats. They looked deserted and spooky and the men couldn't make out the names of the boats until they were almost on top of the pier.

They remained in the car and watched for the man from the shipping office. There was no one in sight but another car was parked not too far from them. When they drove over to it, they saw a man sitting behind the wheel, looking in their direction.

They pulled up and parked their car next to the other one. The man rolled down his side window and shouted something. Through the noise of the rain they could make out their names and Martin Beck nodded 'yes' while he opened his window.

The man introduced himself and suggested that they go on board immediately in spite of the heavy rain.

He was short and heavy and when he hurried off ahead of them toward the *Diana,* he almost seemed to be rolling forward. With a certain amount of trouble, he got over the railing and waited while Martin Beck and Ahlberg climbed after him.

The little man unlocked a door on the starboard side and they walked into some kind of a coatroom. On the other side there was a similar door which led out to the port promenade deck.

54

On the right there were two glass doors leading into the dining room and between the doors was a large mirror. Directly in front of the mirror a flight of stairs led to a lower deck. They followed them and then went down still another flight of stairs which led to four large cabins and a large lounge with lace-covered sofas. The little man showed them how the sofas could be hidden by a curtain.

"When we have deck passengers they can usually sleep here," he said.

The climbed back up the stairs to the next deck where there were cabins for passengers and crew, toilets and bathrooms. The dining room was on the middle deck. There were six round tables which could each accommodate six persons, a buffet toward the stern, a reading and writing room where one could look out through a large window, and a small serving room, with a dumbwaiter, leading to the galley below.

When they went out on the promenade deck again the rain had nearly stopped. They walked toward the stern. On the starboard side there were three doors, the first one led to the serving room and the other two to cabins. On the other side there was a ladder going to the upper deck and on up to the bridge. Next to the ladder was Roseanna McGraw's cabin.

The door to that cabin opened directly toward the stern. The cabin was small, no more than twelve feet long, and lacked ventilation. The back rest on the bed could be lifted up and turned into a top bunk. There was also a wash basin with a mahogany cover which, when down, provided some counter space. On the bulkhead over the wash basin was a mirror with a holder for a glass and toilet articles. The cabin floor was covered with a rug which was tacked down and there was a place for luggage under the bunk. At the end of the bed there was an empty space with some clothing hooks on the bulkhead.

There was hardly room for three people in there which was soon obvious to the man from the shipping office. He went out and sat on a box containing life jackets and looked anxiously at his soaking wet shoes which dangled a good bit above the deck.

Martin Beck and Ahlberg examined the small cabin. They hadn't hoped to find any traces of Roseanna since they knew that the cabin had been cleaned a good number of times since she had occupied it. Ahlberg lay down on the bed

55

carefully and stated that there was hardly enough room in it for an adult person.

They left the cabin door open and went out and sat down beside the man on the life jacket box.

After they had been sitting quietly for a while, looking into the cabin, a large, black car drove up. It was the men from the S.K.A. They carried a large, black case between them and it didn't take long before they had begun to work.

Ahlberg poked Martin Beck in the ribs and nodded his head toward the ladder. They climbed up to the upper deck. There were two lifeboats there, one on each side of the smokestack, and several large containers for deck chairs and blankets, but otherwise the deck was quite empty. Up on the bridge deck were two passenger cabins, a storeroom, and the captain's cabin which was behind the pilot room.

At the foot of the ladder Martin Beck stopped and took out the deck plans which he had received from the canal boat office. Following this, they went through the boat one more time. When they returned to the stern of the middle deck, the little man was still sitting on the box, looking sorrowfully at the men from the S.K.A. who were on their knees in the cabin pulling tacks out of the rug.

It was two o'clock by the time the large, black police car drove off toward the Gothenburg road with a shower of mud spraying from its wheels. The technicians had taken everything that was loose in the cabin with them, although it wasn't very much. They didn't think it would take long for them to have the results of their analysis finished.

Martin Beck and Ahlberg thanked the man from the shipping office and he shook their hands with exaggerated enthusiasm, clearly grateful to be finally getting away from there.

When his car had disappeared round the first bend in the road, Ahlberg said: "I am tired and rather hungry. Let's drive down to Gothenburg and spend the night there. Okay?"

About a half hour later they parked outside of a hotel on Post Street. They took single rooms, rested for an hour, and then went out to eat dinner.

While they were eating Martin Beck talked about boats and Ahlberg talked about a trip he had taken to the Faroe Islands.

Neither of them mentioned Roseanna McGraw.

11

To get from Gothenburg to Motala one takes Route 40 eastward via Borås and Ulricehamn to Jönköping. There, one turns northward onto the European Route 3 and continues on to Ödeshög, and follows Route 50 from there past Tåkern and Vadstena into Motala. It is a distance of approximately 165 miles and on this particular morning it took Ahlberg only about three and a half hours to cover it.

They had started at five-thirty in the morning, just at daybreak, while the garbage trucks were loading and newspaper women and one or two policemen were the only people to be seen on the rain-cleaned streets. A good many flat, gray miles disappeared behind the car before Ahlberg and Martin Beck broke the silence. After they had passed Hindås, Ahlberg cleared his throat and said:

"Do you really think it happened there? Inside that crowded cabin?"

"Where else?"

"With other people only a few inches away, behind the wall in the next cabin?"

"Bulkhead."

"What did you say?"

"Behind the bulkhead, not the wall."

"Oh," said Ahlberg.

Six miles later Martin Beck said:

"With others so close by, he would have to keep her from screaming."

"But how could he stop her? He must have ... been at it rather long?"

Martin Beck did not answer. Each of them was thinking about the small cabin with its few Spartan conveniences. Neither of them could keep their imagination from entering the picture. Both of them were experiencing the same feeling of helpless, creeping unpleasantness. They reached in their pockets for cigarettes and smoked in silence.

When they drove into Ulricehamn, he said: "She could have received some of the injuries after she was already dead, or at least, unconscious. There are things in the autopsy statement that suggest it could have happened that way."

Ahlberg nodded. Without having to talk about it they both knew that such a thought made them feel better.

In Jönköping they stopped at a cafeteria and got some coffee. It didn't sit well with Martin Beck as usual, but at the same time it perked him up a little.

At Gränna, Ahlberg said what they had both been thinking for the last few hours:

"We don't know her."

"No," replied Martin Beck without taking his eyes from the hazy but pretty view.

"We don't know who she was. I mean . . ."

He was silent.

"I know what you mean."

"You do, don't you? How she lived. How she acted. What kind of people she went around with. That kind of thing."

"Yes."

All that was true. The woman on the breakwater had received a name, an address and an occupation. But nothing more. . . .

"Do you think that the technical boys will find something?"

"We can always hope."

Ahlberg gave him a quick look. No, they didn't need fancy phrases. The only thing they could conceivably hope for from the technical report was that it would, at least, not contradict their assumption that cabin A 7 was the scene of the crime. The *Diana* had made twenty-four trips on the canal since the woman from Lincoln had been on board. That would mean that the cabin had been well cleaned at least as many times; that the bedclothes, towels and other paraphernalia which had been there had been washed over and over again and were hopelessly mixed together by now. It also meant that between thirty and forty people had occupied the cabin after Roseanna McGraw. All of them had naturally left their traces.

"We still haven't heard the records of witnesses' examinations," said Ahlberg.

"Yes."

Eighty-five people, one of whom was presumably guilty, and the rest of whom were possible witnesses, each had their small pieces that might fit into the great jig-saw puzzle. Eighty-five people, spread over four different continents. Just

58

to locate them was a Herculean task. He didn't dare think about the process of getting testimony from all of them and collecting the reports and going through them.

"And Roseanna McGraw," said Ahlberg.

"Yes," said Martin Beck.

And after a while:

"I can only see one way."

"The guy in America?"

"Yes."

"What's his name?"

"Kafka."

"That's a strange name. Does he seem competent?"

Martin Beck thought about the absurd telephone conversation a few days earlier and produced the first smile of that dismal day.

"Hard to say," he replied.

Halfway between Vadstena and Motala Martin Beck said, more or less to himself:

"Suitcases. Clothing. Toilet articles, the toothbrush. Souvenirs she had bought. Her passport, money, traveler's checks."

Ahlberg's hands gripped the wheel harder.

"I'll comb the canal carefully," he said. "First between Borenshult and the harbor. Then east of Boren. The locks have already been covered, but . . ."

"Lake Vättern?"

"Yes. We have almost no chance there and maybe not even in Boren if the dredger has buried everything there by now. Sometimes I dream about that damned apparatus and wake up in the middle of the night swearing. My wife thinks that I've gone mad. Poor thing," he said and drove to a stop in front of the police station.

Martin Beck looked at him with a quick, passing feeling of envy, disbelief, and respect.

Ten minutes later Ahlberg was sitting at his desk in his shirtsleeves as usual, talking to the lab. While he was talking, Larsson entered the room, shook hands with Martin Beck and raised his eyebrow questioningly. Ahlberg hung up the receiver.

"There were some traces of blood on the mattress and the rug. Fourteen counting carefully. They are analyzing them."

If these traces of blood had not been found, the theory of cabin number A 7 as the scene of the crime would not have been likely.

The Superintendent didn't seem to notice their relief. Their wordless communication was carried on wave-lengths that were unfamiliar to him. He raised his eyebrow again and said: "Was that all?"

"A few old fingerprints," said Ahlberg. "Not particularly many. They must have cleaned pretty well."

"The Public Prosecutor is on his way here," said Larsson.

"He's most welcome, of course," Ahlberg responded.

Martin Beck left on a 5:20 p.m. train via Mjölby. The trip took four and a half hours and he worked on a letter to America the entire time. When he got to Stockholm, the draft was finished. He wasn't completely satisfied with it but it would have to do. To save time he took a taxi to Nikolai Station, borrowed an examining room, and typed up the letter. While he was reading the finished copy, he heard brawling and swearing nearby and heard a constable say: "Take it easy, boys, take it easy."

For the first time in a long while he remembered his own days as a patrolman and how deeply he had disliked the results of Saturday nights.

At a quarter of eleven he stood in front of the mailbox on Vasa Street. The metal top closed with a bang.

He walked southward in the light rain, past the Hotel Continental and the new, tall department stores. On the escalator down to the subway, he thought about Kafka and wondered if this man, whom he didn't know, would understand what he meant.

Martin Beck was tired and fell asleep soon after he got into the subway, safe in the knowledge that he wouldn't be getting off before the end of the line.

12

Ten days later Martin Beck received a reply from America. He saw it on his desk when he arrived in the morning, even before he had shut the door behind him. While he hung up his coat he glanced at his face in the mirror. He was pale and looked sallow and he had dark circles under his eyes. This was no longer due to the flu but to the fact that he had gone without much sleep. He tore open the large brown envelope and took out two transcripts of examinations, a typewritten letter and a card with biographical data. He thumbed through the papers with curiosity but thwarted his impulse to begin reading them immediately. Instead, he went in to the administrative office and asked for a rapid translation with three copies.

Afterwards he walked up one flight of stairs, opened a door, and walked into Kollberg's and Melander's office. They sat at their desks working, with their backs to one another.

"Have you changed the furniture?"

"It's the only way we can manage," said Kollberg.

He was pale and red-eyed just like Martin Beck. The imperturbable Melander looked no different than usual.

A copy of a report on thin, yellow paper lay in front of Kollberg. He was following each line with his index finger and said:

"Mrs. Lise-Lotte Jensen, sixty-one years old, has told the police in Vejle, Denmark, that it was a wonderful trip. That the smörgåsbord was wonderful, that it rained one whole day and one whole night and that the boat was delayed and that she was seasick the night it rained out in the lake, which was the second night. In spite of all that, the trip was wonderful and all the other passengers were *so* nice. She can't remember the nice girl in the picture. In any case they didn't sit at the same table. But the captain was charming and her husband said that it wasn't possible to eat all that good food so it certainly could have been possible that not everyone went to all the meals. The weather was wonderful except when it rained. They had no idea that Sweden could be so nice! Damn it, I had no idea it could be either," continued Kollberg. "They mostly played bridge with that charming gentleman from South Africa and his wife, Mrs. Hoyt, who came from Durban. Of course the cabins were rather small and the second night—here's something—there was a big, hairy arachnida on the bed. Her husband had a great deal of trouble getting it out of the cabin. Well, does arachnida mean a sex maniac?"

"A spider," said Melander without taking his pipe out of his mouth.

"I love the Danes," Kollberg continued. "They have neither seen nor heard anything unusual and, 'finally,' writes the policeman named Toft in Vejle who conducted the examination, 'there is obviously nothing in the testimony of this delightful, elderly couple which can spread any light on the case.' His art of deduction is crushing."

"Let's see, let's see," Melander grumbled to himself.

"Here's to our Danish brothers," said Kollberg.

Martin Beck leaned over the desk and leafed through the papers. He mumbled something which was inaudible. After ten days of work they had managed to locate two-thirds of the people who had been on board the *Diana*. By one means or another they had contacted more than forty persons and in twenty-three cases, they had regular examination transcripts at their disposal. The results were meager. Of those who had thus far been examined there was no one who could remember anything about Roseanna McGraw other than that they thought they had seen her on board some time during the trip.

Melander took his pipe out of his mouth and said: "Karl-Ake Eriksson, one of the crew. Have we found him?"

Kollberg checked one of his lists.

"A stoker. No, but we know a little about him. He shipped out from the Seamen's House in Gothenburg three weeks ago. On a Finnish freighter."

"Uhum," said Melander. "And he is twenty-two years old?"

"Yes, and what do you mean with that uhum?"

"His name reminded me of something. You ought to remember it too. But he didn't call himself by the same name then."

"Whatever you remember must certainly be right," said Kollberg with resignation.

"That devil has a memory like a circus elephant," he said to Martin Beck. "It's like sharing an office with a computer."

"I know."

"One who smokes the world's worst tobacco," said Kollberg.

"I'll have it in a minute," said Melander.

"Sure, I know. Damn it I'm tired," answered Kollberg.

"You don't get enough sleep," said Melander.

"Yes."

"You ought to see to it that you get plenty of sleep. I sleep eight hours every night. Fall asleep the minute I put my head on the pillow."

"What does your wife say about that?"

"Nothing. She goes to sleep even faster. Sometimes we don't even get to turn out the light."

"Nonsense. No, in any case, I don't get enough sleep these days."

"Why not?"

"I don't know. I just can't sleep."

"What do you do then?"

"Just lie there and think about how dreadful you are."

Kollberg grabbed his letter basket. Melander knocked the ashes out of his pipe and gazed at the ceiling. Martin Beck, who knew him, realized that he had just fed new material into that priceless memory where he stored everything he had ever seen, read, or heard.

A half hour after lunch one of the girls from the administrative office came in with the translations.

Martin Beck took off his jacket, locked his door and began to read.

First the letter. It read:

Dear Martin:

I think I understand what you mean. The transcripts of examinations which I am enclosing have been typed directly from the tapes. I haven't made any changes or shortened them in any way. You can judge the material for yourself. If you would like me to, I can dig up a few more people who knew her but I think that these two are the best. I hope to God that you get the devil that did it. If you get the guy, don't forget to give it to him for me too. I am enclosing a collection of all the biographical data I could get hold of and a commentary on the transcripts.

Sincerely,
Elmer

He laid the letter aside and took out the transcripts. The first one contained the heading:

"Examination of Edgar M. Mulvaney at the office of the District Attorney, Omaha, Nebraska, October 11, 1964. Examining Officer: Detective Lieutenant Kafka. Witness to the Examination: Sergeant Romney.

KAFKA: You are Edgar Moncure Mulvaney, thirty-three years old, living at 12 East Street here in town. You are an engineer and have been employed for one year as an Assistant Department Head at the Northern Electric Company in Omaha. Is that correct?

MULVANEY: Yes, that's right.

K: You are not under oath and your testimony will not be registered with a notary public. Some of the questions that I am going to ask you have to do with intimate details of your private life and you may find them unpleasant. You are being examined for information and none of the things that you say will be made public or will be used against you. I cannot force you to answer but I want to state the following: by answering all the questions fully and truthfully and as explicitly as possible, you can make a contribution which will help to see that the person or persons responsible for the murder of Roseanna McGraw are captured and punished.

M: I'll do my best.

K: You were living in Lincoln until eleven months ago. You also worked there.

M: Yes, as an engineer with the Department of Public Works, the section that took care of street lighting.

K: Where did you live?

M: In a building at 83 Greenrock Road. I shared an apartment with a colleague. We were both bachelors then.

K: When did you get to know Roseanna McGraw?

M: It was nearly two years ago.

K: In other words the autumn of 1962?

M: Yes, in November.

K: Under what circumstances did you meet?

M: We met at the house of one of my colleagues, Johnny Matson.

K: At a party?

M: Yes.

K: Did that Matson go around with Roseanna McGraw?

M: Hardly. It was an open house party where a lot of people came and went. Johnny knew her slightly from the library where she worked. He had invited all kinds of people. Lord knows where he got hold of all of them.

K: How did you meet Roseanna McGraw?

M: I don't know. We simply met there.

K: Had you gone to the party specifically looking for female company?

   (Pause)

K: Will you kindly answer the question.

M: I'm trying to remember. It's possible. I didn't have a particular girl I was going with at that time. But more likely I went there because I didn't have anything better to do.

K: And what happened?

M: Roseanna and I met by sheer chance, so to speak. We talked for a while. Then we danced.

K: How many dances?

M: The first two. The party had hardly begun.

K: Then you met right away?

M: Yes, we must have.

K: And?

M: I suggested that we leave.

K: After only two dances?

M: More exactly, during the second dance.

K: And what did Miss McGraw answer?

M: She said: 'Yes, let's go.'

K: Without any other comment?

M: Yes.

K: How did you presume to make such a suggestion?

M: Do I have to answer questions like that?

K: If you don't, this conversation is meaningless.

M: Okay, I noticed that she was getting excited while we were dancing.

K: Excited? In what way? Sexually?

M: Yes, naturally.

K: How did you know?

M: I can't (pause) exactly explain. In any case it was obvious. It was her behavior. I can't really be more precise.

K: And you? Were you sexually excited?

M: Yes.

K: Had you had anything to drink?

M: One martini, at most.

K: And Miss McGraw?

M: Roseanna never drank liquor.

K: So you left the party together? What happened then?

M: Neither of us had driven there. We took a taxi to the house that she was living in, 116 Second Street. She still lives there. Lived, I mean.

K: She let you go with her—just like that?

M: Oh, we made some conversation. The usual stuff, you know. I don't remember the words. Actually, they seemed to bore her.

K: Did you get close to one another in the taxi?

M: We kissed.

K: Did she object?

M: Not at all. Anyway, I said we kissed.

   (Pause)

K: Who paid the taxi driver?

M: Roseanna. I didn't have time to stop her.

K: And then?

M: We went into the apartment. It was very nice. I remember that I was surprised. She had a lot of books.

K: What did you do?

M: Aw . . .

K: Did you have intercourse?

M: Yes.

K: When?

M: Almost immediately.

K: Will you please give an account, as carefully as possible, of what happened.

M: Say, what the hell are you doing? Is this some kind of private Kinsey Report?

K: I'm sorry. I want to remind you of what I said at the beginning of our conversation. This can be important.

   (Pause)

K: Are you having difficulty remembering?

M: God, no.

   (Pause)

M: It feels strange to sit here and talk about a person who hasn't done any harm and who is dead anyway.

K: I understand your feelings. If I keep on insisting it's only because we need your help.

M: Okay, ask.

K: You came into the apartment together. What happened?

M: She took off her shoes.

66

K: And then?

M: We kissed.

K: And then?

M: She went into the bedroom.

K: And you?

M: I followed her. Do you want the details?

K: Yes.

M: She undressed and lay down.

K: On the bed?

M: No, *in* the bed. Under the sheets and blankets.

K: Was she totally undressed?

M: Yes.

K: Did she seem shy?

M: Not at all.

K: Did she turn out the lights?

M: No.

K: And you?

M: What do you think?

K: Did you have sexual intercourse then?

M: What in hell do you think we did? Crack nuts? Yes, I'm sorry but . . .

K: How long did you stay?

M: I don't know exactly, until one or two. Then I went home.

K: And this was the first time you saw Miss McGraw?

M: Yes, it was the first time.

K: What did you think of her when you left there? And the next day?

(Pause)

M: I thought . . . first I thought that she was just an ordinary, cheap tramp although she had not given that impression at all in the beginning. Then I thought that she was a nymphomaniac. One idea was crazier than the other. Now, here, especially since she is dead, it seems absurd that I ever could have thought either of those things.

(Pause)

K: Listen to me, my friend. I assure you that it is just as painful for me to ask these questions as it is for you to answer them. I would never have done this if there hadn't been a purpose. The worst part of it is that we are not through yet. Not by a longshot.

M: I'm sorry that I got upset just now. It's just that I'm not accustomed to the situation and the surroundings. It seems so crazy to sit here and say things about Roseanna, things I

have never said to anyone, with detectives running around
outside the room and while the tape recorder turns and turns
and the sergeant just sits over there and stares. Unfortunately, I'm not exactly a cynic, particularly when it has to do
with ...
K: Jack, close the Venetian blinds over there. Then wait
outside.
   (Pause)
ROMNEY: Goodbye.
M: I'm sorry.
K: You have nothing to be sorry about. What actually
happened between you and Miss McGraw? After your first
meeting?
M: I telephoned her two days later. She didn't want to see
me then, she said so quite directly. But she said to call again
if I wanted to. The next time I called her—it must have been
about a week later—she invited me up.
K: And you ...
M: Yes, we slept together. Then it continued like that.
Sometimes once a week, sometimes twice. We always met at
her apartment. Often on Saturdays, then we were together on
Sundays if we were both free.
K: How long did this go on?
M: For eight months.
K: Why did it break up?
M: I fell in love with her.
K: I'm afraid that I don't really understand.
M: Actually it's quite simple. To tell the truth I had been
in love with her for a long time. I really loved her. But we
never talked about love, so I said nothing.
K: Why not?
M: Because I wanted to hold her. Then when I told her ...
Well, then it was all over.
K: How did it happen?
M: You have to understand that Roseanna was the most
upright person I have ever met. She liked me a lot and above
all, she liked to sleep with me. But she didn't want to live
with me. She never made any secret of that. Both she and I
knew precisely why we would meet.
K: How did she react when you told her that you loved
her?
M: She was sad. Then she said: 'We'll sleep together one
more time and tomorrow you'll leave here and that's the end.
We are not going to hurt one another.'

K: Did you accept that?

M: Yes. If you had known her as well as I had you would have understood that there wasn't anything else to do.

K: When did this happen?

M: On July 3 last year.

K: And that was the end of all contact between you?

M: Yes.

K: Did she see other men during the period you were going together?

M: Yes and no.

K: In other words, did you have the impression that she was together with other men from time to time?

M: It wasn't a question of impressions. I know. In March I attended a four-week course in Philadelphia. Even before I left, she told me that I couldn't count on her being ... faithful for such a long time. When I came back I asked her and she said that she had done it once, after three weeks.

K: Had sexual intercourse?

M: Yes. Boy, that's a hell of an expression. I asked her with whom, stupidly enough.

K: What did she answer?

M: That it was none of my business. And it wasn't either, especially from her point of view.

K: During the eight months that you saw her did you have intimate ... sleep together regularly? Do I understand you correctly?

M: Yes.

K: But what about the evenings and nights that you weren't together? What did she do then?

M: She was alone. She liked being alone. She read a great deal and, anyway, she sometimes worked evenings. She wrote some, too, but I don't know what. She never mentioned it to me. You understand, Roseanna was very independent. Then too, we really didn't have the same interests. Except for one thing. But we got along well together and that's the truth.

K: How can you be sure that she was alone when you weren't there?

M: I ... I was jealous sometimes. Once in a while when she wouldn't see me I went there and stood outside her apartment house watching. Twice I even stood there from the time she came home until the time that she left in the morning.

K: Did you give her money?

M: Never.

69

K: Why not?

M: She didn't need my money, she told me so from the very beginning. If and when we went out, she always paid for herself.

K: And when you stopped seeing each other? What did she do then?

M: I don't know. I never saw her again. It wasn't too long before I got a new job and moved here.

K: How would you describe her character?

M: She was very independent, as I said earlier. Honest. Completely natural, in every way. For example, she never wore make-up or jewelry. She seemed calm and relaxed for the most part, but once she said that she didn't want to see me too often because she knew that if she did I would get on her nerves. She said everyone did and that in our case it was unnecessary.

K: I am going to ask you some rather intimate questions now.

M: Go ahead. I'll answer anything now.

K: Have you any idea of how many times you were together?

M: Yes. Forty-eight times.

K: Are you sure? Exactly?

M: Yes. I can even tell you why. Every time we met and slept together I drew a small, red ring around the date on my office calendar. Just before I threw it away I counted the days.

K: Would you say that her sexual behavior patterns were normal?

M: She was very sexual.

K: Had you had enough experience to judge that?

M: I was thirty-one years old when we met. A certain amount had happened before that time.

K: Did she usually have an orgasm when you had sexual intercourse?

M: Yes, always.

K: Did you usually have intercourse several times in an evening?

M: No. Never. It wasn't necessary.

K: Did you use contraceptives?

M: Roseanna had some kind of pills. She took one every morning.

K: Did you usually discuss sexual matters?

M: No, never. We knew what we needed to know.

K: Did she often speak about her previous affairs?

M: Never.

K: And you?

M: Only once. She seemed totally uninterested and I never talked about it again.

K: What did you speak about?

M: Anything and everything. Mostly everyday things.

K: Whom did she see, other than you?

M: No one. She had a friend, a girl at the library, but they rarely saw one another outside of work. Roseanna liked to be alone, as I said.

K: But she went to that party where you met?

M: Yes, in order to meet someone to sleep with. She had been . . . abstaining for a long time then.

K: How long?

M: For more than six weeks.

K: How do you know that?

M: She said so.

K: Was she difficult to satisfy?

M: Not for me, in any case.

K: Was she demanding?

M: She wanted what all normal women want. That a man would take her until she didn't have anything left, if I understand you correctly.

K: Did she have any particular habits?

M: In bed?

K: Yes.

M: Harrison's Law isn't valid in Nebraska, is it?

K: No, you don't have to worry about that.

M: It doesn't really matter. She had only one habit which could possibly be called special. She scratched.

K: When?

M: Generally speaking, all the time. Especially when she had an orgasm.

K: How?

M: How?

K: Yes, how did she scratch?

M: I understand. Well, with both hands and all her fingers. Like a claw. From the hips, over the back and all the way up to the neck. I still have marks. It looks like they'll never go away.

K: Did she show much variety in her sexual exertions?

M: What unbelievable expressions you use! No, not at all. She always lay in the same way. On her back with a pillow

71

under her hips and her legs spread wide apart and raised high. She was completely natural and direct and open in this as in everything else. She wanted to do it, she wanted a lot and at one time, without digression or deviations and in the only way that was natural for her.

K: I understand.

M: You ought to understand at this point.

(Pause)

K: Just one more thing. From what you've said I have the impression that during your time together it was you who took the initiative, that it was always you who contacted her. You telephoned and she answered, either that you should come up, or that she didn't care to see you then and that you should call another day. It was always she who decided if and when you would meet?

M: I believe so.

K: Did she ever call you and ask you to come over?

M: Yes, four or five times.

(Pause)

K: Was it hard for you when you broke up?

M: Yes.

K: You have been very helpful. And very honest. Thank you.

M: I hope you understand that this conversation must be confidential. I met a girl here last Christmas and we got married in February.

K: Naturally. I said that in the beginning.

M: Okay, now maybe you can turn off the tape recorder.

K: Of course."

Martin Beck put down the bound report and thoughtfully dried the perspiration from his forehead and palms with a crumpled handkerchief. Before he began to read again he went out to the toilet, washed his face and drank a glass of water.

13

The second report from Kafka was not as long as the first. It also had a rather different tone.

"Examination of Mary Jane Peterson held at Police Headquarters, Lincoln, Nebraska, October 10, 1964. Examining Officer: Detective Lieutenant Kafka. Witness to the Examination: Sergeant Romney.

ROMNEY: This is Mary Jane Peterson. She is single, twenty-eight years old, and lives at 62 South Street. Employed at the Community Library here in Lincoln.

KAFKA: Have a seat, Miss Peterson.

PETERSON: Thank you. What's this all about?

K: Just a few questions.

P: About Roseanna McGraw?

K: That's right.

P: I don't know any more than what I've already said. I received a postcard from her. That's all. Have you brought me here from my work just to hear me say it again?

K: Were you and Miss McGraw friends?

P: Yes, of course.

K: Did you live together before Miss McGraw took her own apartment?

P: Yes, for fourteen months. She came here from Denver and had no place to go. I let her live with me.

K: Did you share the expenses for the apartment?

P: Naturally.

K: When did you separate?

P: More than two years ago. It was sometime during the spring of 1962.

K: But you continued to see one another?

P: We met every day at the library.

K: Did you also see each other in the evening?

P: Not very often. We saw enough of each other during working hours.

K: What did you think of Miss McGraw's character?

73

P: *De mortuis nihil nisi bene.*

K: Jack, take over here. I'll be right back.

R: Lieutenant Kafka asked you what you thought of Miss McGraw's character?

P: I heard him and I answered: *De mortuis nihil nisi bene.* That's Latin and means 'One shouldn't speak ill of the dead.'

R: The question was this: what was her character like?

P: You can ask someone else about that. May I go now?

R: Just try and you'll see.

P: You're a dope. Has anyone ever told you that?

R: If I were in your shoes, God forbid, I'd be pretty careful about talking like that.

P: Why?

R: Maybe because I don't like it.

P: Ha!

R: What was her character like?

P: I think you had better ask someone else about that, you idiot.

K: That's fine, Jack. Now, Miss Peterson?

P: Yes, what is it?

K: Why did you and Miss McGraw separate?

P: We were crowded. Anyway, I can't see that it's any business of yours.

K: You were good friends, weren't you?

P: Yes, of course.

K: I have a report from the police in the third district from the record on April 8, 1962. At ten past two in the morning several tenants in the building at 62 South Street complained of screaming, loud arguments and continuous noise from an apartment on the fourth floor. When police officers Flynn and Richardson got there ten minutes later they were not let into the apartment and had to get the superintendent to open the door with a pass key. You and Miss McGraw were found in the apartment. Miss McGraw had on bathrobe, and you were dressed in high-heeled shoes and what Flynn described as a white cocktail dress. Miss McGraw was bleeding from a scratch on her forehead. The room was disorderly. Neither of you would make a complaint, and order was restored—at least that's what it says here—and the policemen left the apartment.

P: What do you mean by bringing that thing up?

K: The next day Miss McGraw moved to a hotel, and one week later found her own apartment a few blocks up the same street.

P: I'm asking you again. What do you mean by bringing up that old scandal story? As if I haven't had enough unpleasantness already.

K: I am trying to convince you of the necessity of answering our questions. It's also a good idea to tell the truth.

P: Okay, I threw her out. Why not? It was my apartment.

K: Why did you throw her out, as you put it?

P: What difference does that make today? Who would be interested in a three year old fight between two girlfriends?

K: Anything that has to do with Roseanna McGraw is of interest just now. It seems—as you see in the papers—that there's not much to write about her.

P: Do you mean to say that you can blow up this story for the newspapers if you want to?

K: This report is a public document.

P: In that case isn't it odd that they haven't already gotten hold of it.

K: That's partly because Sergeant Romney got hold of it first. The minute he sends it back to the central archives anyone is free to take any part of it.

P: And if he doesn't send it back?

K: Then it's a different story.

P: Will the record of this examination also be available to the public?

K: No.

P: Can I depend on that?

K: Yes.

P: Okay, what do you want to know? Hurry up, though, so I can get out of here before I become hysterical.

K: Why did you force Miss McGraw to leave your apartment?

P: Because she embarrassed me.

K: In what way?

P: Roseanna was trash. She was in heat like a bitch. And I said it to her face.

K: What did she answer to that?

P: My dear Lieutenant, Roseanna didn't answer such commonplace statements. She held herself above them. Just lay naked on the bed as usual and read some philosopher. And then she would look at me. Large-eyed, uncomprehending and indulgent.

K: Was she very temperamental?

P: She had no temperament at all.

K: What was the direct cause of your sudden breakup?

P: You can try to figure that one out yourself. Even you ought to have enough imagination for that.

K: A man?

P: A slob she wanted to sleep with while I sat and waited for him in some hole about thirty miles from here. He had misunderstood in some way—he was pretty dumb too—and thought that he was to pick me up at home. When he got there I'd already left. Roseanna was home, naturally. She was always home. And so whatever happened, happened. Thank God that slob had left by the time I got back. Otherwise I would have been behind bars in Sioux City at this point.

K: How did you find out what had happened?

P: Roseanna. She always told the truth. I asked her why she had done it. She said, 'Now, Mary Jane, I *wanted* to do it.' And besides she was logical: 'Now, Mary Jane, it only shows that he isn't worth putting stock in.'

K: Would you still state that you and Miss McGraw were friends?

P: Yes, oddly enough. If Roseanna ever had a friend it was I. It was better after she moved and we didn't have to see each other day in and day out. When she first came here— from college—she was always alone. Her parents had just died in Denver at almost the same time. She didn't have any brothers or sisters or any other relatives or any friends. She was also short of money. There was something muddled about her inheritance and year after year went by without it being settled. Eventually she got the money, right after she took that apartment.

K: What was her character like?

P: I think that she suffered some kind of independence complex which had some unusual expression. One of her attitudes was to dress sloppily. She took a certain pride in looking horrible. At best she went around in slacks and a large, baggy sweater. It was hard for her to force herself to put on a dress to go to work. She had a lot of strange ideas. She almost never wore a bra and she needed to more than most of us. She hated to wear shoes. In general, she said she didn't like clothing. When she was at home she often ran around naked the entire day. She never wore a nightgown or pajamas. That irritated me terribly.

K: Was she messy?

P: Only with her appearance, but I am sure that was put on. She pretended that she never realized there were such things as cosmetics, hairdressers or nylon stockings. But with

76

other things she was almost meticulous, above all with her books.

K: What kind of interests did she have?

P: She read a lot. Wrote a bit, but don't ask me what because I don't know. In the summer she was often out for hours. She said that she liked to walk. And then men. But she didn't have a lot of interests.

K: Was Miss McGraw an attractive woman?

P: Not at all. You ought to have understood that from what I've said. But she was man crazy and that goes a long way.

K: Did she have any steady man in her life?

P: When she moved out she did go around now and then with a man who worked for the Highway Department for a half a year. I met him a few times. Lord knows how often she cheated on *him*, probably hundreds.

K: While you were living together, did she often bring men to the apartment?

P: Yes.

K: What do you mean by often?

P: What do *you* mean?

K: Did it happen several times a week?

P: Oh, no, there had to be some moderation.

K: How often did it happen? Answer!

P: Don't use that tone of voice.

K: I'll use any tone of voice I want to. How often did she bring men home to the apartment?

P: Once or twice a month.

K: Was it always different men?

P: I don't know. I didn't always see them. As a matter of fact I usually didn't see them. At times she kept pretty much to herself. Often she had people there when I was out dancing or someplace.

K: Didn't Miss McGraw go out with you?

P: Never. I don't even know if she could dance.

K: Can you give me the names of any of the men she went around with?

P: There was a German student whom we met at the library. I introduced them. I remember his name was Mildenberger. Uli Mildenberger. She brought him home three or four times.

K: During how long a period?

P: A month, possibly five weeks. But he telephoned her every day, and between times they certainly met somewhere

77

else. He lived here in Lincoln for several years but went back
to Europe last spring.

K: What did he look like?

P: Handsome. Tall, blond and broad-shouldered.

K: Did you have intimate relations with this Mildenberger?

P: What the hell business is that of yours?

K: How many different men do you think she brought
home during the time you lived together?

P: Oh, six or seven.

K: Was Miss McGraw attracted to a certain type of man?

P: In this instance she was perfectly normal. She wanted
to have good looking guys. The kind that at least looked like
men.

K: What do you know about her trip?

P: Only that she had been planning it for a long time. She
wanted to take the boat over and then travel around Europe
for a month and see as much as possible. Then she thought
she might stay in one place for the rest of the time, in Paris
or Rome or someplace. Why are you asking about all this
anyway? The police over there shot the man that murdered
her.

K: That information was unfortunately incorrect. Due to a
misunderstanding.

P: May I finally go now? *I* actually have work to do.

K: How did you react when you learned what had happened to Miss McGraw?

P: At first it was a real shock but I wasn't terribly surprised.

K: Why not?

P: And you ask that? After you know how she lived?

K: That will be all now. Goodbye Miss Peterson.

P: And you won't forget what you've promised?

K: I haven't promised anything. You can shut off the tape
recorder now, Jack."

Martin Beck swung back in his chair, put his left hand to his
mouth and bit on the knuckle of his index finger. Then he
took the last remaining paper that he had received from
Lincoln, Nebraska, and read through Kafka's explanation
absentmindedly.

"Roseanna Beatrice McGraw. Born, May 18, 1937 in
Denver, Colorado. Father, small-scale farmer. The farm was

78

about twenty miles from Denver. Education: college in Denver and three years at the University of Colorado. Both parents died in the fall of 1960. Inheritance, about $20,000, paid out in July, 1962. Miss McGraw has not left a will and as far as one knows has no heirs.

"As far as the reliability of the witnesses: my impression was that in some way Mary Jane Peterson altered reality and that she held back certain details, obviously ones that might be disadvantageous to her. I have had a chance to check out Mulvaney's testimony on several points. The statement that R. McG. had only met one other man during the period from November 1962 to July 1963 seems to be correct. I got this from some kind of diary that I found in her apartment. The date was March 22 and the man's initials are U. M. (Uli Mildenberger?) She always made a note of her relationships in the same way, a sort of code with the date and the initials. I have not been able to find any untruths or direct lies in Mulvaney's story.

"Regarding the witnesses: Mulvaney is about 6 feet 2 inches tall, quite strong, blue eyed and has dark blond hair. Seems straightforward but a little naive. Mary Jane Peterson is quite a girl, attractive, stylishly dressed, strikingly slender and well developed. Neither of them have a police record, other than the ridiculous story about the trouble in the girls' apartment in 1962.

(signed)"

Martin Beck put on his jacket and set the lock on the door. Then he went back to his desk. He spread Kafka's papers out in front of him and sat completely still with his elbows on the desk and his forehead in his hands.

14

Martin Beck looked up from the records of the examinations when Melander opened the door to his office. This was something that didn't happen very often.

"Karl-Åke Eriksson-Stolt," said Melander. "Do you remember him?"

Martin Beck thought for a moment.

"Do you mean the fireman on the *Diana?* Was that his name?"

"He calls himself Eriksson now. Two and a half years ago he was called Eriksson-Stolt. That's when he was sentenced to a year in prison because he had seduced a girl who was not yet thirteen years old. Don't you remember? A tough, long-haired, fresh guy."

"Yes, I think I remember. Are you sure it's the same fellow?"

"I checked with the Seamen's Association. It's the same guy."

"I don't remember very well how it happened. Didn't he live in Sundyberg?"

"No, in Hagalund, with his mother. It happened one day when his mother was at work. He didn't go to work. He took the janitor's daughter home with him. She wasn't quite thirteen and it was later proven that she was a bit retarded. He managed to get her to drink alcohol, I think it was aquavit mixed with juice and when she was drunk enough, he slept with her."

"Was it her parents who reported him?"

"Yes, and I went out to get him. During the examination he tried to play tough and stated that he had thought that the girl was of age and that she wanted to. She really didn't look a day over eleven and even then she seemed young for her age. The doctor who examined her said that she may have gone through shock, but I don't know. In any case, Eriksson was sentenced to a year of hard labor."

Martin Beck had a chill when he realized that this man

80

had been on board the *Diana* at the same time as Roseanna.

"Where is he now?" he asked.

"On a Finnish freighter. It's called the *Kalajoki*. I'll find out where she is. Notice that I said *she*."

The same minute that Melander closed the door behind him, Martin Beck picked up the telephone and called Ahlberg.

"We've got to get hold of him," said Ahlberg. "Call me as soon as you have talked to the shipping line. I want him here, even if I have to swim after him myself. The other fireman has also shipped out on another boat, but I'll find out where soon. In addition, I ought to talk with the chief engineer again. He's left the sea and is now working for Electrolux."

They hung up. Martin Beck sat unoccupied for a few minutes while he wondered what he should do. Suddenly, he became nervous, left his office, and walked upstairs.

Melander had just finished a telephone conversation when he entered the room. Kollberg wasn't there.

"That boat, the *Kalajoki*. It's just leaving Holmsund. It's tied up at Söderhamn for the night. The shipping line has confirmed the fact that he's on board."

Martin Beck returned to his office and called Ahlberg again.

"I'll take one of my boys with me and drive up and get him," said Ahlberg. "I'll call you when we have got him."

They were silent for a moment. Then Ahlberg said: "Do you think it was he?"

"I don't know. It could be a possibility of course. I have only seen him once, and that was more than two years ago, just before he was sentenced. A pretty twisted type."

Martin Beck spent the rest of the afternoon in his office. He wasn't in the mood to work but he managed to get a number of routine things done. He kept thinking about the Finnish freighter that was on its way to Söderhamn. And about Roseanna McGraw.

When he went home he tried to work on his model ship but after a while he merely sat there with his elbows on the table and his hands clasped in front of him. He could hardly expect to hear anything from Ahlberg before the next morning and finally he went to bed. He slept fitfully and awakened at five o'clock in the morning.

By the time the morning newspaper hit the floor with a

81

thump he was already shaved and dressed. He had read through the sports pages by the time Ahlberg called.

"We have him here now. He's playing hard-boiled. Not saying anything. I can't exactly say that I like him. By the way, I've spoken to the Prosecutor. He says that we need an expert examiner and that I should ask you to come down. I think it's necessary."

Martin Beck looked at his wristwatch. By now he knew the time-table by heart.

"Okay. I can make the seven-thirty train. See you. So long."

He asked the taxi to drive past Kristineberg where he stopped for his file containing the examination records. At twenty-five minutes after seven he was sitting on the train.

Karl-Åke Eriksson-Stolt was born in Katarina parish twenty-two years ago. His father died when he was six years old and the following year his mother had moved to Hagalund. He was an only child. His mother, who was a seamstress, had supported him until he had finished school. The only teacher who had remembered him said that he had been of average intelligence, noisy and insubordinate. After he left school, he had held several different jobs, mostly as a messenger boy or a construction worker. When he was eighteen years old he went to sea, first as an ordinary seaman and then as a fireman. The Seamen's Association had nothing particular to say about him. One year later he moved back to his mother's and let her support him for a year until the State took over that detail. A year and a half ago he was released from the penitentiary.

Martin Beck had studied this record the day before but read through it carefully one more time. There was also a statement from the examining psychiatrist in the folder. It was rather short and mainly spoke about libido, lethargy and frigidity. In addition it stated that Karl-Åke Eriksson-Stolt had psychopathic tendencies and a strongly developed sex drive, a combination that could lead to abnormal expressions.

Martin Beck went directly to the police station from the railroad station and knocked on Ahlberg's door at ten minutes to eleven. Superintendent Larsson was in Ahlberg's office. They looked tired and worried and seemed relieved to pass the ball to someone else. Neither of them had succeeded in getting a word out of Eriksson with the exception of a number of swear words.

Ahlberg looked through the file quickly. When he closed it Martin Beck said: "Did you get hold of the other fireman?"

"Yes, in a way. He's working on a German boat that is in the Hook of Holland right now. I telephoned Amsterdam this morning and spoke with the police superintendent there who knew a little German. You ought to hear my German. If I understood him correctly there is someone in the Hague who speaks Danish who could take care of the official examination. Now if he understood *me* correctly, we ought to hear something from there tomorrow."

Ahlberg sent out for coffee and after Martin Beck had two cups, he said: "Okay. We might as well start now. Where shall we work?"

"In the next room. There's a tape recorder and whatever else you need there."

Eriksson looked just about the way Martin Beck had remembered him. About five feet, eleven inches tall, thin and gangly. A long, thin face with close-set blue eyes under long, curly eyelashes and straight, heavy eyebrows. A straight nose, a small mouth with thin lips and a weak chin. Long whiskers and a little dark mustache which Martin Beck could not remember having seen before. He had bad posture and was round-shouldered. He was dressed in a pair of old blue-jeans, a blue workshirt, black leather vest and black shoes with pointed toes.

"Sit down," said Martin Beck and nodded toward a chair on the other side of the desk. "Cigarette?"

Eriksson took the cigarette, lit it and sat down. He placed the cigarette in the corner of his mouth, slunk down in his chair and raised his right foot on his left knee. Then he put his thumbs inside his belt and tapped his left foot while he looked at the wall above Martin Beck's head.

Martin Beck looked at him for a moment, turned on the tape recorder which was placed on a low table beside him, and began to read some of the papers in his file.

"Eriksson, Karl-Åke. Born November 23, 1941. Seaman, currently employed on the Finnish freighter *Kalajoki*. Home address, Hagalund, Solna. Is that right?"

Eriksson made a small motion with his head.

"I asked you a question. Is that right? Is the information correct? Answer. Yes or no."

E: Yes, damn it.

B: When did you sign on the *Kalajoki?*

E: Three or four weeks ago.

83

B: What did you do before that?

E: Nothing particular.

B: Where did you do nothing particular?

E: What?

B: Where were you living before you signed on the Finnish boat?

E: With a friend in Gothenburg.

B: How long did you stay in Gothenburg?

E: A few days. Maybe a week.

B: And before that?

E: At my old lady's, my mother's.

B: Were you working then?

E: No, I was sick.

B: What was wrong with you?

E: I was just sick. Felt bad and had a fever.

B: Where did you work before you were sick?

E: On a boat.

B: What was the name of the boat?

E: The *Diana*.

B: What kind of job did you have on the *Diana*?

E: Fireman.

B: How long were you on the *Diana*?

E: The whole summer.

B: From . . . ?

E: From the first of July until the middle of September. Then they lay off. They put the boat up, too. They only run in the summer. Back and forth with a bunch of corny tourists. Damn dull. I wanted to sign off the tub but my buddy wanted to stay on, and anyway, I needed the cash.

After that strain on his oratorical powers, Eriksson seemed completely exhausted and sank even further down in his chair.

B: What's your buddy's name? What was his job on the *Diana*?

E: Fireman. There were three of us at the engine. Me, my buddy and the engineer.

B: Did you know any of the other crew members?

Eriksson bent forward and put out his cigarette in the ash tray. "What the hell kind of an examination is this," he said, and threw himself back in his chair. "I haven't done anything. Here I've gone and gotten a job and some damn cops come and . . ."

B: You will answer my questions. Did you know any of the other crew members?

84

E: Not when I started. I only knew my buddy then. But you get to meet the others later. There was a guy who worked on the deck that was kind of fun.

B: Did you meet any girls on the trips?

E: There was only one gal who was anything at all but she went around with the cook. The rest of them were old bags.

B: The passengers then?

E: We didn't see much of them. I really didn't meet any girls.

B: Did you work in shifts, the three of you in the engine room?

E: Yes.

B: Do you remember if anything unusual happened at any time during the summer?

E: No, what do you mean, unusual?

B: If any one trip was different from the rest. Didn't the engine break down at some point?

E: Yes, that's right. A steampipe broke. We had to go into Söderköping for repairs. It took a hell of a long time. But that wasn't my fault.

B: Do you remember when it happened?

E: Just after we'd passed Stegeborg.

B: Yes, but which day did it happen?

E: Who the hell knows. What kind of damn nonsense is this? It wasn't my fault that the engine broke down. Anyway, I wasn't working then. It wasn't my shift.

B: But when you left Söderköping? Was it your shift then?

E: Yes, and before that too. All three of us had to work like hell to get the barge going again. We worked all night and then we worked the next day, the engineer and I.

B: What time did you go off the shift during the day?

E: The day after Söderköping? Quite late in the afternoon, I think.

B: Then what did you do when you were free?

Eriksson looked emptily at Martin Beck and didn't answer.

B: What did you do when you had finished working that day?

E: Nothing.

B: You must have done something? What did you do?

(The same empty look.)

B: Where was the boat when you were free?

E: I don't know. At Roxen, I think.

B: What did you do when you got off the shift?

E: Nothing, I told you.

B: You must have done *something*. Did you meet anyone?
Eriksson looked bored and stroked his neck.

B: Think about it. What did you do?

E: What a lot of garbage. What do you think anyone can do on that damned tub? Play football? The boat was right out in the middle of the water. Now listen, the only things you could do on that tub were eat and sleep.

B: Did you meet anyone that day?

E: Sure, I met Brigitte Bardot. How the hell can I know if I met anyone. It was a few years ago.

B: Okay. We'll start over. Last summer, when you were working on the *Diana*, did you meet anyone or any of the passengers?

E: I didn't meet any passengers. We didn't get to meet the passengers anyway. And even if we had, I wasn't interested. A bunch of snotty tourists. The hell with them.

B: What's the name of your buddy who also worked on the *Diana?*

E: Why? What's this all about anyway? We didn't do anything.

B: What's his name?

E: Roffe.

B: First name and last name.

E: Roffe Sjöberg.

B: Where is he now?

E: He's on some German boat. I don't know where the hell he is. Maybe he's in Kuala Lampur. I don't know.

Martin Beck gave up. He turned off the tape recorder and got up. Eriksson began to stretch slowly to get out of his chair.

"Sit down," roared Martin Beck. "Sit there until I tell you to get up."

He called in to Ahlberg who stood in the doorway five seconds later.

"Get up," said Martin Beck, and went out of the room ahead of him.

When Ahlberg came back to his office Martin Beck was sitting beside his desk. He looked up at him and shrugged his shoulders.

"Let's go and eat now," he said. "I'll try again later."

15

At nine-thirty the next morning Martin Beck sent for Eriksson for the third time. The examination continued for two hours and brought equally poor results.

When Eriksson slouched out of the room escorted by a young constable, Martin Beck put the tape recorder on rewind and went to get Ahlberg. They listened to the tape mostly in silence which was broken only now and then by Martin Beck's short comments.

A few hours later they were sitting in Ahlberg's office.

"Well, what do you think?"

"It wasn't he," said Martin Beck. "I'm almost sure of it. In the first place he isn't intelligent enough to keep up the mask. He simply doesn't understand what it's all about. He's not faking."

"Maybe you're right," said Ahlberg.

"In the second place, and this is only instinct, but I'm convinced of it in any case. We know a little about Roseanna McGraw, don't we?"

Ahlberg nodded.

"So it's very hard for me to believe that she would willingly go to bed with Karl-Åke Eriksson."

"No, that's right. She was willing, but not with just anyone. But who said that she did willingly?"

"Yes. It must have been that way. She met someone that she thought she would like to go to bed with and by the time it had gone far enough for her to discover her mistake, it was too late. But it wasn't Karl-Åke Eriksson."

"It could have happened some other way," said Ahlberg doubtfully.

"How? In that tiny cabin? Someone forced open the door and threw himself on her? She would have fought and screamed like mad and people on board would have heard her."

"He could have threatened her. With a knife or maybe a pistol."

Martin Beck shook his head slowly. Then he got up quick-

87

ly and walked over to the window. Ahlberg followed him with his eyes.

"What should we do with him?" asked Ahlberg. "I can't hold him much longer."

"I'd like to talk with him one more time. I don't think he really knows why he is here. I am going to tell him now."

Ahlberg got up and put on his jacket. Then he went out.

Martin Beck remained seated for a while, thinking. After that he sent for Eriksson, took his briefcase and went into the examining room next door.

"What the hell is all this about?" asked Eriksson. "I haven't done anything. You can't keep me here when I haven't done anything. God damn it. . . ."

"Be quiet until I tell you you can talk. You are here to answer my questions," said Martin Beck.

He took out the retouched photograph of Roseanna McGraw and held it up in front of Eriksson.

"Do you recognize this woman?" he asked.

"No," Eriksson answered. "Who is she?"

"Look carefully at the picture and then answer. Have you ever seen the woman in this photograph?"

"No."

"Are you sure?"

Eriksson placed one elbow on the back of his chair and rubbed his nose with his index finger.

"Yes. I've never laid eyes on the dame."

"Roseanna McGraw. Does that name mean anything to you?"

"What a hell of a name. Is this a joke?"

"Have you heard the name Roseanna McGraw before?"

"No."

"Then I'm going to tell you something. The woman in the photograph is Roseanna McGraw. She was an American and a passenger on the *Diana*'s first trip out of Stockholm on July 3. The *Diana* was delayed on that trip by twelve hours, first due to fog south of Oxelösund and then due to an engine breakdown. You have already said that you were on that trip. When the vessel arrived in Gothenberg ten hours off schedule Roseanna McGraw wasn't on it. She was killed during the night between July 4-5 and was found three days later in the lock chamber at Borenshult."

Eriksson sat straight up in his chair. He grabbed the arm rests and chewed on the left corner of his mouth.

"Is that why . . . ? Do you think that . . . ?"

88

He pressed the palms of his hands together, placed his hands tightly between his knees and bent forward so that his chin nearly rested on the desk. Martin Beck saw how the skin on the bridge of his nose had paled.

"I haven't murdered anyone! I've never seen that dame! I swear!"

Martin Beck said nothing. He kept looking directly at the man's face and saw the fear grow in his enlarged eyes.

When he spoke his voice was dry and toneless.

"Where were you and what were you doing on the night of July 4-5?"

"In my cabin. I swear! I was in my cabin sleeping! I haven't done anything! I've never seen that dame! It isn't true!"

His voice rose to a falsetto and he threw himself back in his chair. His right hand went up to his mouth and he began to bite on his thumb while he stared at the photograph in front of him. Then his eyes narrowed and his voice became thin and hysterical.

"You're trying to trick me. You think you can frighten me, don't you? All that about the girl is fake. You've talked with Roffe and that devil said it was me. He's squealed. He did it, not me. I haven't done anything. That's the truth. I haven't done anything. Roffe said it was me, didn't he? He said it."

Martin Beck didn't take his eyes away from the man's face.

"That bastard. He fixed the lock and he stole the money."

He bent forward and his voice became eager. The words poured out of him.

"He forced me to go along with it. He had worked in that damn building. It was his idea all along. I didn't want to. I said so. I refused. I didn't want to have anything to do with such a thing. But he forced me, that damned louse. He squealed, that ass. . . ."

"Okay," said Martin Beck. "Roffe squealed. You'd better tell me everything now."

One hour later he played back the tape for Larsson and Ahlberg. There was a complete confession of a burglary which Karl-Åke Eriksson and Roffe · Sjöberg had committed in a garage in Gothenburg one month earlier.

When Larsson had left to telephone to the Gothenburg police, Ahlberg said: "In any case we know where we have him for the time being."

He sat quietly for a while and drummed on the desk.

"Now there are about fifty possible suspects left," said Ahlberg. "If we go on the premise that the murderer was among the passengers."

Martin Beck remained silent and looked at Ahlberg who sat with his head down and seemed to be examining his fingernails. He looked just as depressed as Martin Beck had felt when he realized that the examination of Eriksson wasn't leading anywhere.

"Are you disappointed?" he asked.

"Yes, I'll have to admit it. For a while I really thought we were there and now it seems that we have just as far to go."

"We've made some progress in any case. Thanks to Kafka."

The telephone rang and Ahlberg answered it. He sat listening for a long while with the receiver pressed against his ear. Then he cried suddenly:

"Ja, ja, ich bin hier. Ahlberg *hier."*

"Amsterdam," he said to Martin Beck who left the room discreetly.

While he was washing his hands he thought '*an, auf, hinter, in, neben, über, unter, vor, zwischen,*' and he was reminded of the first sticky odor of a room many years ago and of a round table with a baize cloth and an elderly teacher with a thin German grammar book between her fat fingers. When he went back Ahlberg had just put down the phone.

"What a language," he said. "Roffe Sjöberg wasn't on the boat. He had signed on in Gothenburg but he never went on board. Well, that will be Gothenburg's headache now."

Martin Beck slept on the train. He didn't wake up before it arrived in Stockholm. He really only woke up when he got into his own bed at home.

16

At ten minutes after five Melander tapped at the door. He waited about five seconds before he showed his long, thin face in the door opening and said: "I thought I'd leave now. Is that all right?"

He had no official reason for asking but he went through the same process every day. On the other hand, he never bothered to announce his arrival in the morning.

"Certainly," said Martin Beck. "So long."

After a moment he added, "Thanks for your help today."

Martin Beck remained and listened to the work day die away. The telephones were the first to become silent, then the typewriters, and then the sound of voices stopped until finally even the footsteps in the corridors could no longer be heard.

At five-thirty he called home.

"Shall we wait for dinner?"

"No, go ahead and eat."

"Will you be late?"

"I don't know. It's possible."

"You haven't seen the children for ages."

Without doubt he had both seen and heard them less than nine hours ago, but she knew that just as well as he.

"Martin?"

"Yes."

"You don't sound well. Is it anything special?"

"No, not at all. We have a lot to do."

"Is that all?"

"Yes, of course."

Now she sounded like herself again. The moment had passed. A few of her standard phrases and the discussion was over. He had held the receiver to his ears and heard the click when she put hers down. A click, and empty silence and it was as if she were a thousand miles away. Years had passed since they had really talked.

He wrinkled his forehead and sighed and looked at the papers on his desk. Each one of them had something to say about Roseanna McGraw and the last days of her life. He was sure of that. And still, they didn't tell him anything.

It seemed meaningless to read through all of them once again but he probably should do it anyway, and do it now. He would start soon.

He stretched out his hand to get a cigarette but the package was empty. He threw it into the wastepaper basket and reached in the pocket of his jacket for another pack. During the past few weeks he had smoked twice as much as he usually did and he felt it, both in his wallet and in his throat. It seemed that he had used up his reserve pack because the only thing he found in his pockets was something that he did not immediately recognize.

It was a postcard, bought at a tobacco shop in Motala. It showed the lock chamber at Borenshult seen from above. The lake and the breakwater were in the background and two men were in the process of opening the sluice gates for a passenger boat rising in the foreground. The picture was obviously quite old because the ship on the photograph no longer existed. Her name was *Astrea* and she had long since succumbed to the wreckers and the blowtorches.

But then, at the time when the photograph was taken, it had been summer and suddenly he remembered the fresh odor of flowers and wet shrubbery.

Martin Beck opened a drawer and took out his magnifying glass. It was shaped like a scoop and there was an electric battery in the handle. When he pressed the button, the object under study was illuminated with a small bulb. It was a good photograph and he could quite clearly make out the skipper on the port side of the bridge and several of the passengers who were hanging on the railing. The forward deck of the ship was loaded with cargo, still another sign that the picture was far from new.

He had just moved his glance slightly to the right when Kollberg walloped on the door with his fists and walked in.

"Hi, were you frightened?"

"Frightened to death," answered Martin Beck and felt his heart skip a beat.

"Haven't you gone home yet?"

"Sure. I'm sitting three stories up in my apartment and eating chicken."

"By the way, when do we get paid?"

"Tomorrow, I hope."

Kollberg collapsed in the visitor's chair.

They sat quietly for a while. Finally Kollberg said: "That was a flop, wasn't it? Examining that tough guy you went down and mangled?"

"He didn't do it."

"Are you absolutely sure?"

"No."

"Do you *feel* sure?"

"Yes."

"That's good enough for me. When you get right down to it there is a difference between seducing a twelve year old girl and killing a full grown woman."

"Yes."

"And anyway, she would never have gone for a type like that. Not if I've read my Kafka right."

"No," Martin Beck agreed with conviction. "She wouldn't have."

"What did the guy in Motala think? Was he disappointed?"

"Ahlberg? Yes, somewhat. But he's stubborn. What did Melander say, by the way?"

"Nothing. I've know that fellow since our training days and the only thing that ever depressed him was tobacco rationing."

Kollberg took out a notebook with a black cover and thumbed through it thoughtfully.

"While you were away I went through everything again. I tried to make up a summary."

"Yes?"

"I asked myself, for example, the question that Hammar is going to ask us tomorrow: What do we know?"

"And what did you answer?"

"Wait a minute. It's better if you answer. What do we know about Roseanna McGraw?"

"A little. Thanks to Kafka."

"That's right. I would even venture to say that we know all the important factors about her. Further: what do we know about the actual murder?"

"We have the scene of the crime. We also know approximately how and when it happened."

"Do we actually know where it happened?"

Martin Beck drummed his fingers on the top of the desk. Then he said:

"Yes. In cabin 7 on board the *Diana*."

"According to the blood-type that's right. But that would never hold as evidence."

"No, but *we* know it," said Martin Beck quickly.

"Okay. We'll pretend that we know it. When?"

"On the night of July 4. After dark. In any event sometime after dinner which ended at eight o'clock. Presumably sometime between nine o'clock and midnight."

"How? Yes, on that point we have the autopsy report. We can also guess that she undressed herself, of her own free will. Or possibly under threat for her life. But that doesn't seem likely."

"No."

"And so, last but not least, what do we know about the culprit?"

Kollberg answered his own question in twenty seconds: "That the person in question is a sadist and sexually twisted."

"That the person in question is a man," Martin Beck added.

"Yes, most likely. And pretty strong. Roseanna McGraw was clearly not dropped off a wagon."

"We know that he was on board the *Diana*."

"Yes, if we assume that our earlier theory was correct."

"And that he must belong in one of two categories: passengers or the crew."

"Do we really know that?"

It was silent in the room. Martin Beck massaged his hairline with the tips of his fingers. Finally he said: "It must be so."

"Must it?"

"Yes."

"All right, we'll say it is. But on the other hand, we don't have any idea what the murderer looks like or of his nationality. We have no fingerprints and nothing that can tie him to the crime. We don't know if he knew Roseanna McGraw earlier. We don't know where he came from, or where he went or where we could find him today."

Kollberg was very serious now.

"We know damned little, Martin," he said. "Are we even absolutely sure that Roseanna McGraw *didn't* step off the boat in Gothenburg safe and sound? That someone didn't kill her afterwards? Someone who knew where she had come from and who might have transported her body back to Motala and then thrown it in?"

"I've thought of it. But it's too absurd. Things don't happen that way."

"Since we haven't yet received the menu from the boat for

94

those days, it is still theoretically possible. Even if it stretches the imagination. And even if we manage to prove, really prove, that she never got to Gothenburg, there is still another possibility: she could have gone ashore while the boat was in the lock chamber at Borenshult and met some nut who was wandering around in the bushes."

"In that case we ought to have found something."

"Yes, but 'ought to' is a weak concept. There are things in this case that almost drive me crazy. How in hell could she disappear during half the trip without anyone noticing it, not even the room steward or the waiter in the dining room?"

"The person who killed her must have stayed on board. He arranged the cabin to make it look normal and used. It was only a question of one night."

"Where did the sheets go? And the blankets? They must have had blood on them. He couldn't very well just sit down and start doing laundry. And if he had thrown everything in the water, where did he get fresh things from?"

"There wasn't that much blood, the autopsy didn't say so. And if the person who killed her was familiar with the vessel, he could have gotten fresh bedding from the supply closet."

"Would a passenger be that much at home on the boat? And wouldn't someone notice?"

"It isn't so hard. Have you ever been on a passenger ship at night?"

"No."

"Everyone goes to sleep. It's completely quiet and empty. Almost all the closets and cupboards are unlocked. When this boat passed Lake Vättern, during the night watch, there were only three people who were definitely awake. Those on watch, two on the bridge and one in the engine room."

"Shouldn't someone have noticed that she didn't get off in Gothenburg?"

"There is no set procedure for getting off when the boat lands there. They tie up at Lilla Bommen and the passengers grab their things and rush down the gangway. On this particular trip, most people were in a hurry because the ship had been delayed. In addition, contrary to usual, it was dark when they got in."

Martin Beck stopped speaking and gazed at the wall for a while.

"What irritates me most is that the passengers in the next cabin didn't notice anything," he said.

"I can explain that, I found out just two hours ago that a

95

Dutch couple had cabin A 3. Both were over seventy and nearly stone deaf."

Kollberg turned the page and scratched his head.

"Our so-called theory of how, when and where the crime took place is mainly built on principles of probability, logical assumptions and the application of some psychology. It certainly is weak on evidence. We have to hold to it in any case because it's all we have to go on. But we must also appraise the statistics in the same way, right?"

Martin Beck leaned back in his chair and crossed his arms over his chest.

"Let's hear it," he said.

"We know the names of eighty-six people who were on board. Sixty-eight passengers plus the eighteen that made up the crew. Thus far we have located, or in some way been in contact with all of them, with the exception of eleven. But we know the nationalities, sexes, and—with three exceptions —the ages of all of them. Now, let's use a process of elimination. First of all we have to eliminate Roseanna McGraw. That leaves eighty-five. After that, all the women, eight in the crew and thirty-seven among the passengers. That leaves forty. Among these there are four boys under ten and seven men over seventy. That leaves twenty-nine. Furthermore, there was the captain and the helmsman. They were on watch between eight o'clock and midnight, giving each other alibis. They hardly had time to murder anyone. It's a bit less clear with the people in the engine room. Deduct those two and we have a grand total of twenty-seven. We have, however, the names of twenty-seven male persons between the ages of fourteen and sixty-eight. Twelve are Swedish, seven of whom were crew members, five Americans, three Germans, one Dane, one South African, an Englishman, a Frenchman, a Scot, a Turk and a Dutchman. The geographic spread is equally terrifying. One of the Americans lives in Texas, another in Oregon. The Englishman lives in Nassau in the Bahamas, the South African in Durban, and the Turk in Ankara. It's going to be one hell of a trip for whoever examines them. In addition, there are four out of this twenty-seven whom we haven't been able to locate. One Dane, and three Swedes. We haven't been able to show that any of these passengers have traveled with the canal boats earlier, in spite of the fact that Melander has plowed through passenger lists for the past twenty-five years. My own theory is that none of the passengers could have done it. Only four of them were traveling in single cabins. The others ought to have been more or less observed by their spouses or whomever they shared a cabin with. None of them really knew their way around the boat well enough or the routine on board to have done it. That leaves the eight men in the crew, the helmsman, the two firemen, a cook, and three deck boys. We have already eliminated the chief engineer, he fell by the wayside because of his age. My theory is that none of them could have done it either. They were under too much observance by each other and the possibilities of fraternizing with the passengers were quite limited. So my theory says that no one murdered Roseanna McGraw. And it must be wrong. My theories are always wrong. Oh, the perils of thought."

It was quiet for thirty seconds. Then Kollberg said:

"Now if it wasn't that creature Eriksson. . . . Damn, but it was good luck that you got him arrested anyway. . . . By the way, are you listening? Have you heard what I said?"

"Yes, of course," said Martin Beck absentmindedly. "Yes, I'm listening."

It was true. Martin Beck had been listening. But Kollberg's voice had sounded more and more distant during the last ten minutes. Two totally different ideas had suddenly occurred to him. One was an association with something he had heard someone say, and it had immediately penetrated the bottom of his unfulfilled and forgotten thoughts. The other was more tangible, a new plan of attack that could well be worked out.

"She must have met someone on board," he said to himself.

"Unless it was suicide," said Kollberg with a measure of irony.

"Someone who didn't plan to kill her, at least in the beginning, and who also had no reason to keep himself hidden. . . ."

"Sure, that's what we think, but what difference does it make when we don't . . ."

Martin Beck saw clearly a scene from his last July day in Motala. The ugly vessel, *Juno*, as she rounded the dredger and nosed in toward the harbor chamber.

He straightened up, took out the old postcard, and stared at it.

"Lennart," he said to Kollberg. "How many cameras were used during those days? At least twenty-five, more likely thirty, maybe even forty. At each lock, people went on shore to take pictures of the boat and of each other. There must be. pictures from that trip pasted into twenty or thirty family albums. All kinds of pictures. The first ones were probably taken right at the pier in Stockholm, and the last ones in Gothenburg. Let's say that twenty people took thirty pictures each during those three days. That's about one roll per person, and some might have taken more. Lennart, that means there must be at least six hundred photographs. . . . Do you understand . . . six hundred photographs. Maybe even a thousand."

"Yes," said Kollberg slowly. "I understand what you mean."

17

"It will be a terrible job, of course," said Martin Beck.

"No worse than what we're already doing," answered Kollberg.

"Maybe it's only a wild idea. I could be completely wrong."

This was a game that they had played many times before, Martin Beck doubting and needing support. He knew in advance what the answer would be and he also knew that Kollberg knew he knew. Even so, they stuck to their ritual.

"It will have to give us something," said Kollberg stubbornly.

And after a few seconds he added: "Anyway, we have a head start. We already know where they are with a few exceptions, and we've already had contact with most of them."

It was easy for Kollberg to sound convinced. That was one of his specialties.

After a while Martin Beck asked: "What time is it?"

"Ten minutes after seven."

"Is there anyone on the list who lives in the vicinity?"

Kollberg studied his notebook.

"Nearer than you think," he said. "On North Mälarstrand. A retired colonel and his wife."

"Who's been there? You?"

"No, Melander. Nice people," he said.

"Was that all?"

"Yes."

The street was wet and slippery and Kollberg swore bitterly when his back wheels skidded. Three minutes later they were there.

The colonel's wife opened the door.

"Axel, there are two gentlemen from the police here," she called in towards the living room in a very loud voice.

"Ask them to come in," roared the colonel. "Or would you rather I came out and stood in the hall?"

Martin Beck shook the rain off his hat and walked in. Kollberg wiped his feet energetically.

"We are having maneuver weather," bellowed the colonel. "Please excuse me, gentlemen, for not getting up."

On the low table in front of him was a half-played game of dominoes, a cognac glass, and a bottle of Rémy Martin. Nearby, the television was blaring away deafeningly.

"Maneuver weather, as I said. Would you gentlemen like to have some cognac? That's the only thing that helps."

"I'm driving," shouted Kollberg as he looked seriously at the bottle.

It took ten seconds before Martin Beck's feelings of solidarity won out. He shook his head.

"You do the talking," he said to Kollberg.

"What was that?" the colonel screamed.

Martin Beck managed a smile and made a nonchalant gesture. He was convinced that the least attempt to enter into the discussion would ruin his voice for a whole week. The conversation continued.

"Photographs? No, we never take pictures any more. I see so poorly and Axel always forgets to wind the film after he's taken a picture. That nice young man who was here two weeks ago asked the same thing. He was such a nice boy."

Martin Beck and Kollberg exchanged a quick look, not only in astonishment, over the remarkable statement about Melander.

"But strangely enough," thundered the colonel, "Major Jentsch. . . . But of course, naturally you don't know who he is. We sat with him and his wife during the trip. A procurement officer, a most pleasant man. As a matter of fact we were commissioned the same year but the unfortunate end of the campaign against the Bolsheviks put an end to his career. You know, the promotions came quickly as long as the war continued, but after 1945, that was that. Well, it wasn't so serious for Jentsch. He was a procurement officer and they were worth their weight in gold right after the war. I remember he received a Director's position with a food company in Osnabrück. Yes, we had some things in common, a lot to talk about, and the time passed quickly. A great deal, as I said. For nine months, maybe it was eleven as a matter of fact, well, in any case he had been the liaison officer with the Blue Division. You know about the Blue Division? The Spanish élite troops that Franco put in against the opposition. And I must say, we often tear apart the Italians and Greeks

100

and Spaniards and others here at home ... yes, we rip them up pretty well, but I must say, as I have said, that these boys in the Blue Division, in other words, they really could ..."

Martin Beck turned his head and looked with despair at the television screen which was now showing a program that must have been at least one month old about picking beets in southern Sweden. The colonel's wife was watching the program attentively and seemed unconscious of her surroundings.

"I understand," Kollberg screamed.

Then he took a deep breath and with admirable strength of voice and direction continued:

"What was it you began to say about photographs?"

"What? Oh yes, I was saying that strangely enough Major Jentsch was an expert in handling a camera, in spite of the fact that he doesn't hear or see any better than we do. He took a lot of photographs on the trip and just a few days ago we received a whole envelope full of them from him. I think that was very thoughtful of him. It must have been expensive for him to have them printed for us. They are very good photographs. Pleasant memories no matter what."

Martin Beck moved toward the television and lowered the volume a little. It had happened instinctively, in self-protection, without his really having been conscious of what he had done. The colonel's wife looked at him uncomprehendingly.

"What? Yes, naturally. Missan, will you get the photographs we received from Germany. I would like to show them to these gentlemen."

Martin Beck watched the woman who was called Missan from under knotted eyebrows as she got out of her TV chair.

The pictures were in color and about 3 by 4 inches in size. There were about fifteen of them in the envelope and the man in the easy chair held them between his thumb and his index finger. Martin Beck and Kollberg stood bent forward, one on either side of him.

"This is us and here is Major Jentsch's wife, oh yes, and you can see my wife here ... yes, and here am I. This photograph was taken from the command bridge. That was the first day out. I'm talking to the captain, as you probably can see. And here ... unfortunately I don't see too well either ... will you give me the magnifying glass, darling ...?"

The colonel wiped off the magnifying glass slowly and carefully before he continued.

"Yes, here we are. Now you can see Major Jentsch himself, and then me and my wife. . . . Major Jentsch's wife must have taken this photograph. It looks a bit dimmer than the rest. And here we are again, in the same place but from a slightly different angle, it seems to me. And . . . let me see . . . the lady that I am talking to here was a Frau Liebeneiner, she was German too. She ate at our table, too, a very charming and fine woman, but, unfortunately, a bit elderly. She lost her husband at El Alamein."

Martin Beck paid closer attention and saw a very old woman in a flowered dress with a pink hat. She stood next to one of the lifeboats with a cup of coffee in one hand and a piece of pastry in the other.

The inspection continued. The shots were all the same. Martin Beck began to get a pain in his back. He knew now, without doubt, just how Major Jentsch's wife looked.

The last picture lay on the mahogany table in front of the colonel. It was one of those which Martin Beck had already spoken of. The *Diana* seen directly from the stern, tied up at the pier in Stockholm, with the City Hall in the background and two taxis right up at the gangway.

The picture must have been taken just before the boat sailed because there were at lot of people already on board. To the stern of the port lifeboat on the shelter deck, Major Jentsch's wife from Osnabrück could be seen. Directly below her stood Roseanna McGraw. She was bending forward with her arms resting on the railing and her feet spread apart. She had sandals on, and sunglasses. She wore a full yellow dress with shoulder straps. Martin Beck bent as far over as he could and tried to make out the people standing next to her. At the same time he heard Kollberg whistle through his teeth.

"Oh yes, oh yes," said the colonel undisturbed. "This is the ship, here at Riddarholm. There is the City Hall tower. And there is Hildegard Jentsch. That was before we met. And, yes, that was strange. This young girl also sat at our table a few times. She was English or Dutch, I think. They must have moved her to another table later so that we old folks could have a little more room for our elbows."

A strong, wrinkled index finger, with a lot of white hairs enlarged under the magnifying glass, rested on the girl in the sandals and the loose, yellow dress.

Martin Beck took a breath in order to say something, but Kollberg was quicker.

"What?" asked the colonel. "Am I certain? Of course I am certain. She sat at the same table as we did at least four or five times. She never said anything though, if I remember correctly."

"But . . ."

"Yes, of course your colleague showed me her portrait, but you understand, it wasn't her face that I recognized. It's the dress, or more correctly, not exactly the dress, either."

He turned to the left and placed his powerful index finger on Martin Beck's chest.

"It was the décolleté," he said in a thundering whisper.

18

It was a quarter past eleven and they were still sitting in the office at Kristineberg. The breeze was blowing freshly and small drops of rain splashed against the windows.

Twenty photographs were spread out on the table in front of Martin Beck. He had pushed nineteen of them aside and was studying the picture of Roseanna McGraw in the magnifying glass's circle of light for, perhaps, the fiftieth time. She looked just exactly as he had imagined her. Her glance seemed to be directed upward, probably in the direction of Riddarholm's tower. She looked healthy and alert and totally unconscious of the fact that she had only about thirty-six hours left to live. On her left was cabin number A 7. The door was open but the picture didn't show enough for anyone to see how it looked inside.

"Do you realize that we were lucky today," said Kollberg. "It's the first time, too, since we started on this damned case. One usually has some luck, sooner or later. This time though, it was a lot later."

"We've had some bad luck also."

"You mean because she was sitting at a table with two deaf old men and three half-blind women? That's not bad luck. That's just the law of averages. Let's go home and go to bed now. I'll drop you off. Or would you rather take that great gift to humanity, the subway?"

"We have to get a telegram off to Kafka first. We can send the rest of it by letter tomorrow."

They were finished a half hour later. Kollberg drove quickly and carelessly through the rain but Martin Beck didn't seem nervous, in spite of the fact that driving usually put him in a bad mood. They didn't speak at all during the trip. When they pulled up in front of the house where Martin Beck lived, Kollberg finally said: "Now you can go to bed and think about all this. So long."

It was quiet and dark in the apartment but when Martin Beck went past his daughter's room, he heard the sound of radio music. She was probably lying in bed with the transistor radio under her pillow. When he was a boy he had read sea adventure novels with a flashlight under the blankets.

There was some bread and butter and cheese on the kitchen table. He made a sandwich for himself and looked for a bottle of beer in the ice-box. There wasn't any. He stood at the sink, ate his frugal supper, and washed it down with half a glass of milk.

Then he went into the bedroom and got into bed, very carefully. His wife turned toward him, half asleep, and tried to say something. He lay quietly on his back and held his breath. After a few minutes her breath was even and unconscious again. He relaxed, closed his eyes and began to think.

Roseanna McGraw had been in one of the earliest photographs. In addition, these photographs had clearly identified five other people, two retired military couples and the widow Liebeneiner. He could easily expect to receive between twenty-five and thirty more sets of pictures, most of them with more photographs than this one. Each negative would be rooted out, every picture would be studied carefully to find out whom he, or she, knew in each picture. It had to work. Eventually, they could map out Roseanna McGraw's final trip. They should be able to see it in front of them like a film.

A great deal depended on Kafka and what he could obtain from eight households spread across the continent of North America. Americans were wasteful with film. Weren't they known for that? And then, if anyone other than the murderer had been in contact with the woman from Lincoln, wouldn't it very likely have been one of her own countrymen? Maybe they should look for the murderer mainly among the Americans on board. Maybe, one of these days, he would have the telephone pressed against his ear and hear Kafka say: "Yeah, I shot the bastard."

In the middle of this thought Martin Beck fell asleep, suddenly, and without trying.

It rained the next day, too, and it was gray and sprinkling. The last yellow leaves of fall stuck sadly to the walls of the house and to the windowpanes.

Almost as if Martin Beck's night-time thoughts had reached him, Kafka sent a laconic telegram:

SEND AS MUCH MATERIAL AS POSSIBLE.

Two days later, Melander, who never forgot anything, took his pipe out of his mouth and said, tranquilly: "Uli

Mildenberger is in Hamburg. He was there all summer. Would you like to have him examined?"

Martin Beck thought about it for about five seconds. "No."

He was on the point of adding: "Make a note of his address," but stopped himself at the last minute, shrugged his shoulders and went on with his business.

During these days, he often had very little to do. The case had reached a point where it was going on its own pretty much at the same time as it was spreading itself out all over the globe. There was an open "hot line" between himself and Ahlberg in Motala. After that, it was spread like the rays of the sun all over the map from the North Cape in the north to Durban in the south and Ankara in the east. By far, the most important line of contact led to Kafka's office in Lincoln, nearly six thousand miles to the west. From there it branched out to a handful of geographically separated places on the American continent.

With so many widespread informants at their disposal, couldn't they ensnare and catch a murderer? The logical answer, unfortunately, was, No. Martin Beck had painful memories from a case involving another sex murder. It had taken place in a cellar in one of the Stockholm suburbs. The body had been found almost immediately and the police arrived on the scene less than an hour later. Several persons had seen the murderer and gave lengthy descriptions of him. The man had left his footprints, cigarette butts, matches, and even several other objects. In addition, he had handled the body with a particularly idiosyncratic perversity. But they had never been able to get him. Their optimism had slowly turned into frustration at their impotence. All the clues had led to nothing. Seven years later, the man was discovered in the act of attempted rape, and arrested. During the examination that followed, he suddenly broke down and admitted the earlier murder.

That crime and its solution seven years later had been only a small incident on the side for Martin Beck. But it had been of the utmost importance to one of his older colleagues. He remembered so well how that man had sat month after month, year after year, in his office late into the night, going through all the papers and rechecking the testimony for the five hundredth, or possibly the thousandth time. He had met that man many times in unexpected places and in surprising

106

circumstances when the man should have been off duty or on vacation but was, instead, always looking for new angles in the case which had become the tragedy of his life. In time, he had become sick and was given his pension early, but even then, he hadn't given up the search. And then, finally, the case was cleared up when someone burst into tears before an astonished policeman down in Halland and confessed to the seven year old crime of strangulation. Martin Beck sometimes wondered if that solution, which came so late, had really given the old detective any peace.

It could happen that way. But that woman in the cellar had been all the things that Roseanna McGraw wasn't, a rootless, wandering person who was hardly a member of society and whose asociability was as indisputable as the contents of her handbag.

Martin Beck thought a great deal about this while he waited for something to happen.

Meanwhile, in Motala, Ahlberg was occupied in annoying the authorities by insisting that every square inch of the bottom of the canal should be dragged and gone over by frogmen. He rarely got in touch with Martin Beck himself but was constantly waiting for the telephone to ring.

After a week, a new telegram arrived from Kafka. The message was cryptic and surprising:

YOU WILL HAVE A BREAK ANY MINUTE NOW.

Martin Beck telephoned Ahlberg.

"He says that there will be a break for us any time now."

"He probably knows that we need one," said Ahlberg

Kollberg added his dissenting opinion: "The man is nearsighted. He's suffering from the disease we call intuition."

Melander didn't say anything at all.

In ten more days, they had received about fifty pictures and had about three times as many negatives printed. Many of the pictures were of poor quality and they could find Roseanna McGraw in only two of them. Both were taken at the Riddarholm pier and she was still standing alone in the stern of A deck, not very far from her cabin. One of the pictures showed her bending over and scratching her right ankle, but that was all. Otherwise they identified the twenty-three more passengers, bringing the total identified up to twenty-eight.

Melander was in charge of scrutinizing the pictures and after he was through with them, he sent them to Kollberg who tried to place them in some kind of chronological order. Martin Beck studied all of them, hour after hour, but said nothing.

The next few days brought a few dozen more pictures but Roseanna McGraw wasn't to be seen on any of them.

On the other hand a letter arrived from Ankara, at last. It was on Martin Beck's desk the morning of the thirteenth day, but it took two more days before the Turkish Embassy presented them with a translation. Contrary to all expectations the contents of that letter seemed to represent the most progress in a long time.

One of the Turkish passengers, a twenty-two year old medical student named Günes Fratt said that he recognized the woman in the picture but he didn't know her name or her nationality. After a "forceful examination" conducted by a high level police officer with a very long name which seemed made up of only the letters ö, ü, and z, the witness had admitted that he had found the woman attractive and had made two "verbal overtures" to her in English during the first day of the trip, but that he had not been encouraged. The woman had not replied. Somewhat later on the trip, he thought he had seen her with a man and had drawn the conclusion that she was married and that she had only happened to appear alone. The only thing the witness could say about the man's appearance was that he was "presumably tall." During the latter part of the trip, the witness had not seen the woman. Günes Fratt's uncle, who was examined "informally" by the official with that impossible name, stated that he had kept a watchful eye on his nephew during the entire trip and that the boy had not been left alone for more than ten minutes at a time.

The embassy added the comment that both the travelers belonged to wealthy and highly respected families.

The letter did not particularly surprise Martin Beck. He had known all along that a letter containing that kind of information would appear sooner or later. Now they had moved a step forward and while he was getting the information together to send to Motala, he was mostly thinking about how it would feel to be "forcefully examined" by a high official of the Turkish police.

One flight up, Kollberg took the news in his stride.

"The Turks? Yes, I've heard about their methods."
He looked through his lists.
"Picture number 23, 38, 102, 109 . . ."
"That's enough."

Martin Beck looked through the pile of pictures until he found one which showed both of the men very clearly. He looked for a moment at the uncle's white mustache and then moved his eyes to Günes Fratt who was short, elegantly dressed, and had a small, dark mustache and even features. He didn't look so unattractive.

Unfortunately, Roseanna McGraw had thought differently. This was the fifteenth day since they had thought of collecting photographs. By now they had definitely identified forty-one passengers who had appeared in one or another of the pictures. In addition, two more pictures of the woman from Lincoln had been added to the collection. Both of them had been taken while the boat was in the Södertälje canal. Roseanna McGraw was in the background of one of them, out of focus and with her back turned toward the camera. But in the other, she was seen in profile by the railing with a railroad bridge behind her. She was three hours nearer her death, and had taken off her sunglasses and was squinting up at the sun. The wind had blown her dark hair and her mouth was half-open, as if she were on the verge of saying something or had just yawned. Martin Beck looked at her for a long time through the magnifying glass. Finally he said:

"Who took this picture?"
"One of the Danes," answered Melander. "Vibeke Amdal from Copenhagen. She was traveling alone in a single cabin."
"Find out whatever you can about her."

A half hour later the bomb exploded.

"There's a cable from the United States," said the woman on the other end of the telephone. "Shall I read it to you?"

"STRUCK A GOLD MINE YESTERDAY. TEN ROLLS OF EIGHT MILLIMETER COLOR FILM AND 150 STILLS. YOU WILL SEE A LOT OF ROSEANNA MCGRAW. SOME UNKNOWN CHARACTER SEEMS TO BE WITH HER. PAN AMERICAN GUARANTEES DELIVERY STOCKHOLM THURSDAY.

KAFKA

"Shall I try to translate it?"
"No thank you. That's okay for now."

Martin Beck fell into his chair. He rubbed his hairline and looked at his desk calendar. It was Wednesday, November 25.

Outside, it was raining, and it was chilly. It would soon begin to snow.

19

They showed the film at a studio right across the street from the North Station. It was crowded in the screening room and even at that moment Martin Beck had difficulty in getting over his aversion to groups of people.

His chief was there and so were the County Police Superintendent, the Public Prosecutor, Superintendent Larsson and Ahlberg. They had driven up from Motala. In addition, Kollberg, Stenström and Melander were there.

Even Hammar, who had seen more crime in his day than all the others put together, seemed quiet and tense and alert.

The lights were turned out.

The projector started to whirl.

"Oh, yes, yes . . . ah."

As usual it was hard for Kollberg to keep quiet.

The film started with a shot of the king's guard in Stockholm. They passed Gustaf Adolf's Square. Swung toward the North Bridge. The camera panned toward the Opera House.

"No style," said Kollberg. "They look like military police."

The County Police Superintendent whispered "shush."

Then came shots of pretty Swedish girls with turned up noses sitting in the sun on the steps of the Concert Hall. The tall buildings in the center of the city. A tourist poster in front of a Laplander's tent at Skansen's Park. Gripsholm Castle with a group of folk dancers in the foreground. Some middle-aged Americans with violet lips and sunglasses. The Hotel Reisen, Skepps Bridge, the stern of the *Svea Jarl*, shots from a boat trip to Djurgården and of a large passenger ship anchored in Stockholm seen from a sightseeing boat.

"Which boat is that?" asked the County Police Superintendent.

"Moore-McCormack's *Brazil*," said Martin Beck. "It comes here every summer."

"What building is that?" asked the County Police Superintendent a little later.

"It's an old people's home," said Kollberg. "Haile Selassie

saluted it once when he was here before the war. He thought it was the Royal Palace."

Seagulls, gracefully flapping their wings. Shots from the suburb Farsta, lines of people getting onto a bus with a plexiglass roof. Fishermen, sinisterly staring into the camera.

"Who took the pictures?" asked the County Police Superintendent.

"Wilfred S. Bellamy, Jr. from Klamath Falls, Oregon," said Martin Beck.

"Never heard of it," said the County Superintendent.

Svartmans Street, the pump of Brunkeberg Street, underexposed.

"Now," said the County Police Superintendent.

The *Diana* at Riddarholm's pier. Directly from the stern. Roseanna McGraw in a recognizable pose with her eyes looking straight up.

"There she is," said the County Superintendent.

"Oh God," said Kollberg.

The woman with the violet lips moved in from the left, with a toothy smile. Everything except for the shipping company's flag and the City Hall tower could be seen. White dots. Flickerings. Red-brown shadows. Darkness.

The lights were turned on and the man in the white coat glanced at the door.

"Just one second. There's a little trouble with the projector."

Ahlberg turned around and looked at Martin Beck.

"Now it caught fire and burned up," said First Detective Assistant Lennart Kollberg, who was a mind reader.

At the same moment the lights went out.

"Let's get it in focus, now, boys," said the County Superintendent.

Some more shots of the city, the backs of tourists, West Bridge, a pan shot of the bridge. Whitecaps on the water, the Swedish flag, some sailboats in a race. A long sequence of Mrs. Bellamy with her eyes closed sunning herself in a deck chair.

"Watch the background," said the County Police Superintendent.

Martin Beck recognized several of the people on the film: none of them were Roseanna McGraw.

The Södertälje locks, a road bridge, a railroad bridge. The mast seen from below with the shipping line's flag blowing lightly in the breeze against a blue sky. A motor sailer coming toward them with fish piled up on its deck, someone waving. The same motor sailer seen from the stern. Mrs. Bellamy's wrinkled profile to the right in the picture.

Oxelösund, from the water, its modern church tower against the sky, the steel mill with billowing chimneys. The film rose and fell with the boat's slow, soft rolling and had a diffuse, gray-green tone.

"The weather is worse now," said the County Superintendent.

The entire screen looked light gray, a quick turn of the camera, a bit of the bridge deck which was empty. The City of Gothenburg's flag, wet and slack, on the bow ahead in the distance. The helmsman in the picture, balancing a tray on the way down a ladder.

"What now?" asked the County Police Superintendent.

"They're outside of Hävringe," said Martin Beck. "Sometime around five or six o'clock. They've stopped because of the fog."

A shot from the stern of the shelter deck, deserted deck chairs, light gray, damp. No people.

The camera to the right, then with a light turn, back again. Roseanna McGraw on the ladder-way leading up from A deck, still bare-legged and in sandals but with a thin, plastic raincoat over her dress and a scarf drawn over her hair. Past the lifeboat, right into the camera, a quick, indifferent look at the photographer, her face calm and relaxed, out of the picture to the right. A quick turn. Roseanna McGraw from the back, with her elbows on the railing, the weight of her body resting on her right foot, on her toes, scratching her left ankle with her right hand.

Just about twenty-four hours from her death. Martin Beck held his breath. No one in the room said anything. The woman from Lincoln faded away while white spots streamed over the screen. The film had come to an end.

The fog had disappeared. A strained, violet-lipped smile. Shots of an elderly couple in deck chairs with blankets over their knees. There was no sunshine but it was not raining either.

"Who are they?" asked the County Superintendent.

"Two other Americans," said Kollberg. "Their name is Anderson."

The boat in a lock. A picture from the bridge over the forward deck, a lot of backs. A member of the crew on land, bent forward, pushing the wheel for the lock chamber's

113

gates. The camera flew on, the lock gates opened. Mrs. Bellamy's wrinkled, double chin seen from below with the bridge and the name of the ship in the background.

Another shot from the bridge. A new lock. The forward deck full of people. A change of scene to a man talking busily and wearing a straw hat.

"Cornfield, an American. He traveled alone," said Kollberg.

Martin Beck wondered if he had been the only one to see Roseanna McGraw in the scene that had just passed. She had been standing by the starboard railing, leaning on her elbows as usual, dressed in slacks and a dark sweater.

Shots of the locks continued but she was not in any of them.

"Where would that be?" asked the County Superintendent.

"Karlsborg," answered Ahlberg. "Not at Lake Vättern though. This is a bit west of Söderköping. They left Söderköping at a quarter to ten. This ought to have been around eleven o'clock."

A new lock. Another view of the forward deck. There she was again. Her sweater was black and had a turtleneck collar. A lot of people stood near her. She turned her face toward the camera and seemed to laugh. A fast change of scene. A shot of the water. A long sequence with Mrs. Bellamy and the Andersons. At one point the colonel from North Mälarstrand walked by, between the subject and the eye of the camera.

Martin Beck's neck was perspiring. Ten hours left. Had she laughed?

A short shot of the forward deck with only three or four persons on it. The boat was out on a lake. White spots. End of that roll.

The County Police Superintendent turned around.

"Roxen?"

"No, Asplången," said Ahlberg.

A drawbridge. Buildings on the shore. People on shore, waving and staring.

"Norsholm," said Ahlberg. "It's a quarter after three now."

The camera stayed stubbornly on the shore. Trees, cows, houses. A little girl, seven or eight years old, walked on the path along the edge of the canal. A blue cotton summer dress, two pigtails and wooden shoes. Someone on board threw a coin on the path. She picked it up, curtsied shyly, and looked confused. More coins were thrown. The child picked them up. She ran a few steps to keep up. A woman's hand with a shining half-dollar between two sinewy fingers with crimson colored fingernails. The camera came back again. Mrs. Bellamy with an exalted expression, throwing coins. The girl on the shore with her entire right hand full of money, totally confused, with her astonished blue eyes.

Martin Beck didn't see it. He heard Ahlberg take a deep breath, and Kollberg move in his chair.

In back of the do-gooding woman from Klamath Falls, Oregon, Roseanna McGraw had crossed the shelter deck from left to right. She had not been alone. At her left, and pressed closely to her, there had been another person. A man in a sport cap. He was a head taller than she and his profile could be seen during a brief tenth of a second against the light background.

Everyone had seen him.

"Stop the film," said the County Police Superintendent.

"No, no," said Ahlberg.

The camera did not return to the boat. A number of green shores glided past. Meadows, trees, tall grass blowing in the breeze, until the summer countryside faded away behind a lot of white spots.

Martin Beck took his handkerchief out of his breast pocket, crumpled it in his hands, and dried his neck.

The picture that covered the screen was new and surprising. The canal lay before and below them; it curved through a long, soft distance between tree-covered shores. Along the left side ran a path, and far off to the left some horses were grazing behind a fence. A group of people were walking along the path.

Ahlberg spoke before the County Superintendent had a chance to.

"This is west of Roxen now. The boat has passed Berg's locks. The photographer must have gone ahead to Ljungsbro during that time. There is the last lock before the one at Borensberg. It's about seven o'clock in the evening now."

The white bow with the Gothenburg flag appeared in the foreground far ahead. The people on the path came nearer.

"Thank God," said Ahlberg.

Only Martin Beck knew what he meant. The man who took the movie had an alternative. He could have gotten off the boat and gone with a guide who showed people around a monastery in Vreta during the time the boat was in the lock chamber.

115

Now there was a shot of the entire boat, moving slowly along the canal, inertly, with a gray-white plume of smoke which was reflected against the evening light.

But no one in the projection room looked at the boat any longer. The group of passengers on the path had come so close that separate individuals could be discerned. Martin Beck immediately identified Günes Fratt, the twenty-two year old medical student from Ankara. He walked ahead of the others, waving to the person who was following him.

Then he saw her.

About forty-five feet behind the main group there were two figures. One of them was Roseanna McGraw, still wearing light slacks and a dark sweater. Beside her, taking long steps, walked the man in the sport cap.

They were still quite far away.

"Let there be enough film," thought Martin Beck.

They came nearer. The position of the camera did not change.

Could they make out the faces?

He saw the tall man take her by the arm, as if to help her past a puddle of water in the path.

Saw them stop and look at the boat, which passed by and began to hide them from view. They were gone. But Mr. Bellamy from Klamath Falls was more stubborn than ever and held the position of his camera. Roseanna McGraw passed the boat, could be seen completely and clearly down on the path. She stopped walking and nodded her head, stretched out her right arm toward the person who was still hidden, but who then appeared. There.

The change of scene came as a shock. The sluice gate in the foreground, around and about, on the periphery, observers' legs. He thought he saw a pair of light trousers, feet in sandals and a pair of low shoes right beside them.

The picture was gone. It flickered slightly. Several people sighed. Martin Beck twisted his handkerchief between his fingers.

But it wasn't over yet. A somewhat underexposed shot of a face with violet lips and sunglasses filled the screen, and then disappeared to the right. Along the post side of A deck a waitress in a white blouse banged on a gong. Roseanna McGraw stepped out from behind her coming from the door to the dining room, wrinkled her forehead, looked up at the sky, laughed, and turned toward someone who was hidden. Not completely. They could see an arm in speckled tweed, a

116

bit of a shoulder. Then came the white spots, and then the film faded and ended in gray, gray, gray.

She had laughed. He was certain of it. At seven o'clock on the evening of the fourth of July. Ten minutes later she had eaten beefsteak, fresh potatoes, strawberries and milk, while a Swedish colonel and a German major had exchanged viewpoints on the siege of Stalingrad.

The screen was flooded with light. More locks. A blue sky with floating clouds. The captain with his hand on the telegraph machine.

"Sjötorp," said Ahlberg. "Twelve o'clock the next day. Soon they'll be out in Lake Vånern."

Martin Beck remembered all the details. One hour later it had stopped raining. Roseanna McGraw was dead. Her body had been lying naked and violated in the mud near the breakwater at Borenshult for nearly twelve hours.

On the canal boat's deck people were stretched out in deck chairs, talking, laughing, and looking up at the sun. A wrinkled, upper class woman from Klamath Falls, Oregon, smiled violetly toward the camera.

Now they were in Lake Vänern. People moved about here and there. The repulsive young man from the examination room in Motala emptied a sack of ashes into the lake. His face was sooty and he looked angrily at the photographer.

No woman in a dark sweater and light pants and sandals.

No tall man in a tweed jacket and a sport cap.

Roll after roll of film went by. Vänersborg in the evening sun. The *Diana* tied up there at the pier. A shot of a deck boy going on land. The Tröllhatten canal.

"There's a motor bike on the forward deck," said Ahlberg.

The boat lay tied up at Lilla Bomen in Gothenburg in the clear morning sun, at the stern of the full rigger, the *Viking*. A shot of the forward deck, people going down the gangway. The motor bike was no longer there.

Another shot, the woman with the violet lips sitting stiffly in one of Gothenburg's sightseeing boats, a pan over the Garden Association's flowers, white spots running vertically over the screen.

Fade-out. The end. The lights turned on.

After fifteen seconds of total silence Commissioner Hammar got out of his chair, looked from the County Police Superintendent to the Public Prosecutor and over at Larsson.

"Lunchtime, gentlemen. You are guests of the government."

He looked blandly at the others and said: "I guess that you will want to remain here for a little while."

Stenström left too. He was actually working on a different case.

Kollberg looked questioningly at Melander.

"No, I've never seen that man before."

Ahlberg held his right hand in front of his face.

"A deck passenger," he said.

He turned around and looked at Martin Beck.

"Do you remember the man that showed us around the boat in Bohus? The draperies that could be drawn if any of the deck passengers wanted to sleep on one of the sofas?"

Martin Beck nodded.

"The motor bike wasn't there in the beginning. The first time I saw it was in the locks after Söderköping," said Melander.

He took his pipe out of his mouth and emptied it.

"The guy in the sport cap could be seen there too," he said. "Once, from the back."

When they ran the film the next time, they saw that he was right.

20

The first snow of winter had begun to fall. It flew against the windows in large, white flakes which melted immediately and ran down the window panes in broad rills. It murmured in the rain gutters and heavy drops splashed against the metal window sills.

In spite of the fact that it was twelve noon, it was so dark in the room that Martin Beck had to turn on his reading light. It spread a pleasant light over his desk and the open file in front of him. The rest of the room lay in darkness.

Martin Beck put out his last cigarette, lifted up the ash tray and blew the ashes from the top of his desk.

He felt hungry and regretted that he had not gone to the cafeteria with Kollberg and Melander.

Ten days had passed since they had seen Kafka's film and they were still waiting for something to happen. Just as everything else in this case had, the new clue had disappeared in a jungle of question marks and doubtful testimony. Examination of witnesses had been conducted almost completely by Ahlberg and his staff, very carefully and with a great deal of energy. But the results had been meager. The most positive thing that could be said was that they had not heard anything to negate their theory that a deck passenger had come on board the boat in Mem, Söderköping or Norsholm, and had stayed on the boat all the way to Gothenburg. Nor was there anything to contradict their assumption that this deck passenger had been a man of average build, somewhat above average height, and that he had been wearing a sport cap, a gray speckled tweed jacket, gray gabardine trousers, and brownish shoes. Or, in addition, that he had a blue Monark motor bike.

The first mate, whose testimony was the most helpful, thought that he had sold a ticket to someone who reminded him of the man in the pictures. He did not know when. He wasn't even sure if it had been this past summer. It could have been one of the previous summers. He did have a weak recollection, however, that the man, if indeed it was the same one that they meant, could have had a bicycle or a motor bike with him and, in addition, some fishing equipment and other stuff which could point to the fact that he was a sport fisherman.

Ahlberg had heard this testimony himself and had pushed the witness to the boundary of the conceivable. A copy of the record was in Martin Beck's files.

AHLBERG: Is it usual to carry deck passengers on a cruise?
WITNESS: It was more usual in past years but there are always a few.
A: Where do they usually get on?
W: Wherever the boat stops, or at the locks.
A: What is the most natural stretch for deck passengers to stay on board?
W: Any part of the trip. A lot of people on bicycles or hikers get on in Motala or Vadstena to get across Lake Vättern.
A: And others?
W: Yes, what shall I say. We used to take vacationers from Stockholm to Oxelösund, and from Lidköping to Vånersborg, but we stopped that.
A: Why?
W: It got too crowded. The regular passengers have paid a good price. They shouldn't have to be crowded out by a bunch of old women and young people running around with their thermoses and lunch baskets.
A: Is there anything to contradict the fact that a deck passenger could have come on board at Söderöping?
W: Not at all. He could have come on board anyplace. At any lock, too. There are sixty-five locks on the way. In addition, we tie up at several different places.
A: How many deck passengers could you take on board?
W: At one time? Nowadays, seldom more than ten. Most of the time only two or three. Sometimes none at all.
A: What kind of people are they? Are they usually Swedish?
W: No, not at all. They are often foreigners. They can be anyone at all, although most of them are the kind that like boats and take the trouble to find out what the time-table is.
A: And their names are not placed on the passenger lists?
W: No.
A: Do the deck passengers have a chance to eat meals on board?

120

W: Yes, they can eat like the others if they want to. Often, in an extra sitting after the others have finished. There are fixed prices for the cost of the meal. A la carte, so to speak.

A: You said earlier that you haven't the slightest recollection of the woman on this photograph, and now you say that you think you recognize this man. There was no purser on board and as the first mate, didn't you have the responsibility to take care of the passengers?

W: I take their tickets when they come on board and I welcome them. After that they are left in peace. The idea of this trip isn't to shout out a lot of tourist information. They get enough of that in other places.

A: Isn't it odd that you don't recognize these people? You spent nearly three days with them.

W: All the passengers look alike to me. Remember, I see two thousand of them every summer. In ten years that makes twenty thousand. And while I'm working I am on the bridge. There are only two of us who can take watches. That makes twelve hours a day.

A: This trip was a special one, anyway, with unusual events.

W: I still had a watch on the bridge for twelve hours in any case. And, anyway, I had my wife with me on that trip.

A: Her name isn't on the passenger list.

W: No, why should it be? Members of the crew have the right to take their dependents along on some of the trips.

A: Then information that there were eighty-six people on board for this is not reliable. With deck passengers and dependents it could just as well have been one hundred?

W: Yes, of course.

A: Well, the man with the motor bike, the man on this picture, when did he leave the boat?

W: If I'm not even sure that I've seen him, how the devil should I know when he got off? A number of people who were in a hurry to catch trains, or planes, or other boats debarked at three o'clock in the morning as soon as we got to Lilla Bommen. Others stayed on and slept through the night and waited to debark in the morning.

A: Where did your wife get on board?

W: Here in Motala. We live here.

A: In Motala? In the middle of the night?

W: No, on the way up to Stockholm five days earlier. Then she left the boat on the next trip up, the eighth of July at four o'clock in the afternoon. Are you satisfied now?

121

A: How do you react when you think about what happened on that trip?

W. I don't believe that it happened as you say it did.

A: Why not?

W: Someone would have noticed it. Think about it, one hundred people on a small boat which is ninety feet long and fifteen feet wide. In a cabin which is as big as a rat trap.

A: Have you ever had anything other than a professional relationship with the passengers?

W: Yes, with my wife.

Martin Beck took the three photographs out of his inner pocket. Two of them had been made directly from the movie film, one was a partial blow-up of a black and white amateur picture from a group that Kafka had sent. They had two things in common: they depicted a tall man in a sport cap and a tweed jacket and they were both of very poor quality.

At this juncture hundreds of policemen in Stockholm, Gothenberg, Söderköping and Linköping had received copies of these pictures. In addition they had been sent to every public prosecutor's office and almost every police station from one end of the country to the other, and to several places in other countries.

They were poor photographs but anyone who was really acquainted with the man ought to have recognized him.

Maybe. But at their last meeting Hammar had said: "I think it looks like Melander."

He had also said: "This is no case. It is a guessing contest. Have we any reason to believe that the man is a Swede?"

"The motor bike."

"Which we are not sure was his."

"Yes."

"Is that all?"

"Yes."

Martin Beck put the pictures back in his inner pocket. He took Ahlberg's record of the hearing and looked back through several answers until he found the one he was looking for:

W: Yes, they can eat like the others, if they want to. Often, in an extra sitting after the others have finished. . . .

He thumbed through the papers and took out a list of the canal boats' personnel for the last five years. He read through the list, took his pen from the desk holder and placed a mark next to one of the names. It read:

122

Göta Isaksson, waitress, Polhems Street 7, Stockholm. Employed at the SHT Restaurant from October 15, 1964. The *Diana*, 1959-1961, the *Juno*, 1962, the *Diana*, 1963, the *Juno*, 1964.

There was no notation that either Melander or Kollberg had examined her.

Both telephone numbers for the taxi companies were busy and after he had dismissed the thought of getting hold of a radio car, he put on his hat and coat, turned up his collar and walked through the slush to the subway.

The headwaiter at the SHT Restaurant seemed harassed and irritated, but showed him to one of Miss Göta's tables right next to the swinging doors which led to the kitchen. Martin Beck sat down on the banquette and picked up the menu. While he was reading it, he looked out over the restaurant.

Almost all the tables were taken and only a few of the patrons were women. At several tables there were men sitting alone, most of them in late middle age. To judge by their familiar manner with the waitresses most of them ate there quite often.

Martin Beck watched the waitresses who rushed in and out through the swinging doors. He wondered which of them was Miss Göta and it took almost twenty minutes before he found out.

She had a round, friendly face, large teeth, short rumpled hair, the color of which Martin Beck described as "hair color."

He ordered small sandwiches, meatballs and an Amstel beer and ate slowly while he waited for the lunchtime rush to ebb away. When he had finished eating and had downed four cups of coffee, Miss Göta's other tables were empty and she came over to his.

He told her why he had come and showed her the photograph. She looked at it for a while, laid it down on the table, and took a breath before answering.

"Yes," she said. "I recognize him. I don't have any idea of who he is but he has traveled with the boats several times. Both the *Juno* and the *Diana*, I believe."

Martin Beck took the picture and held it up before her.

"Are you certain?" he asked. "The picture isn't very clear, it could be someone else."

"Yes, I'm certain. He was always dressed like that, by the way. I recognize the jacket and that cap."

123

"Do you remember if you saw him this past summer? You were on the *Juno* then, weren't you?"

"Yes. Let me think. I don't really think so. I see so many people. But the summer before last. I know that I saw him several times. Twice, in any case. I was on the *Diana* then and the girl I worked with, the other waitress, knew him. I remember that they used to talk to each other. He wasn't a regular passenger. I think he only went part of the way. He was a deck passenger. In any event he used to eat at the second or third sitting and he didn't come to all of the meals. But I think he usually got off in Gothenburg."

"Where does your friend live?"

"I wouldn't exactly call her my friend, we only worked together. I don't know where she lives, but she usually went to Växjö at the end of the season."

Miss Göta shifted her weight to the other foot and crossed her hands over her stomach as she looked up at the ceiling.

"Yes, that's right. Växjö. I think she lives there."

"Do you know how well she knew this man?"

"No, I really don't. I think she was a bit taken with him. She used to meet him sometimes when we were off duty although we weren't actually supposed to mix with the passengers. He looked quite pleasant. Attractive in a way. . . ."

"Can you describe him? I mean hair color, the color of his eyes, height, age, and so forth."

"Well, he was pretty tall. Taller than you are, I think. Not thin, not fat, but stockily built, one could say. He had rather broad shoulders, and I think he had blue eyes. I'm not sure about that, of course. Light hair, the kind called ash blond, a little lighter than mine. I didn't see his hair very much because he usually had that cap on. And he had nice teeth, I do remember that. His eyes were round . . . I mean I think he was a little popeyed. But he was definitely good looking. He could be between thirty-five and forty."

Martin Beck asked a few more questions but didn't get much more information. When he got back to his office he looked through the list again and soon found the name he was looking for. There was no address given, only a notation that she had worked on the *Diana* from 1960 until 1963.

It took him only a few minutes to find her name in the Växjö telephone book but he had to wait a long time before she answered the telephone. She seemed very unwilling to meet him but she couldn't really refuse.

124

Martin Beck took the night train and arrived in Växjö at 6:30 a.m. It was still dark and the air was mild and hazy. He walked through the streets and watched the city awaken. At a quarter of eight he was back at the railroad station. He had forgotten his galoshes and the dampness had begun to penetrate the thin soles of his shoes. He bought a newspaper at the kiosk and read it, sitting on a bench in the waiting room with his feet up against a radiator. After a while he went out, looked for a cafe which was open, drank some coffee and waited.

At nine o'clock he got up and paid his check. Four minutes later he was standing in front of the woman's door. The name Larsson was on a metal plate and above it was a calling card with the name Siv Svensson printed in an ornate style.

The door was opened by a large woman in a light blue bathrobe.

"Miss Larsson?" said Martin Beck.

The woman tittered and disappeared. From inside the apartment he heard her voice: "Karin, there's a man at the door asking for you."

He didn't hear an answer but the large woman came back and asked him to come in. Then she disappeared.

He stood in the small, dark hall with his hat in his hand. It was several minutes before a pair of drapes were pushed aside and a voice said to him, "Come in."

"I wasn't expecting you this early," said the woman who was standing inside.

She had gray streaks in her dark hair which was swept up sloppily from her neck. Her face was thin and seemed small in relation to her body. Her features were even and pretty but her skin was sallow and she had not had time to put on any make-up. There were still traces of mascara around her eyes, which were brown and slightly slanted. Her green jersey dress was tight across her breasts and her broad hips.

"I work late every night so I usually sleep late in the morning," she said with some annoyance.

"I beg your pardon," said Martin Beck. "I have come to ask your help in a matter which has a connection with your employment on the *Diana*. Did you work there last summer too?"

"No, last summer I was on a boat that went to Leningrad," answered the woman.

She was still standing up and looked at Martin Beck

cautiously. He sat down in one of the flowery easy chairs. Then he gave her the picture. She took it and looked at it. A nearly imperceptible change crossed her face, her eyes widened for a fraction of a second, but when he handed the picture back to him her face was stiff and dismissing.

"Yes?"

"You know this man, don't you?"

"No," she answered, without the slightest hesitation.

She walked across the room and took a cigarette out of a glass box which lay on the tile table in front of the window. She lit the cigarette and sat down on the sofa across from Martin Beck.

"What do you mean? I've never seen him. Why are you asking?"

Her voice was calm. Martin Beck looked at her for a while. Then he said:

"I know that you know him. You met him on the *Diana* the summer before last."

"No, I've never seen him. You had better go now. I have to get some sleep."

"Why are you lying?"

"You have no right to come here and be impertinent. You had better leave now, as I said."

"Miss Larsson. Why won't you admit that you know who he is? I know that you are not telling the truth. If you don't tell the truth now, it could be unpleasant for you later on."

"I don't know him."

"Since I can prove that you have been seen with this man several times, it would be better to tell the truth. I want to know who the man on the photograph is and you can tell me. Be reasonable."

"This is a mistake. You must be wrong. I don't know who he is. Please leave me alone."

During the conversation Martin Beck looked steadily at the woman. She was sitting on the edge of the sofa and constantly tapping her index finger against her cigarette although there wasn't any ash to knock off. Her face was tense and he saw how her jawbones moved under her skin.

She was frightened.

He stayed in the flowery chair and tried to get her to talk. But now, she said nothing at all, only sat stiffly on the sofa and peeled pieces of orange colored nail polish off her fingernails. Finally she got up and walked back and forth across the room. After a while Martin Beck also got up, took his

126

hat, and said goodbye. She didn't answer. She stood there stiff and dismissing with her back turned toward him.

"You will hear from me again," he said.

Before he left he laid his card on the table.

It was evening before he got back to Stockholm. He went directly to the subway and went home.

The next morning he telephoned Göta Isaksson. She wasn't going to work until the afternoon shift so that he was welcome to stop by whenever he wanted. One hour later he sat in her small apartment. She made some coffee in the kitchenette and when she had poured it and sat down opposite him, he said:

"I went down to Växjo yesterday and talked with your colleague. She denied that she had known the man. And she seemed frightened. Do *you* know why she won't admit that she knew him?"

"I have no idea. I actually know very little about her. She wasn't particularly talkative. We did work together for three summers but she seldom said anything about herself."

"Do you remember if she used to talk about men during the time you were together?"

"Only one. I remember that she said she had met a nice man on the boat. That must have been the second summer we worked together."

She cocked her head and counted to herself.

"Yes, it must have been the summer of '61."

"Did she speak about him often?"

"She mentioned him from time to time. It seemed as if she was seeing him too now and then. He must have been on several trips or else have met her in Stockholm or Gothenburg. Maybe he was a passenger. Maybe he was there because of her. What do I know?"

"You never saw him?"

"No. I've really never thought about it until now when you started asking questions. It *could* have been the same man as the one in the picture although it seemed as if she hadn't met him until two summers ago. And then she never said anything."

"What did she say about him the first summer? 1961?"

"Oh, nothing special. That he was nice. I think that she said that he was refined in some way. I suspect that she meant that he was well mannered and polite and so forth, as if ordinary people weren't good enough for her. But then she

127

stopped talking about him. I think it was over or else something happened between them because she seemed rather depressed toward the end of that summer."

"The following summer, did you see each other then?"

"No, she was still on the *Diana* then and I was working on the *Juno*. We saw each other a few times in Vadstena, I think. The boats meet there, but we never spoke. Won't you have some more coffee?"

Martin Beck could feel his stomach reacting but he couldn't bring himself to say no.

"Has she done anything? I mean, you're asking so many questions."

"No," said Martin Beck. "She hasn't done anything but we want to get hold of the man in the photograph. Do you remember if she said or did anything the summer before last which could have any connection with the man in this picture?"

"No, not that I remember. We shared a cabin and she was sometimes out at night. I suspect that she was meeting some man, but I'm not the type that meddles in other people's business. But I know that she wasn't particularly happy. I mean that if she was in love with someone, she should have seemed happy. But she wasn't. To the contrary, she was nervous and sad. Almost a bit strange. But that could have been because she was sick. She quit before the end of the season, a month early, I think. She just didn't show up one morning and I had to work alone the whole day before they found a replacement. They said that she had gone to the hospital, but no one knew what was wrong with her. She didn't come back that summer in any event. I haven't seen her since."

She poured some more coffee and offered Martin Beck some cookies, while she continued to talk, freely and a great deal, about her work routine, her fellow employees, and some passengers she remembered. It was another full hour before he left there.

The weather had gotten better. The streets were nearly dry and the sun shone down from a clear sky. Martin Beck didn't feel too well, due to the coffee, and he walked back to his office at Kristineberg. While he walked along the water at North Mälarstrand he thought about what he had learned of the two waitresses.

He hadn't learned anything at all from Karin Larsson but

128

the visit to Växjö had convinced him that she knew the man but didn't dare talk about it.

From Göta Isaksson he had learned that:

Karin Larsson had met a man on board the *Diana* during the summer of 1961. Probably a deck passenger, who had possibly traveled with the boat several times that summer.

That two summers later, the summer of 1963, she had met a man, probably a deck passenger, who traveled with the boat now and then. The man could well have been identical to the one on the photograph, according to Göta Isaksson.

That she had seemed depressed and nervous that summer and had quit her job before the end of the season sometime at the beginning of August, and had gone into the hospital.

He didn't know why. Nor did he know which hospital she had gone to and how long she had stayed. The only chance seemed to be to ask her directly.

He dialed the number in Växjö as soon as he got back to his office but didn't get any answer. He suspected that she was asleep or else was working on an early shift.

During the course of the afternoon he called again several times and also a few times during the evening.

On his seventh attempt at two o'clock in the afternoon the following day, a voice which he thought belonged to the large woman in the blue bathrobe answered.

"No, she's away."

"When?"

"She left last night. Who's calling?"

"A good friend. Where did she go?"

"She didn't say. But I heard her call and ask about the trains to Gothenburg."

"Did you hear anything else?"

"It sounded as if she was thinking about working on some boat."

"When did she decide to go?"

"She must have decided awfully quickly. There was some man here yesterday morning and right after that she made up her mind to leave. She seemed changed."

"Do you know which boat she was going to begin working on?"

"No, I didn't hear."

"Will she be gone long?"

"She didn't say. Can I give her any message if I hear from her?"

129

"No, thank you."

She had gone away, in a great hurry. He was sure that she was already on some boat going far out of reach. And now he was certain of what had before been only a guess.

She was frightened to death of someone or something and he had to find out why.

21

The office at the Växjö hospital was quick in getting the information.

"Larsson, Karin Elisabeth, yes, that's right, someone by that name did enter the women's clinic on August 9 and stayed until October 1 last year. For what? You will have to talk to the doctor about that."

The doctor at the women's clinic said: "Yes, it's quite possible that I remember. I'll call you back after I've looked at the records."

While Martin Beck waited he looked at the photographs and read through the description which they had made up after his conversation with Göta Isaksson. It was imperfect but a great deal better than the one they had a few hours earlier.

Height: approximately 6' 1". Body build: normal. Hair color: ash blond. Eyes: presumably blue (green or gray), round, slightly protrudent. Teeth: white, healthy.

The phone call came an hour later. The doctor had located the records.

"Yes, it was just as I thought. She came here on her own the evening of August 9. I remember that I was just going to go home when they called me to take a look at her. They had taken her into the examining room and she was bleeding pretty heavily from her genitals. She had obviously been bleeding heavily for quite a while because she had lost a lot of blood and was in pretty bad shape. No direct danger of course. When I asked her what had happened, she refused to answer. It is not unusual in my department that the patient won't discuss the reason for their bleeding. You can figure the reason out yourself and anyway, it usually comes out sooner or later. But this one didn't say anything at all in the beginning and later on she lied. Do you want me to read directly from the record for you? Otherwise I can tell you in layman's language."

"Yes, please do," said Martin Beck. "My Latin isn't very good."

"Mine neither," said the doctor.

He came from southern Sweden and spoke calmly, evenly and methodically.

"As I said, she bled profusely and had pain, so we gave her an injection. The bleeding came partially from the mouth of the uterus and partly from a wound in the vagina. At the mouth of the uterus and on the back part of the walls of the vagina were wounds which must have been made by a hard, sharp object. Around the muscles at the opening of the vagina there were splits which showed that the instrument must also have been terribly coarse. It isn't unusual for a woman who has undergone a careless or badly performed abortion, or has tried to do the abortion herself, to end up with bad wounds. But I can state that I have never seen anything like her condition in connection with an abortion. It seems totally impossible that she could have made such an attack on herself."

"Did she say that she had, that she had done it herself?"

"Yes, that's what she claimed when she finally said something. I tried to get her to tell me how it had happened but she kept on saying that she had done it herself. I didn't believe her and she knew that I didn't believe her and finally she didn't even try to convince me but just kept repeating what she had already said; 'I did it myself, I did it myself' like a broken phonograph record. The strange part of it was that she hadn't even been pregnant. The uterus was damaged but if she had been pregnant it must have been in such an early stage that she couldn't possibly have known it herself."

"What do you think had happened?"

"Some perverse maniac. It sounds crazy to say it right out but I am almost sure she was trying to protect someone. I was worried about her so we kept her here until October 1 although we could well have let her go earlier. In addition, I hadn't given up hope that she might speak up and tell us about it. But she kept on denying everything else and finally we had to let her go home. There was nothing more I could do. I did speak about it to some acquaintances in the police force here, and they must have done something, but never came up with anything."

Martin Beck said nothing.

"As I told you I don't know exactly what happened," said the doctor. "But it was some kind of a weapon, it's not easy to say what. Maybe a bottle. Has something happened to her?"

132

"No, I only wanted to talk with her."

"That isn't going to be particularly easy."

"No," said Martin Beck. "Thank you for the help."

He put his pen back in his pocket without having made a single note.

Martin Beck rubbed his hairline with the tips of his fingers while he looked at the picture of the man in the sport cap.

He thought about the woman in Växjö whose fear had caused her to hide the truth so stubbornly and carefully and had now driven her to flee from all questions. He stared at the photograph and mumbled, "Why?" But he knew already that there was only one answer to that question.

The telephone rang. It was the doctor.

"I forgot something that might be of interest to you. The patient in question had been in the hospital earlier, at the end of December 1962, to be exact. I forgot it, partly because I was on vacation then, partly because she was in another section of the hospital. But I read about it in her record when I took care of her. That time she had broken two fingers, the index finger and the middle finger on her left hand. That time, too, she refused to say how it had happened. Someone asked her if she had fallen down some stairs and at first she had replied that it had happened that way. But according to the doctor who took care of her at the time, that wasn't likely. The fingers had been broken backwards, toward the back side of her hand, but otherwise there were no other wounds at all. I don't know much more than that. She was treated as usual with gypsum and the like and she healed normally."

Martin Beck thanked him and hung up the receiver. He picked it up immediately again and dialed the number of the SHT Restaurant. He heard a lot of noise from the kitchen and someone calling out "Three beef à la Lindström!" right next to the receiver. A few minutes later Göta Isaksson answered.

"It's so noisy here," she said. "Where were we when she got sick? Yes, I do remember that. We were in Gothenburg then. She wasn't there when the boat left in the morning and then they didn't get a replacement for her until we got into Töreboda."

"Where did you stay in Gothenburg?"

"I used to stay at the Salvation Army Hotel on Post Street but I don't know where she stayed. Presumably on board or

133

at some other hotel. I'm sorry but I have to go now. The customers are waiting."

Martin Beck called Motala and Ahlberg listened silently.

"She must have gone to the hospital in Växjö directly from Gothenburg," he said, finally. "We had better find out where she stayed on the night of the eighth and ninth of August. It must have happened then."

"She was in pretty bad shape," said Martin Beck. "It's strange that she could get herself to Växjö in that condition."

"Maybe the man that did it lived in Gothenburg. In that case it must have happened in his house."

He was silent for a moment. Then he said:

"If he does it one more time, we'll get him. Even though she wouldn't say who he was, she knew his name."

"She's frightened," said Martin Beck. "Frightened to death as a matter of fact."

"Do you think it's too late to get hold of her?"

"Yes," replied Martin Beck. "She knew what she was doing when she ran off. As far as we are concerned she can be out of reach for years. We also know what she did."

"What did she do?" asked Ahlberg.

"She fled for her life," said Martin Beck.

22

The trampled, dirty snow was packed on the streets. Melting snow fell from the rooftops and dropped from the large, yellow star which hung between the buildings on either side of Regering Street. The star had been hanging there for a few weeks in spite of the fact that Christmas was still almost a month away.

Hurried people crowded the sidewalks and a steady stream of traffic filled the streets. Now and then a car would increase its speed and sneak into an opening in the line of cars, spraying muddy snow with its wheels.

Patrolman Lundberg seemed to be the only person who was not in a hurry. With his hands behind his back he walked down Regering Street toward the south staying close to the rows of Christmas decorated windows. Melting snow from the rooftops fell in heavy drops on his patrolman's hat and the slush squeaked under his galoshes. Near NK, he turned off onto Småland Street where the crowds and the traffic weren't as heavy. He walked carefully down the hill and outside of the house where the Jakob Police Station once stood. He stopped and shook the water from his hat. He was young and new to the police force and didn't remember the old police station which had been torn down several years ago and whose district is now part of the Klara Police Station.

Constable Lundberg belonged to the Klara police force and had an errand on Småland Street. At the corner of Norrland Street was a cafe. He entered it. He had been told to collect an envelope from one of the waitresses there.

While he waited, he leaned against the counter and looked around. It was ten o'clock in the morning and only three or four tables were occupied. Directly across from him, a man was sitting with a cup of coffee. Lundberg thought that his face looked familiar and searched his memory. The man began to reach for money in his trouser pocket, and while he was doing so he looked away from the constable.

Lundberg felt the hair on his neck stiffen.

The man on the Göta Canal!

He was almost sure that it was he. He had seen the photograph up at the station house several times and his picture was etched in his memory. In his eagerness he almost forgot the envelope, which was given to him the same second as the man got up and left a few coins on the table. The man was bare-headed and wasn't wearing an overcoat. He moved toward the door and Lundberg established that he was the same height and had the same build and hair coloring as the description.

Through the glass doors he could see the man turn to the right and, with a quick tip of his hat to the waitress, he hurried after him. About thirty feet up the street the man went into a driveway door and Lundberg reached it just in time to see the door close after the man. There was a sign on the door which said: J. A. ERIKSSON MOVING COMPANY./OFFICE. In the upper part of the door there was a glass window. Lundberg went up to the doorway slowly. He tried to look into the glass window as he went by but was only able to make out another glass window at a right angle to the door. Inside were two trucks with J. A. ERIKSSON MOVING COMPANY painted on their doors.

He passed the office door again, more slowly this time. With his neck outstretched, he looked in more carefully. Inside the glass windows were two or three partitions with doors leading to a corridor. On the nearest door which led to the smallest partitioned area and had a window in the glass, he could read the word CASHIER. On the next door there was a sign saying OFFICE—Mr. F. Bengtsson.

The tall man was standing there behind the counter, talking on the telephone. He stood turned toward the window with his back to Lundberg. He had changed from his jacket into a thin, black office coat and was standing with one hand in his pocket. A man in a windbreaker and a fur cap came in through the door farthest back on the short side of the corridor. He had some papers in his hands. When he opened the office door he looked toward the outer door and saw Lundberg who continued calmly out the doorway.

He had done his first shadowing.

"Now damn it," said Kollberg. "We can begin."

"Presumably he has his lunch hour at twelve o'clock," said Martin Beck. "If you hurry, you can get there. Clever boy, that Lundberg, if he's right. Call in when you can this afternoon so that Stenström can relieve you."

"I think I can manage myself today. Stenström can jump in this evening. So long."

At a quarter of twelve Kollberg was at his place. There was a bar right across the street from the moving company and he sat down there by the window. On the table in front of him was a cup of coffee and a small, red vase with a tired tulip in it, a twig of evergreen, and a dusty, plastic Santa Claus. He drank his coffee slowly and never took his eyes off the driveway across the street. He guessed that the five windows to the left of the driveway door belonged to the moving company, but he couldn't distinguish anything behind the glass due to the fact that the bottom halves of the windows were painted white.

When a truck with the moving company's name on the doors came out of the driveway, Kollberg looked at the clock. Three minutes to twelve. Two minutes later the office door opened and a tall man in a dark gray coat and a black hat came out. Kollberg put the money for his coffee on the table, got up, took his hat as he followed the man with his eyes. The man stepped off the curb, and crossed the street past the bar. When Kollberg came out on to the street he saw the man turn the corner onto Norrland Street. He followed him but didn't have to go far. There was a cafeteria about sixty feet from the corner which the man entered.

There was a line in front of the counter where the man waited patiently. When he got there he took a tray, grabbed a small container of milk, some bread and butter, ordered something at the window, paid, and sat down at an empty table with his back to Kollberg.

When the girl at the window shouted "One salmon!" he got up and went to get his plate. He ate slowly and with concentration and only looked up when he drank his milk. Kollberg had gotten a cup of coffee and placed himself so that he could see the man's face. After a while he was even more convinced that this really was the man on the film.

He neither drank coffee nor smoked after his meal. He wiped his mouth carefully, took his hat and coat and left. Kollberg followed him down to Hamn Street where he crossed over to the King's Gardens. He walked rather quickly and Kollberg stayed about sixty feet behind through the East Allé. At Mollin's fountain he turned to the right, passed the fountain which was half filled with dirty, gray snow, and continued up on the West Allé. Kollberg followed him past the "Victoria and Blanche" cafe, across the street to NK, down Hamn Street to Småland Street, where he crossed the street and disappeared into the driveway door.

"Oh yes," thought Kollberg, "that was certainly exciting."

He looked at his watch. Lunch and the walk had taken exactly three-quarters of an hour.

Nothing particular happened during the afternoon. The trucks returned, still empty. People went in and out of doors. A station wagon drove out and came back. Both trucks went out again and when one of them came back it almost collided with the station wagon which was on its way out.

Five minutes before five one of the truck drivers came out of the driveway door with a heavy, gray-haired woman. At five o'clock the other driver came out. The third had still not come back with his truck. Three more men followed him out and crossed the street. They entered the bar and loudly ordered their beers which they received and drank in silence.

Five minutes after five, the tall man came out. He stood in front of the door, took out a key ring from his pocket, and locked the door. Then he placed the key ring back in his pocket, checked to see if the door was properly locked, and walked out onto the street.

While Kollberg was putting his coat on he heard one of the beer drinkers say: "Folke's going home now."

And one of the others: "What does he have to do at home when he isn't hooked. He doesn't know how good he has it. You should have heard my old lady when I came home last night. ... What a time just because a man goes and has a few beers before he goes home after work. I swear. ..."

Kollberg didn't hear any more. The tall man who, without a doubt, was named Folke Bengtsson had disappeared out of sight. Kollberg caught up with him on Norrland Street again. The man was walking through the crowds toward Hamn Start and he continued on to the bus stop right across the street from NK.

By the time Kollberg got there four people were in line behind Bengtsson. He hoped that the bus wouldn't be too full to take them both. Bengtsson looked straight ahead of him the entire time and seemed to be looking at the Christmas decorations in NK's windows. When the bus arrived he hopped up on the step and Kollberg just managed to get on himself before the doors closed.

The man got off at St. Erik's Square. The traffic was tight and it took him a few minutes to get by all the traffic lights and cross to the other side of the square. On Rörstand Street he walked into a supermarket.

He continued along Rörstand Street, passed Birk Street, slunk across the street and went through a door. After a while Kollberg followed him and read the names on the mailboxes. There were two entrances to the house, one from the street and the other from the garden. Kollberg congratulated himself and his luck when he saw that Bengtsson lived in an apartment facing the street, two flights up.

He stationed himself in a doorway across the street and looked up at the third floor. In four of the windows there were frilly tulle curtains and a number of potted plants. Thanks to the man in the bar, Kollberg knew that Bengtsson was a bachelor and doubted that these windows belonged to his apartment. He concentrated his attention on the other two windows. One of them was open and while he was watching it, a light was turned on in the second one, which he presumed was the kitchen window. He saw the ceiling and the upper part of the walls which were white. A few times he could see someone moving about inside but not quite clearly enough to be sure it was Bengtsson.

After twenty minutes it was dark in the kitchen and a light was turned on in the other room. A little later Bengtsson appeared in the window. He opened it wide and leaned out. Then he closed it again, and closed the Venetian blinds. They were yellow and let light come through and Kollberg saw Bengtsson's silhouette disappear inside the room. The windows were without drapes because on both sides of the blinds broad streams of light appeared.

Kollberg went and telephoned to Stenström.

"He's home now. If I don't call you back before nine come and take over."

Eight minutes after nine, Stenström arrived. Nothing had happened except that the light had been turned off at eight o'clock and after that there had been only a weak, cold blue stream of light from between the blinds.

Stenström had an evening paper in his pocket and announced that the man was probably looking at a long, American film on the television.

"That's fine," said Kollberg. "I saw it ten or fifteen years ago. It has a wonderful ending. Everyone dies except the girl. I'll run along now and maybe I'll get to see some of it. If you call me before six I'll come over here."

It was a cold and clear morning. Ten hours later Stenström hurried off toward St. Erik's Square. Since the light had been turned off at ten-thirty in the room on the third floor, nothing had happened.

"Be careful that you don't freeze," Stenström had said before he left. When the door opened and the tall man came out, Kollberg was thankful for a chance to move.

Bengtsson had on the same overcoat as he had the day before but he had changed his hat to a gray Crimea cap. He walked quickly and the breath from his mouth looked like white smoke. At St. Erik's Square he took a bus to Hamn Street and a few minutes before eight Kollberg saw him disappear behind the door to the moving company.

A few hours later he came out again, walked the few steps to the cafe in the house next door, drank a cup of coffee and ate two sandwiches. At twelve o'clock he went to the cafeteria and when he had eaten, he took his walk through the city and went back to his office. At a few minutes after five he locked the door behind him, took the bus to St. Erik's Square, bought some bread in a bakery, and went home.

At twenty minutes after seven he came out of his front door again. At St. Erik's Square he walked to the right, and continued over the bridge and finally swung in to Kungsholm Street where he disappeared into a doorway. Kollberg stood for a while outside the door where the word BOWLING shone in large, red letters. Then he opened the door and went in.

The bowling hall had seven lanes and in back of a railing was a bar with small, round tables and some chairs. Echoes of voices and laughter filled the room. Now and then he heard the sound of rolling balls and the bang that followed.

Kollberg couldn't see Bengtsson anywhere. On the other hand he immediately spotted two of the three men from the bar the previous day. They sat at a table in the bar and Kollberg drew back toward the door in order not to be recognized. After a while the third man came toward the table together with Bengtsson. When they had begun to bowl, Kollberg left.

After a few hours the four bowlers came out. They separated at the trolley stop at St. Erik's Square and Bengtsson walked back the way he had come, alone.

At eleven o'clock it got dark in Bengtsson's apartment but by that time Kollberg was already home and in bed, while his bundled up colleague paced back and forth on Birk Street. Stenström had a cold.

The next day was a Wednesday and it went by pretty

much as the earlier days. Stenström nursed his cold and spent the major part of the day in the cafe on Småland Street.

That evening Bengtsson went to the movies. Five rows in back of him Kollberg watched while a blond, half naked Mr. America struggled with an ancient monster in cinemascope.

The next two days were similar. Stenström and Kollberg took turns following the man's uneventful and highly regimented life. Kollberg visited the bowling alley again and found out that Bengtsson played well and that for years he had played every Tuesday with his three friends from work.

The seventh day was a Sunday and according to Stenström the only interesting thing that happened during the entire day was a hockey match between Sweden and Czechoslovakia which, together with Bengtsson and ten thousand others, he attended.

Kollberg found a new door to stand in on Sunday night.

When, for the second Saturday in a row, he saw Bengtsson come out of his office, lock the door at two minutes after twelve and begin to walk toward Regering Street, he thought: "Now we'll go to the Löwenbräu, and have a beer." When Bengtsson opened the door to the Löwenbräu, Kollberg stood at the corner of Drottning Street and hated him.

That evening he went up to his office at Kristineberg and looked at some pictures from the film. He didn't know how many times he had looked at them.

He looked at each picture for a long time and very carefully, but in spite of the fact that it was hard to believe, he still saw the man whose quiet life he had witnessed for two weeks.

23

"It must be the wrong guy," said Kollberg.

"Are you getting tired?"

"Don't misunderstand me. I have nothing against standing and sleeping in a doorway on Birk Street night after night, but . . ."

"But what?"

"For ten out of fourteen days this is exactly what has happened: at seven o'clock he opens the blinds. At one minute after seven he opens the window. At twenty-five minutes to eight he shuts the window. At twenty minutes to eight he walks out of his front door, walks over to St. Erik's Square and takes the number 56 bus to the corner of Regering Street and Hamn Street, walks to the moving company and unlocks the door at one half minute before eight. At ten o'clock he goes down to the City Cafe, drinks two cups of coffee and eats a cheese sandwich. At one minute after twelve he goes to either one of two cafeterias. He eats. . . ."

"What does he eat?" asked Martin Beck.

"Fish or fried meat. He is finished at twenty minutes past twelve, takes a quick walk through the middle of town, and goes back to work. At five minutes past five he locks up and goes home. If the weather is terrible he takes the number 56 bus. Otherwise he walks up Regering Street, King Street, Queen Street, Barnhus Street, Uppland Street, Observatory Street, through Vasa Park, across St. Erik's Square, past Birk Street and home. On the way he sometimes shops in some supermarket where there aren't too many people. He buys milk and cake every day and every few days he gets bread, butter, cheese and marmalade. He has stayed home and looked at the boob tube eight evenings out of the fourteen. On Wednesdays he has gone to the seven o'clock show at the movies. Fanciful nonsense films, both times. I was the one that had to sit through them. On the way home he stuffs a frankfurter into himself, with both mustard and catsup. Two Sundays in a row he has taken the subway to the stadium to see the ice hockey games. Stenström got to see those. Two

Tuesdays in a row he has gone bowling with three men from his company. On Saturdays he works until twelve. Then he goes to the Löwenbräu and drinks a stein of beer. In addition, he eats a portion of frankfurter salad. Then he goes home. He doesn't look at the girls on the street. Sometimes he stops and looks at the posters in front of the movie houses or in the shop windows, mostly sporting goods and hardware stores. He doesn't buy any newspapers and doesn't subscribe to any either. On the other hand he does buy two magazines, *Rekord-Magasinet* and some kind of fishing magazine. I've forgotten what it is called. Garbage! There is no blue Monark motor bike in the cellar of the apartment house he lives in but there is a red one made by Svalen. It's his. He rarely gets any mail. He doesn't mix with his neighbors but does greet them on the stairs."

"What is he like?"

"How the devil should I know?" Kollberg said.

"Seriously."

"He seems healthy, calm, strong and dull. He keeps his window open every night. Moves naturally and without trouble, dresses well, doesn't seem nervous. He never seems to be in a hurry but doesn't drag. He ought to smoke a pipe. But doesn't."

"Has he noticed you?"

"I don't think so. Not me, in any case."

They sat quietly for a while watching the snow which came down in large, wet flakes.

"You understand," Kollberg said, "I have a feeling that we could keep on like this right up until he has his vacation next summer. It is a fascinating act, but can the country afford to keep two supposedly capable detectives . . ."

He stopped in the middle of the sentence.

"Capable, yes, by the way, last night there was a drunk who said "boo" to me while I stood there and watched the apartment. I almost got a heart attack."

"Is it the right guy?"

"He sure looks like it judging from the film."

Martin Beck rocked in his chair.

"Okay, We'll bring him in."

"Now?"

"Yes."

"Who?"

"You. After work. So that he doesn't neglect anything.

143

Take him up to your office and get the personal information. When you've got that, call me."

"Soft line?"

"Definitely."

It was nine-thirty on December 14. Martin Beck had suffered through the National Police's Christmas party with doughy cake and two glasses of almost alcohol free glögg.

He called the Public Prosecutor in Linköping and Ahlberg in Motala and was surprised to hear them both say: "I'm coming."

They arrived around three o'clock. The Public Prosecutor had come up via Motala. He exchanged a few words with Martin Beck and then went into Hammar's office.

Ahlberg sat in Martin Beck's visitor's chair for two hours but they only exchanged a few remarks of interest. Ahlberg said:

"Do you think it was he?"

"I don't know."

"It must be."

"Yes."

At five minutes after five they heard a knock on the door. It was the Public Prosecutor and Hammar.

"I am convinced that you are right," said the Prosecutor. "Use whatever method you like."

Martin Beck nodded.

"Hi," said Kollberg. "Have you time to come up? Folke Bengtsson, who I've mentioned to you, is here."

Martin Beck put down the receiver and got up. When he got to the doorway he turned around and looked at Ahlberg. Neither of them said anything.

He walked slowly up the stairs. In spite of the thousands of examinations he had conducted, he had a funny, bad feeling in his stomach and in the left part of his chest.

Kollberg had taken off his jacket and stood with his elbows on the desk, calm and jovial. Melander sat with his back to them, tranquilly occupied with his papers.

"This is Folke Bengtsson," said Kollberg, and stood up.

"Beck."

"Bengtsson."

They shook hands. Kollberg put his jacket on.

"I'll run along now. So long."

"So long."

Martin Beck sat down. There was a sheet of paper in

Kollberg's typewriter. He pulled it up a bit and read: "Folke Lennart Bengtsson, Office Manager, Born 6/8/1926 in Gustaf Vasa's parish, Stockholm. Unmarried."

He looked at the man. Blue eyes, a rather ordinary face. A few streaks of gray in his hair. No nervousness. In general, nothing special.

"Do you know why we have asked you to come here?"

"As a matter of fact, no."

"It is possible that you can help us with something."

"What would that be?"

Martin Beck looked toward the window and said:

"It's beginning to snow heavily now."

"Yes, it is."

"Where were you during the first week of July last summer? Do you remember?"

"I ought to. I was on vacation then. The company that I am with closes down for four weeks right after midsummer."

"Yes?"

"I was in several different places, two weeks on the West Coast, among others. I usually go fishing when I'm off. At least one week in the winter too."

"How did you get there? By car?"

The man smiled.

"No, I don't have a car. Not even a driver's license. I went on my motor bike."

Martin Beck sat quietly for a second.

"There are worse ways to travel. I had a motor bike too for a few years. What kind do you have?"

"I had a Monark then, but I got a new one this past fall."

"Do you remember how you spent your vacation?"

"Yes, of course. I spent the first week at Mem, that's on the Östogöta coast, right where the Göta Canal begins. Then I went on to Bohuslän."

Martin Beck got up and went over to the water pitcher which stood on top of a file near the door. He looked at Melander. Walked back. He lifted the hood off the tape recorder and plugged in the microphone. The man looked at the apparatus.

"Did you go by boat between Mem and Gothenburg?"

"No, from Söderköping."

"What was the name of the boat?"

"The *Diana*."

"Which day did you travel?"

"I don't remember exactly. One of the first days in July."

145

"Did anything special happen during the trip?"

"No, not that I can remember."

"Are you sure? Think about it."

"Yes, that's right. The boat had some engine trouble. But that was before I went on board. It had been delayed. Otherwise I wouldn't have made it."

"What did you do when you got to Gothenburg?"

"The boat got in very early in the morning. I went up to a place called Hamburgsund. I had reserved a room there."

"How long did you stay?"

"Two weeks."

"What did you do during those two weeks?"

"Fished as often as I could. The weather was poor."

Martin Beck opened Kollberg's desk drawer and took out the three photographs of Roseanna McGraw.

"Do you recognize this woman?"

The man looked at the pictures, one after the other. His expression didn't change in the slightest.

"Her face looks familiar in some way," he said. "Who is she?"

"She was on board the *Diana*."

"Yes, I think I remember," the man said indifferently.

He looked at the pictures again.

"But I'm not sure. What was her name?"

"Roseanna McGraw. She was an American."

"Now I remember. Yes, that's right. She was on board. I talked with her a few times. As well as I could."

"You haven't seen or heard her name since then?"

"No, actually not. That is to say, not before now."

Martin Beck caught the man's eyes and held them. They were cold and calm and questioning.

"Don't you know that Roseanna McGraw was murdered during that trip?"

A slight shift of expression crossed the man's face.

"No," he said, finally. "No . . . I really didn't know that."

He wrinkled his forehead.

"Is it true?" he said suddenly.

"It seems very strange that you haven't heard anything about it. To be blunt, I don't believe you."

Martin Beck got the feeling that the man had stopped listening.

"Naturally, now I understand why you have brought me here."

"Did you hear what I just said? It seems very strange that

146

you haven't heard anything about it in spite of everything that's been written about this case. I simply don't believe you."

"If I had known anything about it I certainly would have come in voluntarily."

"Come in voluntarily?"

"Yes, as a witness."

"To what?"

"To say that I had met her. Where was she killed? In Gothenburg?"

"No, on board the boat, in her cabin. While you were on board."

"That doesn't seem possible."

"Why not?"

"Someone must have noticed it. Every cabin was fully occupied."

"It seems even more impossible that you never heard anything about it. I find that hard to believe."

"Wait, I can explain that. I never read the newspapers."

"There was a lot about this case on the radio, too, and on the television news programs. This photograph was shown on Aktuellt. Several times. Don't you have a television?"

"Yes, of course. But I only look at nature programs and at movies."

Martin Beck sat quietly and stared at the man. After a minute he said:

"Why don't you read the papers?"

"They don't contain anything that interests me. Only politics and . . . yes, things like you just mentioned, murders and accidents and other miseries."

"Don't you ever read anything?"

"Yes, of course. I read several magazines, about sports, fishing, outdoor life, maybe even a few adventure stories sometimes."

"Which magazines?"

"*The Sportsman*, just about every issue. *All-Sport* and *Rekord-Magazine*, I usually buy them, and *Lektyr*. I've read that one since I was little. Sometimes I buy some American magazines about sport fishing."

"Do you usually talk about the events of the day with your fellow workers?"

"No, they know me and know that I'm not interested. They talk about things with each other, of course, but I seldom listen. That's actually true."

Martin Beck said nothing.

"I realize that this sounds strange, but I can only repeat that it's true. You have to believe me."

"Are you religious?"

"No, why do you ask?"

Martin Beck took out a cigarette and offered the man one.

"No thank you. I don't smoke."

"Do you drink?"

"I like beer. I usually take a glass or two on Saturdays after work. Never anything stronger."

Martin Beck looked at him steadily. The man made no attempt to avoid his glance.

"Well, we found you finally, anyway. That's the main thing."

"Yes. How did you do that, figure out that I was on board, I mean?"

"Oh, it was accidental. Someone recognized you. It's like this: so far you are the only person we have been in contact with who has spoken to this woman. How did you meet her?"

"I think that ... now I remember. She happened to be standing next to me and asked me something."

"And?"

"I answered. As well as I could. My English isn't that good."

"But you often read American magazines?"

"Yes, and that's why I usually take an opportunity to talk with Englishmen and Americans. To practice. It doesn't happen very often. Once a week I usually go to see an American film, it doesn't matter which. And I often look at detective films on the television, although the subject doesn't interest me."

"You spoke with Roseanna McGraw. What did you talk about?"

"Well ..."

"Try to remember. It could be important."

"She talked a bit about herself."

"What, for example?"

"Where she lived, but I don't remember what she said."

"Could it have been New York?"

"No, she named some state in America. Maybe Nevada. I actually don't remember."

"What else?"

"She said that she worked in a library. I remember that

148

very well. And that she had been to the North Cape and in Lapland. That she had seen the midnight sun. She also asked about a number of things."

"Were you together a lot?"

"No, I couldn't say that. I spoke with her three or four times."

"When? During which part of the trip?"

The man didn't answer immediately.

"It must have been the first day. I actually remember that we were together between Berg and Ljungsbro, where the passengers usually get off the boat while the boat is in the locks."

"Do you know the canal area well?"

"Yes, rather well."

"Have you been on it before?"

"Yes, several times. I usually plan to ride part of the way on the boats when it fits in with my vacation plans. There aren't too many of those old boats left and it really is a fine trip."

"How many times?"

"I can't exactly say right away. Maybe if I think about it, but it must have been at least ten times over the years. Different stretches. I only rode the whole way once, from Gothenberg to Stockholm."

"As a deck passenger?"

"Yes, the cabins are booked well in advance. In addition, it's rather expensive to go as a cruise passenger."

"Doesn't it get uncomfortable without a cabin?"

"No, not at all. You can sleep on a sofa in the salon under the deck if you want to. I am actually not terribly fussy about those things."

"So, you met Roseanna McGraw. You remember that you were with her at Ljungsbro. But later in the trip?"

"I think that I spoke with her again on some other occasion, in passing."

"When?"

"I don't actually remember."

"Did you see her during the latter part of the trip?"

"Not that I can remember."

"Did you know where her cabin was?"

No answer.

"Did you hear the question? Where was her cabin?"

"I'm really trying to remember. No, I don't think I ever knew."

149

"You were never inside her cabin?"

"No. The cabins are usually terribly small and anyway, they are double cabins."

"Always?"

"Well, there are a few singles. But not many. They are quite expensive."

"Do you know if Roseanna McGraw was traveling alone?"

"I haven't thought about it. She didn't say anything about it, as far as I can remember."

"And you never went with her to her cabin?"

"No, actually not."

"At Ljungsbro, what did you talk about there?"

"I remember that I asked her if she wanted to see the church at the Vreta monastery, which is right near there. But she didn't want to. And anyway, I'm not sure that she understood what I meant."

"What else did you talk about?"

"I don't actually remember. Nothing in particular. I don't think we spoke that much. We walked part of the way along the canal. A lot of other people did too."

"Did you see her with anyone else?"

The man sat quietly. He looked toward the window expressionlessly.

"This is a very important question."

"I understand that. I'm trying to remember. She must have spoken with other people while I stood next to her, some other American or Englishman. I don't remember anyone in particular."

Martin Beck got up and walked over to the water pitcher.

"Do you want something to drink?"

"No thank you. I'm not thirsty."

Martin Beck drank a glass of water and walked back, pressed a button under the desk, stopped the tape recorder and took off the tape.

A minute later Melander came in and went to his desk.

"Will you take care of this, please," he said.

Melander took the tape and left.

The man called Folke Bengtsson sat completely straight in his chair and looked at Martin Beck with blue, expressionless eyes.

"As I said before, you are the only person we know who remembers, or will admit that he has talked to her."

"I understand."

"It wasn't possibly you that killed her?"

150

"No, as a matter of fact, it wasn't. Do you believe that?"

"Someone must have done it."

"I didn't even know that she was dead. And not even what her name was. You surely don't believe that . . ."

"If I had thought that you would admit it, I wouldn't have asked the question in that tone of voice," said Martin Beck.

"I understand . . . I think. Were you fooling?"

"No."

The man sat quietly.

"If I told you that we know for a fact that you were inside that woman's cabin, what would you say?"

He didn't answer for about ten seconds.

"That you must be wrong. But you wouldn't say that if you weren't certain, isn't that right?"

Martin Beck said nothing.

"In that case I must have been there without knowing what I was doing."

"Do you usually know what you are doing?"

The man lifted his eyebrow slightly.

"Yes, I usually do," he said.

Then he said, positively:

"I wasn't there."

"You understand," said Martin Beck. "This case is highly confusing."

"Thank God that isn't going on the tape," he thought.

"I understand."

Martin Beck stuck a cigarette in his mouth and lit it.

"Are you married?"

"No."

"Have you a steady relationship with any woman?"

"No. I'm a confirmed bachelor, I'm used to living alone."

"Have you any brothers or sisters?"

"No, I was an only child."

"And grew up with your parents?"

"With my mother. My father died when I was six. I hardly remember him."

"Have you no relationships with women?"

"Naturally, I'm not totally inexperienced. I am going on forty."

Martin Beck looked steadily at him.

"When you need female company do you usually turn to prostitutes?"

"No, never."

"Can you name some women who you have been with for either a longer or shorter period of time?"

"Maybe I can, but I don't choose to."

Martin Beck pulled out the desk drawer a little bit and looked down into it. He rubbed his index finger along his lower lip.

"It would be best if you named someone," he said haltingly.

"The person who I'm thinking of at the moment, with whom my relationship was . . . most lasting, she . . . Yes, she's married now and we aren't in contact with one another any more. It would be painful for her."

"It would still be best," said Martin Beck without looking up.

"I don't want to bring her any unpleasantness."

"It won't be unpleasant for her. What's her name?"

"If you can guarantee . . . her married name is Siv Lindberg. But I ask you really . . ."

"Where does she live?"

"Lidingö. Her husband is an engineer. I don't know the address. Somewhere in Bodal I think."

Martin Beck took a last glance at the picture of the woman from Lincoln. Then he closed the drawer again and said:

"Thank you. I am sorry that I have to ask these kinds of questions. But, unfortunately, it's part of my job."

Melander came in and sat down at his desk.

"Would you mind waiting a few minutes," Martin Beck said.

In the room one flight below, the tape recorder played back the last replies. Martin Beck stood with his back against the wall and listened.

"Do you want something to drink?"

"No thank you. I'm not thirsty."

The Public Prosecutor was the first person to say something.

"Well?"

"Let him go."

The Public Prosecutor looked at the ceiling, Kollberg at the floor, and Ahlberg at Martin Beck.

"You didn't press him very hard," said the Prosecutor. "That wasn't a very long examination."

"No."

"And if we hold him?" asked the Prosecutor.

"Then we have to let him go by this time on Thursday," Hammar replied.

"We don't know anything about that."

"No," said Hammar.

"All right," said the Prosecutor.

Martin Beck nodded. He walked out of the room and up the stairs and he still felt ill and had some discomfort in the left part of his chest.

Melander and the man called Folke Bengtsson seemed as if they hadn't moved at all since he had left them.

"I am sorry that it was necessary to bother you. Can I offer you transportation home?"

"I'll take the subway, thank you."

"Maybe that's faster."

"Yes, actually."

Martin Beck walked with him to the ground floor out of routine.

"Goodbye then."

"Goodbye."

An ordinary handshake.

Kollberg and Ahlberg were still sitting and looking at the tape recorder.

"Shall we continue to tail him?" asked Kollberg.

"No."

"Do you think he did it?" asked Kollberg.

Martin Beck stood in the middle of the floor and looked at his right hand.

"Yes," he said. "I'm sure he did."

24

The apartment house reminded him, in a basic way, of his own in the southern part of Stockholm. It had narrow flights of stairs, standardized nameplates on the doors and incinerator doors between each floor. The house was on Fredgat Road in Bodal and he took the Lidingö train to get there.

He had chosen the time carefully. At a quarter past one, Swedish office workers are sitting at their desks and small children are having their afternoon naps. Housewives have turned on some music on the radio and sit down to have a cup of coffee with saccharin tablets.

The woman who opened the door was small, blond, and blue-eyed. Just under thirty and rather pretty. She held on to the doorknob anxiously, as if prepared to close the door immediately.

"The police? Has anything happened? My husband. . . ."

Her face was frightened and confused. It was also fetching, Martin Beck thought. He showed her his identification, which seemed to calm her.

"I don't understand how I can help you but, by all means, come in."

The furniture arrangement was nondescript, gloomy and neat. But the view was marvelous. Just below lay Lilla Värtan and two tugboats were in the process of bringing a freighter to the pier. He would have given a lot to have traded apartments with her.

"Do you have children?" he asked as a diversion.

"Yes, a little girl ten months old. I've just put her in her crib."

He took out the photographs.

"Do you know this man?"

She blushed immediately, looked away, and nodded uncertainly.

"Yes, I knew him. But—but it was several years ago. What has he done?"

Martin Beck didn't answer at once.

"You understand, this is very unpleasant. My husband . . ."

She was searching for the right words.

"Why don't we sit down," said Martin Beck. "Forgive me for suggesting it."

"Yes. Yes, of course."

She sat down on the sofa, tense and straight.

"You have no reason to be afraid or worried. The situation is this: we are interested in this man, for several reasons, as a witness. They have nothing to do with you, however. But it is important that we get some general information about his character from someone who has, in one way or another, been together with him."

This statement didn't seem to calm her particularly.

"This is terribly unpleasant," she said. "My husband, you understand, we have been married for nearly two years now, and he doesn't know anything ... about Folke. I haven't told him, about that man ... but, yes, naturally, as you can understand, he must surely have known that I had been with someone else ... before. ..."

She was even more confused and blushed profusely.

"We never speak about such things," she said.

"You can be completely calm. I am only going to ask you to answer some questions. Your husband will not know what you say, or anyone else for that matter. In any case, no one that you know."

She nodded but continued to look stubbornly to the side.

"You knew Folke Bengtsson?"

"Yes."

"When and where did you know him?"

"I ... we met more than four years ago, at a place, a company where we both worked."

"Eriksson's Moving Company?"

"Yes, I worked there as a cashier."

"And you had a relationship with him?"

She nodded with her head turned away from him.

"For how long?"

"One year," she said, very quietly.

"Were you happy together?"

She turned and looked at him uncertainly and raised her arms in a helpless gesture.

Martin Beck looked over her shoulder and out the window toward a dismal, gray winter sky.

"How did it begin?"

"Well, we ... saw each other every day and then we began

to take our coffee breaks together and then lunches. And ...
yes, he took me home several times."

"Where did you live?"

"On Uppland Street."

"Alone?"

"Oh no. I was still living with my parents then."

"Did he ever come upstairs with you?"

She shook her head, energetically, still without looking at
him.

"What else happened then?"

"He invited me to the movies a few times. And then ...
yes, he asked me to dinner."

"At his house?"

"No, not at first."

"When?"

"In October."

"How long had you been going out with him by then?"

"Several months."

"And then you began a real relationship?"

She sat quietly for a long while. Finally she said: "Do I
have to answer that question?"

"Yes, it is important. It would be better if you answer here
and now. It would save a great deal of unpleasantness."

"What do you want to know? What is it that you want me
to say?"

"You had intimate relations with one another, didn't you?"
She nodded.

"When did it begin? The first time you were there?"
She looked at him helplessly.

"How often?"

"Not particularly often, I think."

"But every time you were there?"

"Oh, no. Not at all."

"What did you usually do when you were together?"

"Well . . . oh, everything, have something to eat, talk, look
at TV and the fish."

"Fish?"

"He had a large aquarium."

Martin Beck took a deep breath.

"Did he make you happy?"

"I . . ."

"Try to answer."

"You ... you are asking such difficult questions. Yes, I
think so."

"Was he brutal to you?"

"I don't understand."

"I mean when you were together. Did he hit you?"

"Oh, no."

"Did he hurt you in any other way?"

"No."

"Never?"

"No, he never did. Why should he have?"

"Did you ever talk about getting married and living together?"

"No."

"Why not?"

"He never said anything about it, never a word."

"Weren't you afraid of becoming pregnant?"

"Yes. But we were always so careful."

Martin Beck managed to make himself look at her. She still sat completely straight on the edge of the sofa, with her knees tightly together and the muscles in her legs strained. She was not only red in the face but even her neck was red, and there were small, fine drops of perspiration along her hairline.

He started again.

"What kind of a man was he? Sexually?"

The question came as a total surprise to her. She moved her hands worriedly. Finally she said:

"Nice."

"What do you mean by nice?"

"He . . . I mean that I think he needed a lot of tenderness. And I, I am, I was the same."

Even though he was sitting less than five feet from her he had to strain to hear what she had said.

"Did you love him?"

"I think so."

"Did he satisfy you?"

"I don't know."

"Why did you stop seeing each other?"

"I don't know. It just ended."

"There is one more thing I must ask you to answer. When you had intimate relations, was it always he who took the initiative?"

"Well . . . what do you want me to say . . . I suspect that it was so, but it usually is that way. And I always agreed."

"How many times would you say it happened?"

"Five," she whispered.

157

Martin Beck sat quietly and looked at her. He should have asked: Was he the first man you slept with? Did you usually take all your clothes off? Did you have the lights on? Did he ever . . .

"Goodbye," he said, and got up. "Forgive me for having bothered you."

He closed the door after himself. The last thing he heard her say was:

"Forgive me, I'm a little shy."

Martin Beck walked back and forth in the slush on the platform while he waited for the train. He kept his hands in his coat pockets and hunched his shoulders, whistled absent-mindedly and off key.

Finally, he knew what he was going to do.

25

Hammar was doodling old men on a piece of scratch paper while he listened. This was supposed to be a good sign. Then he said:

"Where will you get the woman from?"

"There must be someone on the force."

"You had better find her first."

Two minutes later Kollberg said: "Where are you going to get the girl from?"

"Is it you or I who has spent eighteen years with his rear end on the edge of other people's desks?"

"It won't do to get just anybody."

"No one knows the force better than you do."

"Well, I can always look around."

"Right."

Melander appeared totally uninterested. Without turning around or taking his pipe out of his mouth, he said: "Vibeke Amdal lives on Toldebod Street, is fifty-nine years old and the widow of a brewer. She can't remember having seen Roseanna McGraw other than on the picture she took at Riddarholm. Karin Larsson ran away from her boat in Rotterdam, but the police say that she isn't there. Presumably, she took another boat with false papers."

"Foreign ones, of course," said Kollberg. "She knows all about that. It can take a year before we find her. Or five. And then she might not say anything. Has Kafka answered?"

"Not yet."

Martin Beck went upstairs and called Motala.

"Yes," said Ahlberg calmly. "I guess it is the only way. But where are you going to get the girl from?"

"From the police force. Yours, for example."

"No, she doesn't fit."

Martin Beck hung up. The telephone rang. It was a man from the regular patrol force at the Klara Station.

"We did exactly as you said."

"And?"

"The man seems sure enough, but believe me, he's on the

alert. He's watchful, turns around, stops often. It would be hard to tail him without his noticing it."

"Could he have recognized any of you?"

"No, there were three of us and we didn't follow him. We just stood still and let him walk by. Anyway, it's our job not to be recognized. Is there anything else we can do for you?"

"Not for the moment."

The next telephone call came from Adolf Fredrik's Station.

"This is Hansson in the fifth. I watched him at Bråvalla Street both this morning and now when he came home."

"How did he act?"

"Calm, but I have an idea that he was being careful."

"Did he notice anything?"

"Not a chance. This morning I was sitting in the car, and the second time there was a real crowd. The only time I was near him was just now at the newspaper stand on St. Erik's Square. I stood two places behind him in the line."

"What did he buy?"

"Newspapers."

"Which ones?"

"A whole bunch. All four morning papers and both of the evening rags."

Melander tapped on the door and stuck his head in.

"I think I'll go home now. Is that all right? I have to buy some Christmas presents," he explained.

Martin Beck nodded and hung up the phone and thought, "Oh God, Christmas presents," and immediately forgot what he had been thinking.

He went home late but even so he didn't manage to avoid the crowd. The Christmas rush was on and all the stores were open later than usual.

At home his wife said that he seemed absentminded, but he didn't hear her and didn't reply.

At breakfast she said: "Will you be off between the holidays?"

Nothing happened before a quarter after four when Kollberg thundered in and said: "I think I have one who will do."

"On the force?"

"Works at Berg Street. She's coming here at nine-thirty tomorrow morning. If she seems right, Hammar can fix it so that we can borrow her."

"What does she look like?"

"I think that she looks like Roseanna McGraw in some way. She's taller, a little prettier, and presumably shrewder."

"Does she know anything?"

"She's been with the police force for several years. A calm and good girl. Healthy and strong."

"How well do you know her?"

"Hardly at all."

"And she isn't married?"

Kollberg took a piece of paper out of his pocket.

"Here's everything you need to know about her. I'm leaving now. I have to go Christmas shopping."

"Christmas presents," thought Martin Beck and looked at the clock. Four-thirty, and struck by a thought, he grabbed the telephone and called the woman in Bodal.

"Oh, is it you. Yes, Mr. . . ."

"Am I calling at a bad time?"

"No, it's not . . . my husband doesn't get home before a quarter of six."

"Just one simple question. Did the man we spoke about yesterday ever get anything from you? I mean any present, a souvenir or something like that?"

"No, no presents. We never gave each other any. You understand. . . ."

"Was he tight?"

"Economical, I would rather say. I am too. The only . . ."

Silence. He could almost hear her blushing.

"What did you give him?"

"A . . . a little amulet . . . or trinket . . . just an inexpensive little thing. . . ."

"When did you give it to him?"

"When we parted. . . . He wanted to have it . . . I always used to have it with me."

"He took it from you?"

"Well, I was glad to give it to him. One always wants a souvenir . . . even if . . . above all, I mean. . . ."

"Thank you very much. Goodbye."

He telephoned Ahlberg.

"I've talked to Larsson and the Commissioner. The Public Prosecutor is sick."

"What did they say?"

"Okay. They realized that there isn't any other way. It's certainly unorthodox, but . . ."

"It's been done many times before, even in Sweden. What I plan to suggest to you now is a great deal more unorthodox."

"That sounds good."

"Give out the news to the press that the murder is almost cleared up."

"Now?"

"Yes, immediately. Today. You understand what I mean?"

"Yes, a foreigner."

"Right. Like this, for example: 'According to the latest announcement a person, who has been searched for by Interpol for a long time for the murder of Roseanna McGraw, has finally been arrested by the American police.'"

"And we have known all along the murderer was not in Sweden?"

"That's only an example. The main thing is to get it out fast."

"I understand."

"Then I think you'd better come up here."

"Immediately?"

"Just about."

A messenger came into the room. Martin Beck gripped the telephone tightly with his left shoulder and ripped open the cable. It was from Kafka.

"What does he say?" asked Ahlberg.

"Only three words: 'Set a trap.'"

26

Policewoman Sonja Hansson was actually not unlike Roseanna McGraw. Kollberg had been right.

She sat in Martin Beck's office with her hands crossed lightly in her lap and looked at him with calm gray eyes. Her dark hair was combed into a page-boy and her bangs softly over her left eyebrow. Her face was healthy and her expression was open. She didn't seem to use make-up. She looked no more than twenty years old but Martin Beck knew that she was twenty-five.

"First of all I want you to understand that this is voluntary," he said. "You can say no if you want to. We have decided to ask you to take on this assignment because you have the best qualifications to handle it, mainly because of your looks."

The girl in the chair pushed the hair off her forehead and looked questioningly at him.

"Then too," Martin Beck continued, "you live in the middle of the city and you're not married or living with anyone, as it's so nicely put these days. Is that right?"

Sonja Hansson shook her head.

"I hope I can help you," she said. "But what's wrong with my looks?"

"Do you remember Roseanna McGraw, the girl from America, who was murdered on the Göta Canal last summer?"

"Do I? I'm in the Missing Persons Bureau and worked on the case for a while."

"We know who did it and we know that he's here in the city. I've examined him. He admits that he was on the boat when it happened and that he had met her, but says he doesn't even know about the murder."

"Isn't that a rather improbable statement? I mean there was so much about it in the papers."

"He says that he doesn't read newspapers. We couldn't get anything out of him. He acted totally forthright and seemed to answer all our questions honestly. We couldn't hold him and we have stopped tailing him. Our only chance is that he will do it again and that's where you come in. If you are willing, and think you can handle it, of course, you shall be his next victim."

"How nice," said Sonja Hansson and reached for a cigarette from her purse.

"You are rather like Roseanna and we want you to act as a decoy. It would be like this: he works as an office manager for a moving company on Småland Street. You go there and say that you want to have something moved, flirt with him and see that he gets your address and telephone number. You must get him interested in you. Then, we have to wait and hope."

"You say that you've already examined him? Won't he be on his guard?"

"We have leaked some information that ought to have quieted him."

"Am I also supposed to vamp him? How the devil will that be? And if I succeed?"

"You don't need to be afraid. We will always be in the vicinity. But you have to learn everything about the case first. Read all the material we have. You must be Roseanna McGraw. Be like her, I mean."

"Of course I acted in school plays but mostly as angels or mushrooms."

"Well, then. You'll manage."

Martin Beck sat quietly for a few seconds. Then he said:

"This is our only chance. He only needs an impulse and we must provide it for him."

"Okay, I'll try. I hope I can handle it. It isn't going to be easy."

"You'd better start going through everything, reports, films, the examination reports, letters, photographs. After that we can talk about it again."

"Now?"

"Yes, today. Commissioner Hammar will arrange for you to be relieved of your other work until this is settled. And one more thing. We have to go to your apartment and see what it looks like. We have to arrange for duplicate keys as well. We'll get to the rest later."

Ten minutes later he left her in the room next to Kollberg's and Melander's office. She sat with her elbows on the table reading the first report.

Ahlberg arrived that afternoon. He had hardly sat down

164

when Kollberg stormed in and thumped him on the back so hard that he almost fell out of the visitor's chair.

"Gunnar's going home tomorrow," said Martin Beck. "He ought to get a look at Bengtsson before he goes."

"It had better be a pretty careful look," said Kollberg. "But then we had better get going immediately. Every person in town plus half the population in general is running around buying Christmas presents."

Ahlberg snapped his fingers and struck his forehead with the palm of his hand.

"Christmas presents. I had completely forgotten."

"Me too," said Martin Beck. "That is to say I think of it from time to time but that's all that ever gets done about it."

The traffic was terrible. Two minutes before five they dropped Ahlberg at Norrmalms Square and watched him disappear into the crowds.

Kollberg and Martin Beck sat in the car and waited. After twenty-five minutes Ahlberg returned and climbed into the back seat. He said:

"It sure is the guy on the film. He took the number 56 bus."

"To St. Erik's square. Then he'll buy milk, bread and butter and go home. Eat, look at the boob tube, go to bed and fall asleep," said Kollberg. "Where shall I drop you?"

"Here. Now we have our big chance to go Christmas shopping," Martin Beck said.

One hour later in the toy department, Ahlberg said: "Kollberg was wrong. The other half of the population is here too."

It took them nearly three hours to finish their shopping and another hour to get to Martin Beck's home.

The next day Ahlberg saw the woman who was to be their decoy for the first time. She had still only managed to get through a small part of the case material.

That evening Ahlberg went home to Motala for Christmas. They had agreed to start the plan working right after the new year.

27

It was a gray Christmas. The man called Folke Bengtsson spent it quietly at his mother's house in Södertälje. Martin Beck thought unendingly about him, even during the Christmas service in church and in a bath of perspiration under his Santa Claus mask. Kollberg ate too much and had to spend three days in the hospital.

Ahlberg called the day after Christmas and was not sober.

The newspapers contained several differing and unengaging articles which pointed to the fact that the Canal Murder was almost cleared up and that the Swedish police no longer had any reason to bother with the case.

There was the traditional new year's murder in Gothenburg which was solved within twenty-four hours. Kafka sent a tremendously large repulsive postcard, which was lilac colored and portrayed a deer against a sunset.

January 7 arrived and looked like January 7. The streets were full of gray, frozen people without money. The sales had begun but even so, the stores were nearly empty. In addition, the weather was hazy and freezing cold.

January 7 was D-Day.

In the morning Hammar inspected the troops. Then he said:

"How long are we going to carry on with this experiment?"

"Until it succeeds," said Ahlberg.

"So *you* say."

Hammar thought about all the situations which might possibly arise. Martin Beck and Kollberg would be needed for other tasks. Melander and Stenström should, at least part of the time, be working on other cases. Soon, the Third District would begin to complain because the borrowed girl never came back.

"Good luck, children," he said.

A little later, only Sonja Hansson was there. She had a cold and sat in the visitor's chair and sniffled. Martin Beck looked at her. She was dressed in boots, a gray dress and long black tights.

"Do you plan to look like that?" he said sourly.

"No, I'll go home and change first. But I want to point out one thing. On July 3 last year, it was summertime and now it's winter. It might look a bit odd if I ran into a moving company office just now in sunglasses and a thin dress and asked if they could move a bureau for me."

"Do the best you can. The important thing is that you understand the main point."

He sat quietly for a while.

"If, indeed, *I* have understood it," he said.

The woman looked thoughtfully at him.

"I think I understand," she said, finally. "I have read every word that has been written about her, over and over again. I've seen the film at least twenty times. I have chosen clothing that would seem to fit and I have practiced in front of the mirror for hours. But I'm not starting off with much. My personality and hers are completely different. Her habits were different too. I haven't lived as she did and I'm not going to either. But I'll do the best I can."

"That's fine," said Martin Beck.

She seemed unapproachable and it wasn't easy to get through to her. The only thing he knew about her private life was that she had a daughter who was five years old and lived in the country with her grandparents. It seemed that she had never been married. But in spite of the fact that he didn't know her very well, he thought a great deal of her. She was shrewd, and down to earth, and dedicated to her job. That was a lot to say about someone.

It was four o'clock in the afternoon before he heard from her again.

"I've just been there. I went directly home afterwards."

"Well, he isn't going to come and break down the door right away. How did it go?"

"I think it went well. As well as one could wish. The bureau will be delivered tomorrow."

"What did he think of you?"

"I don't know. I got the feeling that he lit up a little bit. It's hard to say when I don't really know how he acts."

"Was it difficult?"

"To be honest, it wasn't very hard. I thought he seemed rather nice. He's attractive, too, in some way. Are you sure that he's the right guy? That's not to say that I have had a great deal of experience with murderers, but I find it difficult to think of him as the man who murdered Roseanna McGraw."

"Yes, I'm sure. What did he say? Did he get your telephone number?"

"Yes, he wrote the address and telephone number down on a loose sheet of paper. And I told him that I have a house phone but that I don't answer it if I am not expecting someone so that it's best to telephone ahead. In general, he didn't say very much."

"Were you alone in the room with him?"

"Yes. There was a fat, old lady on the other side of the glass partition but she couldn't hear us. She was talking on the telephone and I couldn't hear her."

"Did you get a chance to talk with him about anything other than the bureau?"

"Yes, I said that the weather was miserable and he said, it certainly was. Then I said that I was glad Christmas was over and then he said that he was too. I added that when one was alone as I was, Christmas could be sad."

"What did he say then?"

"That he, too, was alone and thought that it was rather dismal at Christmas, even though he usually spent it with his mother."

"That sounds fine," said Martin Beck. "Did you talk about anything else?"

"No, I don't think so."

It was silent on the other end of the telephone for a while. Then she added: "Yes, I asked him to write down the address and telephone number of the company for me so that I wouldn't have to look it up in the telephone book. He gave me a printed business card."

"And then you left?"

"Yes, I couldn't stand around and chatter any longer but I took my time leaving. I had opened my coat and so forth. To show my tight sweater. Yes, by the way, I said that if they didn't get there with the bureau during the day, it didn't make any difference to me since I was almost always home at night waiting for someone to call. But he thought that the bureau would get there during the morning."

"That's fine. Listen, we thought we'd have a rehearsal this evening. We are going to be at the Klara Police Station. Stenström will play Bengtsson and telephone you. You answer, call me at Klara, and we'll come to your house and wait for Stenström. Do you follow me?"

"Yes, I understand. I'll telephone you as soon as Stenström has called. About what time?"

"I'm not going to tell you. You won't know what time Bengtsson will call."

"No, you are right. And, Martin."

"Yes."

"He was actually charming in some way. Not at all unpleasant or snappy. Although it's certain that Roseanna McGraw must have thought so too."

The day room in the Fourth District Station House at Regering Street was neat and proper although it offered very few possibilities for entertainment.

It was a quarter past eight and Martin Beck had read the evening paper twice, just about everything except the sport pages and the classified advertisements. For the past two hours Ahlberg and Kollberg had been playing chess, which obviously took away any desire they might have had to talk. Stenström was sleeping in a chair near the door with his mouth open. He could be excused because he had been working on another case the night before. Anyway, he was there to play the villain and didn't need to be on the alert.

At twenty minutes past eight Martin Beck went over to Stenström and poked him.

"Let's start now."

Stenström got up, went over to the telephone, and dialed a number.

"Hi," he said. "Can I come over? Yes? Fine."

Then he went back to his chair and fell asleep.

Martin Beck looked at the clock. Fifty seconds later the telephone rang. It was tied into a direct line and reserved for their use. No one else could use it.

"This is Beck."

"It's Sonja, hi. He just called. He's coming in a half an hour."

"I got it."

He put down the phone.

"Now let's get started, boys."

"You can just as well give up," said Ahlberg across the chess board.

"Okay," said Kollberg. "One to nothing, in your favor."

Stenström opened one eye.

169

"Which way shall I come from?"

"Any way you want to."

They went down to the car which was parked in the police station's driveway. It was Kollberg's own car and he drove. When he swung out onto Regering Street he said: "Can I be the one to stand in the closet?"

"Oh, no. That's Ahlberg's job."

"Why?"

"Because he's the only one who can go into the house without the risk of being recognized."

Sonja Hansson lived on Runeberg Street, three flights up in the house on the corner facing Eriksberg Square.

Kollberg parked between the Little Theater and Tegner Street. They separated. Martin Beck crossed the street, went into the shrubbery and hid himself in the shadow of Karl Staaff's statue. From there he had a fine view of her house and also of Eriksberg Square as well as of the most important parts of the surrounding streets. He saw Kollberg walk casually down the south side of Runeberg Street with exquisite nonchalance. Ahlberg determinedly held his course toward the front door, opened it, and went in, as if he were a tenant on his way home. Forty-five seconds from now Ahlberg would be in the apartment and Kollberg in his place in the arch under Eriksberg Street. Martin Beck pushed his stop watch and looked at the time. It had been exactly five minutes and ten seconds since he had hung up the telephone after his conversation with Sonja Hansson.

It was raw and he turned up his coat collar and mumbled threateningly at a drunk who tried to bum a cigarette from him.

Stenström had really done his best.

He arrived twelve minutes early and from a completely unexpected direction. He sneaked around the corner from the Eriksberg Park stairs and walked with a group of moviegoers. Martin Beck didn't see him until he slunk into the house.

Kollberg had also functioned satisfactorily because he and Martin Beck met in front of the door.

They went in together, unlocked the inner glass doors, and neither of them said anything.

Kollberg took the stairs. He was supposed to stand a half a flight below the apartment and not advance before he received the signal. Martin Beck tried to get the elevator down by pressing the button but it didn't come. He ran up the stairs and passed the surprised Kollberg on the second floor. The elevator was up on the third floor. Stenström had put it out of commission by not closing the inside door. Thus he had succeeded in ruining that part of the plan which had Martin Beck taking the elevator to the floor above the apartment and arriving at it from above.

It was still quiet in the apartment but Stenström must have depended upon speed, because after only thirty seconds they heard a muffled shriek and some noise. Martin Beck had his key ready and ten seconds later he was in Sonja Hansson's bedroom.

The girl sat on the bed. Stenström stood in the middle of the floor and yawned while Ahlberg held his right arm loosely against his back.

Martin Beck whistled and Kollberg thundered into the apartment like an express train. In his haste he knocked over the table in the hall. He hadn't had any doors to open.

Martin Beck rubbed his nose and looked at the girl.

"Good," he said.

She had chosen the realistic style he had hoped for. She was barefoot and bare-legged and had on a thin, short-sleeved cotton robe which stopped just above her knees. He was sure that she didn't have anything on underneath.

"I'll put something else on and make some coffee," she said.

They went into the other room. She came in almost immediately, dressed in sandals, jeans and a brown sweater. Ten minutes later the coffee was ready.

"My door key sticks," said Ahlberg. "I have to wiggle it like the devil."

"That doesn't matter so much," said Martin Beck. "You won't ever be in as much of a hurry as we are."

"I heard you on the stairs," said Stenström. "Just as she opened the door."

"Rubber soles," said Kollberg.

"Open it faster," said Martin Beck.

"The key hole in the closet is great," said Ahlberg. "I saw you almost the entire time."

"Take the key out next time," said Stenström. "I really wanted to lock you in."

The telephone rang. They all stiffened.

The girl picked up the receiver.

171

"Yes, hello . . . hi . . . no, not tonight . . . well, I'm going to be busy for a while . . . have I met a man? . . . yes, you could say that."

She hung up and met their glances.

"That was nothing," she said.

28

Sonja Hansson stood in the bathroom rinsing out her washing. When she turned off the water she heard the telephone ringing in the living room. She ran in and picked up the receiver without even taking time to dry her hands.

It was Bengtsson.

"Your bureau is on the way," he said. "The truck ought to be there in about fifteen minutes."

"Thanks. It was nice of you to call. Otherwise, I wouldn't open the door, as I told you. I didn't think you would get it here so early. Shall I come down to your office and pay the bill or . . ."

"You can pay the driver. He has the invoice with him."

"Fine. I'll do that, Mr. . . . ?"

"The name's Bengtsson. I hope you'll be satisfied with our service. The truck will be there in fifteen minutes, as I said."

"Thank you. Goodbye."

When she hung up she dialed Martin Beck's number.

"The bureau will be here in fifteen minutes. He just telephoned. I almost missed the call. It was just luck that I heard the phone. I didn't think of it before, but when the water's running in the bathtub I can't hear the phone."

"You had better not bathe for a while," Martin Beck replied. "Seriously, though, you have to be near the telephone all the time. You can't go up to the attic or down to the laundry or anything like that."

"No. I know. Shall I go down to his office as soon as the bureau has come?"

"Yes, I think so. Then call me."

Martin Beck sat in the same room with Ahlberg. As he hung up the phone. Ahlberg looked at him questioningly.

"She's going there in about a half an hour," Martin Beck told him.

"We'll just have to wait then. She's a great gal. I like her."

When they had waited for over two hours Ahlberg said: "Surely nothing could have happened to her now . . ."

"Keep calm," Martin Beck answered. "She'll call."

She called after they had waited another half hour.

"Have you been waiting long?"

Martin Beck grimaced:

"What happened?" he said, and cleared his throat.

"I'll start at the beginning. Two drivers came with the bureau twenty minutes after I talked with you. I hardly glanced at it and told the men where it should go. After they left I noticed it was the wrong bureau and I went down to the office to complain."

"You were there quite a long time."

"Yes. He had a customer when I arrived. I waited outside the counter and he looked at me several times. It seemed as if he was trying to hurry the customer. He was very distressed about the bureau and I said that the mistake was mine, not the firm's. We almost got into an argument about whose fault it was. Then he went to find out if someone could bring the right bureau this evening."

"Yes?"

"But he couldn't arrange it. He promised to see that it would be delivered tomorrow morning, though. He said that he would have liked to bring it himself, and I said that was too much to ask although it certainly would have been pleasant."

"Okay. Did you leave then?"

"No. Of course I stayed on."

"Was he hard to talk to?"

"Not particularly. He seemed a little shy."

"What did you talk about?"

"Oh, about how terrible the traffic is and how much better Stockholm was before. And then I said that it was no city to be alone in, and he agreed, although he said he rather liked to be alone."

"Did he seem pleased to talk to you?"

"I think so. But I couldn't hang around forever. He mentioned that he liked to go to the movies but other than that he didn't go out very much. Then, there wasn't much more to say. So I left. He walked out to the door with me and was very polite. What do we do now?"

"Nothing. Wait."

Two days later Sonja Hansson went back to the moving company again.

"I wanted to thank you for your help and tell you that I received the bureau. I'm sorry to have caused so much trouble."

174

"It was no trouble at all," Folke Bengtsson said. "Welcome back. What can I do for you?"

A man walked into the room and interrupted. He was clearly the head of the firm.

When she left the office she knew Bengtsson was looking at her over the counter and before she reached the outer door, she turned and met his glance.

A week went by before the experiment was repeated. Once again the pretext was a transportation problem. She hadn't been in her apartment on Runeberg Street very long and she was still in the process of gathering some furniture from the attics of various relatives.

After still another five days she stood in his office again. It was just before five o'clock and because she was passing by, she thought she'd drop in.

Sonja Hansson sounded annoyed when she telephoned in.

"He still isn't reacting?" Martin Beck asked.

"Only moderately. You know, I don't believe it's him."

"Why not?"

"He seems so shy. And rather disinterested. I've pressed hard these last few times, practically given him an open invitation. Seven out of ten men would have been sitting outside my door howling like wolves by now. I guess I just don't have any sex appeal. What should I do?"

"Keep on."

"You ought to get someone else."

"Keep on."

Continue. But how long? Hammar's look became more questioning each day that passed. And each time Martin Beck looked in the mirror the face that he met was more and more haggard.

The electric clock on the wall at the Klara Police Station ticked away another three uneventful nights. Three weeks had passed since the dress rehearsal. The plan was well conceived but it didn't seem as if they would ever have the chance to put it into effect. Absolutely nothing had happened. The man called Folke Bengtsson lived a quiet, routine life. He drank his buttermilk, went to work, and slept nine hours each night. But they were almost losing contact with their normal environments and the outer world. The hounds chased themselves to death without the fox even noticing it, Martin Beck thought.

He stared angrily at the black telephone which hadn't rung for three weeks. The girl in the apartment on Runeberg

Street knew that she should only use it for one specific situation. They called her twice each evening to check. Once at six o'clock and again at midnight. That was the only thing that happened.

The atmosphere in Martin Beck's home was strained. His wife didn't say anything but the doubting look in her eyes was more and more unmistakable each time he looked at her. She had given up faith in this project a long time ago. It had not produced results and kept him away from home night after night. And he neither could nor would explain.

It was somewhat better for Kollberg. At least Melander and Stenström relieved him every third night. Ahlberg kept occupied by playing chess by himself. That was called solving problems! All topics of conversation had long since been pre-empted.

Martin Beck had lost the train of thought in the newspaper article he was pretending to read. He yawned and looked at his exemplary colleagues who, eternally silent, sat directly opposite each other, their heads heavy with profound thoughts.

He looked at the clock. Five to ten. Yawning again, he got up stiffly and went out to the toilet. He washed his hands, rinsed his face with cold water, and went back.

Three steps from the door he heard the telephone ring.

Kollberg had already finished the conversation and hung up.

"Has he . . . ?"

"No," said Kollberg. "But he's standing outside on the street."

This was unexpected, but actually, it changed nothing. During the next three minutes Martin Beck analyzed the plan in detail. Bengtsson couldn't force the downstairs door and even if he managed to, he would hardly have time to get upstairs before they got there.

"We had better be careful."

"Yes," said Kollberg.

They drove to a fast stop in front of the Little Theater. They separated.

Martin Beck stood, watched Ahlberg go through the door, and looked at his watch. It was exactly four minutes since she had called. He thought about the woman alone in the apartment two flights above. Folke Bengtsson was not in sight.

Thirty seconds later a light was turned on in a window on

176

the third floor. Someone came to the window and seemed to look out, but disappeared almost immediately. The light went off. Ahlberg was in his place. They waited in silence by the bedroom window. The room was dark but a narrow stream of light came through the door. The lamp in the living room was lit to show that she was home. The living room window looked out on the street and from the bedroom they could see several of the cross streets leading to the intersection.

Bengtsson stood by the bus stop directly across the street. He looked up at her window. He was the only person there and after he had stood for a while he looked up and down the block. Then he walked slowly to the island that separated the street's traffic. He disappeared in back of a telephone booth.

"Here it comes," said Ahlberg and motioned in the dark.

But the telephone didn't ring and after several minutes Bengtsson could be seen walking up the street.

Along the sidewalk there was a low, stone wall which ran all the way to the building below her window. In back of it was an area planted with grass and low shrubbery which led to the house.

Once again, the man stopped on the sidewalk and looked up toward her house. Then he began to walk toward her door slowly.

He disappeared out of sight and Ahlberg stared out over the square until he caught sight of Martin Beck who stood completely still by a tree in the planted area. A trolley on Birger Jarls Street hid him for several seconds and after it had passed, he was gone.

Five minutes later they saw Bengtsson again.

He had been walking so close to the wall that they hadn't seen him until he stepped out into the street and began to walk toward the trolley stop. At a kiosk, he stopped and bought a frankfurter. While he ate it, he leaned against the kiosk and stared up at her window constantly. Then he began to pace back and forth with his hands in his pockets. Now and then he looked up at her window.

Fifteen minutes later Martin Beck was behind the same tree again.

The traffic was heavier now and a stream of people crowded the streets. The movie had ended.

They lost sight of Bengtsson for a few minutes but then saw him in the midst of a group of moviegoers on the way home. He walked toward the telephone booth but stopped again a few feet from it. Then suddenly, he walked briskly toward the planted area. Martin Beck turned his back and slowly moved away.

Bengtsson passed the little park, crossed the street toward the restaurant and disappeared down Tegner Street. After a few minutes he appeared again on the opposite sidewalk and began to walk around Eriksberg Square.

"Do you think that he's been here before?" asked the woman in the cotton dressing gown. "I mean, it's only pure chance that I saw him tonight."

Ahlberg stood with his back against the wall near the window and smoked a cigarette. He looked at the girl beside him who was turned toward the window. She stood with her feet apart and had her hands in her pockets. In the weak light reflected from the street, her eyes looked like dark holes in her pale face.

"Maybe he's been here every night," she said.

When the man below had completed his fourth swing around the square, she said: "If he's going to tramp around like this the whole night I'll go crazy and Lennart and Martin will freeze to death."

At 12:25 he had gone around the square eight times, each time moving faster. He stopped below the steps leading to the park, looked up at the house, and half-ran across the street to the trolley stop.

A bus drove in to the bus stop, and when it moved on, Bengtsson was no longer there.

"Look. There's Martin," Sonja Hansson said.

Ahlberg jumped at the sound of her voice. They had been whispering to one another all along and now she spoke in her normal voice for the first time in two hours.

He saw Martin Beck hurry across the street and jump into a car which had been waiting in front of the theater. The car started even before he managed to close the door and drove off in the same direction as the bus.

"Well, thanks for your company tonight," Sonja Hansson said. "I think I'll go to sleep now."

"Do that," said Ahlberg.

He would have liked some sleep too. But ten minutes later he walked through the door at Klara Police Station. Kollberg arrived shortly after.

They had made five moves in their chess game when Martin Beck came in.

"He took the bus to St. Erik's Square and went home. He

178

put out the light almost immediately. He's probably asleep by now."

"It was mere chance that she caught sight of him," said Ahlberg. "He could have been there several times before."

Kollberg studied the chess board.

"And if he was? That wouldn't prove anything."

"What do you mean?"

"Kollberg's right," Martin Beck answered.

"Sure," said Kollberg. "What would it prove? Even I have roamed around like an alley cat outside of the houses of willing girls."

Ahlberg shrugged his shoulders.

"Although I was younger, a lot younger."

Martin Beck said nothing. The others made a half-hearted attempt to concentrate on their game. After a while, Kollberg repeated a move which caused a draw, in spite of the fact that he had been winning.

"Damn," he said. "That chatter makes me lose my train of thought. How much are you leading by?"

"Four points," said Ahlberg. "Twelve and a half to eight and a half."

Kollberg got up and paced around the room.

"We'll bring him in again, make a thorough search of his house, and rough him up as much as we can," he said.

No one answered.

"We ought to tail him again, with new guys."

"No," said Ahlberg.

Martin Beck continued biting on his index finger knuckle. After a while he said: "Is she getting frightened?"

"It doesn't seem so," Ahlberg answered. "That girl doesn't get nervous easily."

"Neither did Roseanna McGraw," Martin Beck thought.

They didn't say much more to one another but were still wide awake when the noise of the morning traffic on Regering Street indicated that although their work day had ended, it was just beginning for others.

Something had happened, but Martin Beck didn't know exactly what.

Another twenty-four hours passed. Ahlberg increased his lead by another point. That was all.

The following day was a Friday. Three days were left before the end of the month and the weather was still mild. It had been rainy and misty most of the time and at twilight the fog had rolled in.

179

At ten minutes after nine the sound of the telephone broke the silence. Martin Beck picked up the receiver.

"He's here again. He's standing by the bus stop."

They got there fifteen seconds faster than the last time in spite of the fact that Kollberg had parked on the street. After another thirty seconds they saw the signal indicating that Ahlberg was in his place.

The repetition was almost frightening. The man named Folke Bengtsson wandered around Eriksberg Square for four hours. Four or five times, he hesitated outside the telephone booth. Once he stopped and ate a frankfurter. Then he rode home. Kollberg followed him.

Martin Beck had been very cold. He walked quickly back to the police station with his hands in his pockets and his eyes on the ground.

Kollberg arrived a half hour later.

"Everything's quiet."

"Did he see you?"

"He was like a sleepwalker. I don't think he would have seen a hippopotamus three feet in front of him."

Martin Beck dialed Policewoman Sonja Hansson's number. He felt that he must think about her in terms of her job and her rank. Otherwise, he couldn't stand it.

"Hello. It's Saturday tomorrow, or more correctly, today. He works until noon. Be there when he finishes work. Rush past him as if he were on your way somewhere. Take hold of his arm and say: 'Hi, I've been waiting for you. Why haven't I heard from you?' or something like that. Don't say any more. Then take off. Leave your coat open too."

He paused briefly.

"You have to do your very best this time."

He hung up. The others stared at him.

"Which one of you is the best tail?" he said absently.

"Stenström."

"Okay. From the minute he leaves his house early tomorrow morning I want him followed. Stenström can do it. Report all his movements. Here. On the other telephone. Two of us must be here all the time."

Ahlberg and Kollberg were still staring at him but he didn't notice.

At twenty-two minutes to eight Bengtsson walked out of his front door and Stenström's assignment had begun.

He stayed near the moving company's office on Småland

180

Street until quarter after eleven when he went into a cafe and sat down by the window waiting.

At five minutes to twelve he saw Sonja Hansson on the corner.

She was dressed in a thin, blue tweed coat which was open. He could see that her belt was drawn tightly around her waist. Under the coat she had on a black turtleneck sweater. She was bare-headed and carried gloves but no pocketbook. Her stockings and black pumps seemed much too thin for the weather.

She continued across the street and disappeared out of his sight.

The moving company's employees began to leave the office and finally the man named Bengtsson came out and locked the door. He ambled along the sidewalk and when he had moved a few feet, Sonja Hansson came running toward him. She greeted him, took hold of his arm, and said something to him as she looked in his eyes. She let go of his arm almost immediately and continued talking while she took a few steps away from him. Then she turned on her heels and ran on.

Stenström had seen her face. It had expressed eagerness, pleasure and appeal. Silently he applauded her performance.

The man remained where he was and watched her run down the street. He moved slightly, as if to follow her, but changed his mind, put his hands in his pockets and walked off slowly with his head lowered.

Stenström got his hat, paid the cashier, and looked out the door carefully. When Bengtsson had turned the corner, Stenström left and followed him.

At the Klara Police Station Martin Beck stared dismally at the telephone. Ahlberg and Kollberg had temporarily given up their chess game and sat silently behind their newspapers. Kollberg was working on a crossword puzzle and chewing frantically on a pencil.

When the telephone finally rang, he bit so hard on the pencil that it broke in two.

Martin Beck had the receiver at his ear before the first ring ended.

"Hi. It's Sonja. I think it went well. I did exactly as you said."

"Good. Did you see Stenström?"

"No, but I guess he was there someplace. I didn't dare turn around so I just kept on going for several blocks."

"Are you nervous?"

181

"No. Not at all."

It was a quarter after one before the telephone rang again.

"I'm in a tobacco shop on Järn Square," said Stenström. "Sonja was great. She must have put a few bees in his bonnet. We've walked through the center of town, over the main bridge and now he's wandering around in the Old City."

"Be careful."

"No problem. He's walking like a zombie. He doesn't see or hear anything around him. I've got to take off now so that I don't lose him."

Ahlberg got up and walked back and forth on the floor.

"It's not exactly a pleasant job we've given her," he said.

"She'll do fine," said Kollberg. "She'll take care of the rest of it well too. I hope Stenström doesn't scare him off though."

"Stenström's okay," he said, after a while.

Martin Beck said nothing.

It was a few minutes after three when they heard from Stenström again.

"Now we're on Folkung Street. He just keeps going up and down the streets. He never stops and never looks around. He seems apathetic in some way."

"Just keep on," Martin Beck replied.

Normally, it would take a lot to break down Martin Beck's calm exterior. But after he had looked from the clock to the telephone for forty-five minutes and no one in the room had uttered a word, he suddenly got up and went out.

Ahlberg and Kollberg looked at one another. Kollberg shrugged his shoulders and began to set up the chess board.

Out in the washroom Martin Beck rinsed his hands and face with cold water and dried himself carefully. When he walked out into the corridor, a policeman in shirtsleeves told him that he had a telephone call.

It was his wife.

"I haven't seen hide nor hair of you for an eternity and now I'm not even supposed to call you. What are you doing? When are you coming home?"

"I don't know," he said tiredly.

She continued to talk and her voice became harsh and shrill. He broke in and interrupted her in the middle of a sentence.

"I don't have time now," he said irritably. "Goodbye. Don't call any more."

He regretted his tone before he put down the receiver but shrugged his shoulders and went back to his chess-playing colleagues.

Stenström's third call came from Skepps Bridge. By then it was twenty minutes to five.

"He went into a restaurant for a while. He's sitting alone in a corner drinking a beer. We've walked around the entire southern part of the city. He still seems strange."

Martin Beck realized that he hadn't eaten anything all day. He sent out for some food from the cafeteria across the street. After they had eaten Kollberg fell asleep in his chair and began to snore.

When the telephone rang he woke up with a start. It was seven o'clock.

"He's been sitting here until now and he's had four beers. He's just left and is on his way toward the center of the city again. He's walking faster now. I'll call in as soon as I can. So long."

Stenström sounded out of breath as if he had been running and he hung up the phone before Martin Beck had a chance to say anything.

"He's on his way there," said Kollberg.

The next call came at half past seven and was even shorter and just as one-sided.

"I'm at Englebrekts Square. He's walking on Birger Jarls Street at a pretty fast pace."

They waited. They watched the clock and the telephone in turn.

Five after eight. Martin Beck picked up the receiver in the middle of the ring. Stenström sounded disappointed.

"He's swung onto Eriksberg Street and crossed the viaduct. We're on Oden Street now. I guess he's going home. He's walking slowly again."

"Damn it! Call me when he's home."

A half hour went by before Stenström called again.

"He didn't go home. He turned onto Uppland Street. He doesn't seem to realize that he has feet. He just walks and walks. Mine won't hold up much longer."

"Where are you now?"

"North Ban Square. He's passing the City Theater now."

Martin Beck thought about the man who had just passed the City Theater. What was he thinking about? Was he really thinking at all; or was he just walking around unconscious

183

of his surroundings, withdrawn and with one thought or possibly one decision ripening within him?

During the next three hours Stenström telephoned four times from different places. The man stayed on the streets near Eriksberg Square but never went really close to her house.

At 2:30 a.m. Stenström reported that Bengtsson had finally gone home and that the light in his room had just gone out.

Martin Beck sent Kollberg as a replacement.

At eight o'clock on Sunday morning Kollberg came back, awakened Ahlberg who was sleeping on a sofa, threw himself down on it and slept.

Ahlberg went over to Martin Beck who sat brooding by the telephone.

"Has Kollberg arrived?" he asked and looked up with bloodshot eyes.

"He's sleeping. Out like a light. Stenström's on watch."

They only had to wait two hours for the first telephone call of the day.

"He's gone out again," Stenström reported. "He's walking toward the bridge to Kungsholm."

"How does he look?"

"Just the same. Even the same clothes. God knows if he even took them off."

"Is he walking fast?"

"No, rather slowly."

"Have you slept?"

"Yes, a little. But I don't exactly feel like a man of steel."

Between ten in the morning and four in the afternoon Stenström called in approximately every hour. Except for two short breaks in a coffee shop, Folke Bengtsson had been walking for six hours. He had wandered around Kungsholm, the old part of the city, and southern Stockholm. He hadn't gone anywhere near Sonja Hansson's apartment.

At five-thirty Martin Beck fell asleep in his chair by the telephone. Fifteen minutes later Stenström's call awakened him.

"I'm at Norrmalms Square. He's walking toward her part of the city. He seems different now."

"In what way?"

"It's as if he's come to life. He seems compelled in some way."

Eight-fifteen.

"I have to be more careful now. He's just swung onto Sveavägen still headed in her direction. He's looking at girls now."

Nine-thirty.

"Sture Street. He's going slowly toward Sture Square. He seems calmer and is still looking at the girls."

"Take it easy," Martin Beck said.

Suddenly he felt fresh and rested in spite of the fact that he hadn't really slept for forty-eight hours.

He stood and looked at the map on which Kollberg was trying to follow Bengtsson's wandering with a red pen. The phone rang again.

"That's the tenth time he's called today," said Kollberg.

Martin Beck picked up the receiver and looked at the clock. One minute to eleven.

It was Sonja Hansson. Her voice was hoarse and quivered a little.

"Martin! He's here again."

"We'll be right there," he said.

Sonja Hansson pushed the telephone away and looked at the clock. One minute after eleven. In four minutes Ahlberg would come through the door and relieve her of that helpless, creeping feeling of unpleasantness she had at the thought of being alone. She wiped her perspiring palms on her cotton dressing gown. The cloth clung to her hips with the dampness.

She walked softly into the dark bedroom and over to the window. The parquet floor felt cold and hard under her bare feet. She stood on her toes, supported herself with her right hand against the window frame, and peeked carefully through the thin curtains. A number of people were on the street, several of them in front of the restaurant across the way but she didn't see Bengtsson for at least a minute and a half. He turned off of Runeberg Street and continued straight out onto Birger Jarls Street. Right in the middle of the trolley tracks he turned sharply to the right. After about half a minute, he disappeared from her sight. He had moved very fast, with long, gliding steps. He looked directly in front of him as if he didn't see anything around him or was concentrating on something in particular.

She went back into the living room which seemed welcoming with its light and warmth and the familiar accessories she liked. She lit a cigarette and inhaled deeply. In spite of the

185

fact that she was fully conscious of what she had taken on, she was also a little relieved when he walked by and didn't stop at the telephone booth. She had already waited too long for that clanging telephone ring which would smash her peace of mind into splinters and bring an irrational and unpleasant element into her home. Now she hoped that it would never come, that everything was wrong, that she could go back to her regular work routine and never have to think about that man again.

She picked up the sweater she had been knitting for the last three weeks, walked over to the mirror and held it to her shoulders. It would soon be finished. She looked at the clock again. Ahlberg was now about ten seconds late. He wouldn't break any records today. She smiled because she knew that would irritate him. She met her own calm smile in the mirror and saw the small beads of perspiration that glittered along her hairline.

Sonja Hansson walked through the hall and into the bathroom. She stood with her feet spread apart on the cool tile floor, bent forward and washed her face and hands with cold water.

When she turned off the tap she heard Ahlberg clattering with his key in the front door. He was already more than a minute late.

With the towel still in her hand she stepped out into the hall, stretched out her other hand, unlocked the safety latch, and threw open the door.

"Thank God. I'm so glad that you're here," she said.

It wasn't Ahlberg.

With a smile still on her lips she backed slowly into the apartment. The man called Folke Bengtsson didn't let go of her with his eyes as he locked the door behind him and put on the safety chain.

186

29

Martin Beck was the last man out and already through the door when the telephone rang again. He ran back and grabbed the receiver.

"I'm in the lobby of the Ambassador Hotel," said Stenström. "I've lost him. Somewhere outside here in the crowd. It can't have been more than four or five minutes ago."

"He's already on Runeberg Street. Get there as fast as you can."

Martin Beck threw the phone down and rushed out to the stairs after the others. He climbed in the car past the back of Ahlberg's front seat. They always sat in the same places. It was important that Ahlberg got out first.

Kollberg put the car in gear but had to release the clutch immediately and swerve to avoid a gray police truck which was coming in. Then he got underway and turned up Regering Street between a green Volvo and a beige Volkswagen. Martin Beck supported his arms on his knees and stared out at the cold gray drizzle. He was excited and alert both mentally and physically but felt collected and well prepared like a well trained athlete before a try for a new record.

Two seconds later the green Volvo ahead of them collided with a small delivery truck which came out of a one-way street, the wrong way. The Volvo swung sharply to the left one second before the collision and Kollberg, who had already started to pass, was also forced to turn to the left. He reacted quickly and didn't even touch the car in front of him but the other cars came to a stop right across the intersection and very close to each other. Kollberg had already put his car in reverse when the beige Volkswagen smashed into their left front door. The driver had stopped suddenly, which was a grave error in terms of the congestion at the intersection.

It was not a serious accident. In ten minutes several traffic policemen would be there with their tape measures. They would write down the names and the license numbers, ask to see drivers' licenses, identity cards and radio licenses. Then they would write "body damage" in their official books, shrug their shoulders and go away. If none of the drivers who were now yelling and shaking their fists at one another smelled of whisky, they would then get back into their cars and drive off in their own directions.

Ahlberg swore. It took ten seconds for Martin Beck to understand why. They couldn't get out. Both doors were blocked as effectively as if they had been soldered together.

In the same second that Kollberg took the desperate decision to back out of the confusion, a number 55 bus stopped in back of them. With that, the only way of retreat was cut off. The man in the beige Volkswagen had come out into the rain, clearly furious and loaded with arguments. He was out of sight and was probably somewhere behind the other two cars.

Ahlberg pressed both of his feet against the door and pushed until he groaned, but the beige colored car was still in gear and couldn't be budged.

Three or four nightmare-like minutes followed. Ahlberg yelled and waved his arms. The rain lay like a frozen gray membrane over the back window. Outside a shadowy policeman could be seen in a shining dark raincoat.

Finally several observers seemed to understand the situation and began to push the beige Volkswagen away. Their movements were fumbling and slow. A policeman tried to stop them. Then, after a minute he tried to help them. Now there was a distance of three feet between the cars but the hinge had stuck and the door wouldn't move. Ahlberg swore and pushed. Martin Beck felt the perspiration run from his neck, down under his collar, and collect in a cold runnel between his shoulder blades.

The door opened, slowly and creakingly.

Ahlberg tumbled out. Martin Beck and Kollberg tried to get out of the door at the same time and somehow managed to do so.

The policeman stood ready with his pad in his outstretched hand.

"What happened here?"

"Shut up," Kollberg screamed.

Fortunately he was recognized.

"Run," yelled Ahlberg, who was already fifteen feet ahead of them.

Groping hands tried to stop them. Kollberg ran into an old man selling frankfurters from a box resting on his stomach.

Four hundred and fifty yards, Martin Beck thought. That

would take a trained sportsman only a minute. But they weren't trained sportsmen. And they weren't running on a cinder track, but on an asphalt street in below freezing rain. Ahlberg was still fifteen feet ahead of them at the next corner when he tripped and nearly fell. That cost him his lead and they continued, side by side down the slope. Martin Beck was beginning to see stars. He heard Kollberg's heavy panting right behind him.

They turned the corner, crashed through the low shrubbery, and saw it, all three of them at the same time. Two flights up in the apartment house on Runeberg Street the weak, light rectangle which showed that the lamp in the bedroom was on and the shades were drawn.

The red stars before his eyes had disappeared and the pain in his chest was gone. When Martin Beck crossed the street he knew that he was running faster than he had ever run in his life even though Ahlberg was nine feet ahead of him and Kollberg by his side. When he got to the house, Ahlberg already had the downstairs door open.

The elevator was not on the ground floor. They hadn't thought about using it anyway. On the first flight landing he noted two things: he no longer was getting air in his lungs and Kollberg was not at his side. The plan worked, the damned perfect plan, he thought as he climbed the last stairs with the key already in his hand.

The key turned once in the lock and he pushed against the door which opened a few inches. He saw the safety chain stretched across the crevice and from inside the apartment heard no human sound, only a continuous, peculiarly metallic telephone signal. Time had stopped. He saw the pattern on the rug in the hall, a towel and a shoe.

"Move away," said Ahlberg hoarsely but surprisingly calmly.

It sounded as if the whole world had cracked into pieces when Ahlberg shot through the safety chain. He was still pushing against the door and fell, rather than rushed, through the hall and the living room.

The scene was as unreal and as static as a tableau in Madame Tussaud's Chamber of Horrors. It seemed as immutable as an overexposed photograph, drowned in flooding white light, and he took in every one of its morbid details.

The man still had his overcoat on. His brown hat lay on the floor, partly hidden by the torn, blue and white dressing gown.

189

This was the man who had killed Roseanna McGraw. He stood bent forward over the bed with his left foot on the floor and his right knee on the bed, pressed heavily against the woman's left thigh, just above her knee. His large, sunburned hand lay over her chin and mouth with two fingers pressed around her nose. That was his left hand. His right hand rested somewhat lower down. It sought her throat and had just found it.

The woman lay on her back. Her wide-open eyes could be seen through his outstretched fingers. A thin stream of blood ran along her cheek. She had brought up her right leg and was pressing against his chest with the sole of her foot. She was naked. Every muscle in her body was straining. The tendons in her body stood out as clearly as on an anatomical model.

A hundredth of a second, but long enough for each detail to become etched into his consciousness and remain there always. Then the man in the overcoat let go his grip, jumped to his feet, balanced himself and turned around, all in a single, lightning quick movement.

Martin Beck saw, for the first time, the person he had hunted for six months and nineteen days. A person called Folke Bengtsson who only slightly reminded him of the man he had examined in Kollberg's office one afternoon shortly before Christmas.

His face was stiff and naked; his pupils contracted; his eyes flew back and forth like those of a trapped animal. He stood leaning forward with his knees bent and his body swaying rhythmically.

But once again—only a tenth of a second—he cast himself forward with a choked, gurgling sob. At the same moment Martin Beck hit him on the collarbone with the back side of his right hand and Ahlberg threw himself over him from behind and tried to grab his arms.

Ahlberg was hindered by his own pistol and Martin Beck was caught unawares by the strength of the attack, partly because the only thing he could think about was the woman on the bed who didn't move and just lay there, stretched out and limp, with her mouth open and her eyes half-closed.

The man's head hit him in the diaphragm with an amazing force and he was thrown backwards against the wall at the same time as the madman broke out of Ahlberg's incomplete grip and rushed for the door, still crouching and with a speed

190

in his long stride that was just as unbelievable as everything else in this absurd situation.

The entire time the unceasing telephone signal continued.

Martin Beck was never nearer to him than a half a flight of stairs and the distance kept increasing.

Martin Beck heard the fleeing man below him but didn't see him at all until he reached the ground floor. By that time the man had already gone through the glass door near the entry and was very close to the relative freedom of the street.

But Kollberg was there. He took two steps away from the wall and the man in the overcoat aimed a powerful blow at his face.

One second later Martin Beck knew that the end was finally here. He heard very clearly the short, wild scream of pain when Kollberg grabbed the man's arm and bent it all the way up to his shoulder with a fast, merciless twist. The man in the overcoat lay powerless on the marble floor.

Martin Beck stood leaning against the wall and listened to the police sirens which seemed to be coming from several directions at the same time. A picket had already been set up and out on the sidewalk several uniformed policemen were warding off the stubborn group of curious bystanders.

He looked at the man called Folke Bengtsson who was half lying where he had fallen with his face against the wall and the tears streaming down his cheeks.

"The ambulance is here," said Stenström.

Martin Beck took the elevator up. She sat in one of the easy chairs dressed in corduroy slacks and a woolen sweater. He looked at her unhappily.

"The ambulance is here. They'll be right up."

"I can walk myself," she said, tonelessly.

In the elevator she said, "Don't look so miserable. It wasn't your fault. And there's nothing seriously wrong with me."

He wasn't able to look her in the eye.

"Had he tried to rape me I might have been able to cope with him. But it wasn't a question of that. I had no chance, none at all."

She shook her head.

"Ten or fifteen seconds more and ... Or if he hadn't started to think about the downstairs telephone, that disturbed him. Broke the isolation in some way. Ugh! God, it's awful."

191

When they went out to the ambulance she said: "Poor man."

"Who?"

"Him."

Fifteen minutes later only Kollberg and Stenström were left outside the house on Runeberg Street.

"I came just in time to see how you fixed him. Stood on the other side of the street. Where did you learn to do that?"

"I was a parachute jumper. I don't use it very often."

"That's the best I've ever seen. You can take anyone with that."

> "In August was the jackal born,
> The rains fell in September.
> 'Now such a fearful flood as this,'
> Says he, 'I can't remember!' "

"What is that?"

"A quote," said Kollberg. "Someone named Kipling."

30

Martin Beck looked at the man who sat slouched before him with one arm in a sling. He kept his head bowed and didn't look up.

This was the moment he had waited for for six and a half months. He leaned over and turned on the tape recorder.

"Your name is Folke Lennart Bengtsson, born in Gustaf Vasa's parish on the sixth of August, 1926, now living at Rörstand Street in Stockholm. Is that correct?"

The man nodded almost imperceptibly.

"You must answer out loud," Martin Beck said.

"Yes," said the man called Folke Bengtsson. "Yes that's correct."

"Do you admit that you are guilty of murder and sexual assault of the American citizen Roseanna McGraw on the night of July 4-5 last year?"

"I haven't murdered anyone," Folke Bengtsson said.

"Speak up."

"No, I didn't do it."

"Earlier you have admitted that you met Roseanna McGraw on July 4 last year on board the passenger ship *Diana.* Is that correct?"

"I don't know. I didn't know what her name was."

"We have evidence that you were with her on July 4. That night you killed her in her cabin and threw her body overboard."

"No, that's not true!"

"Killed her the same way you tried to kill the woman on Runeberg Street?"

"I didn't want to kill her."

"Who didn't you want to kill?"

"That girl. She came to me several times. She asked me to come to her apartment. She didn't mean it seriously. She only wanted to humiliate me."

"Did Roseanna McGraw also want to humiliate you? Was that why you killed her?"

"I don't know."

"Were you inside her cabin?"

"I don't remember. Maybe I was. I don't know."

Martin Beck sat quietly and studied the man. Finally he said: "Are you very tired?"

"Not really."

"Does your arm hurt?"

"Not any more. They gave me a shot at the hospital."

"When you saw that woman last night, didn't she remind you of the woman last summer, the woman on the boat?"

"They aren't women."

"What do you mean? Of course they're women."

"Yes but . . . like animals."

"I don't understand what you mean."

"They are like animals, completely given over to . . ."

"Given over to what? To you?"

"For God's sake don't mock me. They were given over to their lust. To their shamelessness."

Thirty seconds of silence.

"All true human beings must think so, except for the most decadent and depraved."

"Didn't you like those women? Roseanna McGraw and the girl on Runeberg Street, whatever her name was. . . ."

"Sonja Hansson."

He spat out the name.

"Yes, that's right. Didn't you like her?"

"I hate her. I hated the other one too. I don't remember very well. Don't you see how they act? Don't you understand what it means to be a man?"

He spoke quickly and eagerly.

"No. What do you mean?"

"Ugh! They're disgusting. They sparkle and exult with their decadence, and later they're insolent and offensive."

"Do you visit prostitutes?"

"They aren't as disgusting, not as shameless. And then they take money. At least there's a certain honor and honesty about them."

"Do you remember what you answered when I asked you the same question the last time?"

The man seemed confused and anxious.

"No. . . ."

"Do you remember that I asked you if you went to prostitutes?"

"No, did you do that?"

Martin Beck sat quietly for a moment again. He rubbed his nose.

"I want to help you," he said finally.

"With what? Help me? How can you help me? Now, after this?"

"I want to help you to remember."

"Yes."

"But you must try, too."

"Yes."

"Try to remember what happened after you went on board the *Diana* in Söderköping. You had your motor bike and fishing things with you and the boat was a lot behind schedule."

"Yes, I remember. The weather was beautiful."

"What did you do when you went on board?"

"I think I ate breakfast. I hadn't eaten earlier because I remember that I planned to eat on board."

"Did you talk with the people at your table?"

"No, I think I was alone. The others had already eaten."

"And then? After you had eaten?"

"I suspect I went out on the deck. Yes, that's what I did. The weather was good."

"Did you talk to anyone?"

"No, I stood by myself up in the bow. Then it was time for lunch."

"Did you eat alone then too?"

"No, there were others at the table, but I didn't talk to anyone."

"Was Roseanna McGraw at your table?"

"I don't remember. I didn't think much about who sat there."

"Do you remember how you met her?"

"No, actually not."

"Last time you said that she asked you about something and that you began to have a conversation."

"Yes, that's right. Now I remember. She asked me what was the name of the place we were passing."

"What was it called?"

"Norsholm, I think."

"And then she stayed there and talked to you?"

"Yes. I don't remember much of what she said."

"Did you think badly of her immediately?"

"Yes."

"Why did you talk with her then?"

"She forced herself on me. She stayed there and talked and laughed. She was like all the others. Shameless."

"What did you do then?"

"Then?"

"Yes, didn't you go on land together?"

"She followed me when I left the boat for a while."

"What did you talk about?"

"I don't remember. Everything and anything. Nothing in particular. I remember thinking that it was good practice for my English."

"When you went back on board, what did you do then?"

"I don't know. I really don't remember. Maybe we ate dinner later."

"Did you meet her later that evening?"

"I remember that I stood in the bow for a while after it got dark. But I was alone then."

"Didn't you meet her that evening? Try to remember."

"I think so. I don't really know, but I think that we sat on a bench in the stern and talked. I really wanted to be left in peace but she forced herself on me."

"Didn't she invite you into her cabin?"

"No."

"Later that evening you killed her, isn't that so?"

"No, I didn't do anything like that."

"Do you really not remember that you killed her?"

"Why are you plaguing me? Stop repeating that word all the time. I didn't do anything."

"I don't want to plague you."

Was that the truth? Martin Beck didn't know. Anyway he suspected that the man was on the defensive again, that his barriers against the outer world were on the point of functioning again, and that it would be more difficult to breach them the more he tried to break them down.

"Well, it's not so important."

The look in the man's eyes once again lost its sharpness and became frightened and roaming.

"You don't understand me," he said thickly.

"I'm trying to. I understand that you don't like a number of people. That you find them repulsive."

"Don't you understand that? People can be disgusting."

"Yes, I understand. You think particularly badly of a certain category, especially the women who you call shameless. Is that right?"

The man didn't say anything.

196

"Are you religious?"

"No."

"Why not?"

He shrugged his shoulders confusedly.

"Do you read religious books or magazines?"

"I've read the Bible."

"Do you believe in it?"

"No, there's too much in it that can't be explained and is passed over."

"What, for example?"

"All the dirtiness."

"Do you think that women like Roseanna McGraw and Miss Hansson are dirty?"

"Yes. Don't you agree? Look at all the disgusting things that happen all around us. I read the newspapers for a few weeks at the end of the year and they were full of disgusting things every day. Why do you think that is?"

"And you don't want to have anything to do with these dirty people?"

"No, I don't."

He held his breath for a second and added: "Absolutely not."

"Okay, so you don't like them. But don't women like Roseanna McGraw and Sonja Hansson have a great deal of attraction for you? Don't you want to look at them and touch them? Feel their bodies?"

"You don't have the right to say such things to me."

"Don't you want to look at their legs and arms? To feel their skin?"

"Why are you saying these things?"

"Don't you want to feel them? Take off their clothes? See them naked?"

"No, no, that's not so."

"Don't you want to feel their hands on your body? Don't you want them to touch you?"

"Be quiet," screamed the man, and started to get out of his chair.

His sudden movement caused him to pant and he grimaced badly. Probably it had hurt his wounded arm.

"Oh well, there's nothing unusual about that. Actually it is really very normal. I have the same thoughts when I see certain women."

The man stared at him.

"Are you saying that I am not normal?"

197

Martin Beck said nothing.

"Are you stating that I would be abnormal just because I had a few shameful feelings in my body?"

No answer.

"I have a right to my own life."

"Yes, but not to the lives of others. Last night I saw with my own eyes how you nearly killed another human being."

"You did not. I didn't do anything."

"I never say anything I'm not sure of. You tried to kill her. If we hadn't gotten there in time, you would have had a human life on your conscience now. You would have been a murderer."

Strangely enough this made a strong impression on him. He moved his lips for a long time. Finally he said, almost inaudibly:

"She deserved it. It was her fault, not mine."

"Sorry, I didn't hear you."

Silence.

"Will you please repeat what you said."

The man looked sulkily at the floor.

Suddenly Martin Beck said: "You're lying to me."

The man shook his head.

"You say that you only buy magazines about sports and fishing. But you also buy magazines with pictures of naked women in them."

"That's not true."

"You forget that *I* never lie."

Silence.

"There are over one hundred such magazines stuffed in the back of your closet."

His reaction was very strong.

"How do you know that?"

"We've had men searching your apartment. They found the magazines in the back of your closet. They found a lot of other things also, for example, a pair of sunglasses that actually belonged to Roseanna McGraw."

"You break into my home and violate my private life. What's the reason for that?"

After a few seconds he repeated his last sentence and added: "I don't want to have anything to do with you. You're detestable."

"Well, it isn't forbidden to look at pictures," said Martin Beck. "Not at all. There's nothing wrong with that. The women in these magazines look like any other women.

There's no great difference. If the pictures had shown, for example, Roseanna McGraw or Sonja Hansson or Siv Lindberg. . . ."

"Be quiet," the man screamed. "You shouldn't say that. You have no right to mention that name."

"Why not? What would you do if I told you that Siv Lindberg has been photographed in magazines like that?"

"You lying devil."

"Remember what I said before. What would you do?"

"I would punish . . . I would kill you also because you had said it. . . ."

"You can't kill me. But what would you do with that woman, what is her name now, oh yes, Siv. . . ."

"Punish, I would, I would . . ."

"Yes?"

The man opened and closed his hands time after time.

"Yes, that's what I would do," he said.

"Kill her?"

"Yes."

"Why?"

Silence.

"You shouldn't say that," the man said.

A tear ran down his left cheek.

"You destroyed many of the pictures," said Martin Beck quietly. "Cut them with a knife. Why did you do that?"

"In my home . . . you have been inside my home. Searched and snooped. . . ."

"Why did you cut up the pictures?" Martin Beck said very loudly.

"That's none of your business," said the man hysterically. "You devil! You debauched swine!"

"Why?"

"To punish. And I'll punish you too."

Two minutes of silence followed. Then Martin Beck said in a friendly tone: "You killed the woman on the boat. You don't remember it yourself but I shall help you remember. The cabin was small and narrow. It was poorly lit inside. The boat was going through a lake, isn't that right?"

"It was at Boren," said the man.

"And you were in her cabin and you took off her clothes."

"No. She did that herself. She began to undress. She wanted to infect me with her dirtiness. She was disgusting."

"Did you punish her?" said Martin Beck calmly.

"Yes. I punished her. Don't you understand? She had to be punished. She was debauched and shameless."

"How did you punish her? You killed her, didn't you?"

"She deserved to die. She wanted to make me dirty too. She gloried in her shamelessness. Don't you understand," he screamed. "I had to kill her. I had to kill her dirty body."

"Weren't you afraid that someone would see you through the ventilator?"

"There wasn't any ventilator. I wasn't afraid. I knew that I was doing the right thing, she was guilty. She deserved it."

"After you had killed her? What did you do then?"

The man sank into his chair and mumbled.

"Don't plague me any more. Why do you have to talk about it all the time. I don't remember."

"Did you leave the cabin when she was dead?"

Martin Beck's voice was soft and calm.

"No. Yes. I don't remember."

"She lay naked on the bunk, didn't she? And you had killed her. Did you remain in the cabin?"

"No, I went out. I don't remember."

"Where on the boat was the cabin located?"

"I don't remember."

"Was it far below decks?"

"No, but it was quite far back ... farthest back ... the last one toward the stern on the deck."

"What did you do with her after she was dead?"

"Don't ask me about that all the time," he said, whining like a little child. "It wasn't my fault. It was her fault."

"I know that you killed her and you have said that you did it. What did you do with her afterwards?" asked Martin Beck in a friendly voice.

"I threw her in the lake. I couldn't stand to look at her," the man screamed loudly.

Martin Beck looked at him calmly.

"Where?" he said. "Where was the boat then?"

"I don't know. I only threw her in the lake."

He collapsed in his chair and began to cry.

"I couldn't stand to look at her. I couldn't stand looking at her," he said in a monotone with the tears running down his cheeks.

Martin Beck turned off the tape recorder, picked up the telephone and called for a police constable.

When the man who had killed Roseanna McGraw was

taken away, Martin Beck lit a cigarette. He sat completely still and stared in front of him.

Things looked crooked in front of his eyes and he rubbed them with his thumb and index finger.

He reached for a pencil in the holder on the desk and wrote:

GOT HIM. CONFESSED ALMOST EMMEDIATELY, IMIDIAE-MED. . . .

He put the pencil back, crumpled up the paper and threw it in the wastebasket. He decided to telephone Kafka when he had gotten some sleep and was rested.

Martin Beck put on his hat and coat and left. It had begun to snow at two o'clock and by now the ground was covered with a blanket of snow several inches thick. The flakes were large and wet. They dipped down in long, listless swirls, tight and abundant, dampening all sound and making the surroundings remote and unattainable. The real winter had arrived.

Roseanna McGraw had come to Europe. At a place called Norsholm she had met a man who was travelling to Bohuslän to fish. She wouldn't have met him if the boat hadn't had an engine breakdown or if the waitress hadn't moved her to another table in the dining room. Later, he had happened to kill her. She could just as easily have been run over on King Street in Stockholm or fallen down her hotel stairs and broken her neck. A woman named Sonja Hansson might possibly never again feel completely calm or sleep soundly and dreamless with her hands between her knees as she did when she was a little girl. Even so, she had actually not had anything to do with all this. They had all sat in their offices in Motala and Stockholm and Lincoln, Nebraska, and solved this case by means that could never be made public. They would always remember it, but hardly with pride.

Round-shouldered and whistling Martin Beck walked through the pulsing, white mist to the subway station. People looking at him would probably have been surprised if they knew what he was thinking.

Here comes Martin Beck and it's snowing on his hat. He walks with a song; he walks with a sway! Hello friends and brothers; it squeaks underfoot. It is a winter night. Hello to you all; just give a call and we'll go home to southern Stockholm! By subway. To my part of town.

He was on the way home.

201

PER WAHLÖÖ and MAJ SJÖWALL, his wife and co-author, wrote ten Martin Beck mysteries. Mr. Wahlöö, who died in 1975, was a reporter for several Swedish newspapers and magazines and wrote numerous radio and television plays, film scripts, short stories and novels. Maj Sjöwall is also a poet.